The Garden in the Darkness

✦ A Strange Space Novel ✦

KATIE SILVERWINGS

Memphis, TN

PepTalk Productions, LLC

Copyright © 2024 Katie Silverwings. All rights reserved. This is a work of fiction. The characters and events in this book are entirely fictional. Any resemblance to actual events or persons, living or dead, is entirely coincidental.

Publisher's Cataloging-in-Publication Data
provided by Five Rainbows Cataloging Services

Names: Silverwings, Katie, 1991- author.
Title: The garden in the darkness : a strange space novel / Katie Silverwings.
Description: Second edition. | Memphis, TN : PepTalk Productions, 2025. | Series: Strange space adventures, bk. 4.
Identifiers: LCCN 2024924094 (print) | ISBN 978-1-959922-38-4 (paperback) | ISBN 978-1-959922-39-1 (hardcover) | ISBN 978-1-959922-40-7 (ebook) | ISBN 978-1-959922-41-4 (audiobook)
Subjects: LCSH: Fighter pilots--Fiction. | Space travelers--Fiction. | Extraterrestrial beings--Fiction. | Families--Fiction. | Science fiction. | Illustrated works. | BISAC: FICTION / Science Fiction / Space Exploration. | FICTION / Science Fiction / Action & Adventure. | FICTION / Science Fiction / Alien Contact. | FICTION / Family Life / General. | GSAFD: Science fiction.
Classification: LCC PS3619.I58 G37 2025 (print) | LCC PS3619.I58 G37 2025 (ebook) | DDC 813/.6--dc23.

Published by PepTalk Productions, LLC 2024
Memphis, Tennessee, USA
www.PepTalkProductionsLLC.com

Cover art © 2024 Katie Silverwings. All rights reserved.
www.KatieSilverwings.com

To the ones who share my adventure.

Books by Katie Silverwings

FEATHERED FRIENDSHIP
✶ A Strange Space™ Novella ✶

CELADON
✶ A Strange Space™ Novel ✶

HOW OCEAN MERLANI STOLE THEIR NAVIGATOR
✶ A Strange Space™ Novel ✶

WARMTH AND DARKNESS
✶ A Strange Space™ Novella ✶

THE GARDEN IN THE DARKNESS
✶ A Strange Space™ Novel ✶

TALES OF THE NAVIGATORS: VOLUME 1
✶ Strange Space™ Short Stories ✶

ON THE SUBJECT OF KITTENS AND MITTENS
✶ A Strange Space™ Novella ✶

The printing of this edition of *The Garden in the Darkness* was made possible through the generous support of the members of the Strange Space Fan Club, including:

Astral Navigator

Sharon T. Hinton

Space Adventurer (1 Year)

Tabitha

Thank you so much to all of my Fan Club members and supporters! I couldn't do this without you.

To find out more about the Strange Space Fan Club and join for free, visit:

www.KatieSilverwings.com/Fan-Club

Characters Appearing in this Story

The following list of characters is divided by species and arranged in order of their appearance in the narrative. Only characters with significant "speaking roles" have been detailed here. Characters who are mentioned but do not appear are not included. Listed family connections are not exhaustive.

Florivans

MIRAWYND

They/them. Also known as "Wyndi." An orphaned survivor-smallest kitten. 2nd Darter Squadron mascot. Counterpart and ward of **Julian Potts**. Great-grandkitten of **Elder Marine**.

NYX YRITAL

They/them. A botanist, formerly of the staff at the Mayview Outpost. Kitten of **Elder Caeruleus**. Heart's-sibling of **Reba Kiely**.

ELDER CELADON TOREVAL

They/them. Also known as "Dons." Primary Quantum Space Drive Engineer, SCV *Aegolius*. Youngest of the Florivan Council of Elders; Defense Fleet Elder. Counterpart to **Lt. Hsu Li**. Adoptive entile of **Mirawynd** and heart's-sibling to **Ocean Marbree** and **Elias Rudolph**.

OCEAN MARBREE

They/them. Also known as "Breezy." Secondary Quantum Space Drive Engineer, SCV *Gymnasio*. Adjunct officer to **Colonel Esteban Vasquez** of the

6th Darter Squadron. Counterpart to **Pilot-Corporal George Barker.** Heart's-sibling to and member of the household of **Elder Celadon.**

Teryin and Tesnee

They/them. The youngest kittens of **Elder Celadon.**

Humans

Pilot-Sergeant Julian Potts

He/him. Also known as "Sarge." 2nd Darter Squadron pilot, assigned to SCV *Surnia.* Counterpart and guardian to **Mirawynd.**

Pilot-Major Abigail Ioane

She/her. 2nd Darter Squadron pilot, assigned to SCV *Surnia.* Former Project Snail Darter test pilot.

Dr. Reba Kiely

She/her. A civilian physician who did her residency at the Teegarden Shipyards medical facility. Childhood best friend of **Julian Potts.** Heart's-sister of **Nyx Yrital.**

Pilot-Major Anna Toussaint

She/her. 2nd Darter Squadron pilot, assigned to SCV *Surnia.* Former Project Snail Darter test pilot.

Pilot-Major Penny Albright

She/her. 2nd Darter Squadron pilot, assigned to SCV *Surnia.* Former Project Snail Darter test pilot.

Petty Officer 3rd Class Elias Rudolph

He/him. Also known as "Rudy." Darter Maintenance Technician, 2nd Darter Squadron, assigned to SCV *Surnia.* Husband of **Hsu Li** and heart's-brother of **Celadon Toreval.**

Pilot-Corporal George Barker

He/him. 6th Darter squadron pilot and Secondary Astral Navigator (in training), SCV *Gymnasio*. Counterpart of **Ocean Marbree**.

Colonel Esteban Vasquez

He/him. Lead pilot of the 6th Darter Squadron, assigned to SCV *Gymnasio*. Former Project Snail Darter test pilot.

Lt. Hsu Li

He/him. Lead Astral Navigator, SCV *Aegolius*. Former personal assistant to **Admiral Marvin**. Called "Beacon" by Florivans. Husband of **Elias Rudolph** and counterpart to **Elder Celadon**.

Contents

Characters Appearing in this Story ⋯⋯ ix

Part 1: An Unscheduled Landing

1 ⋯⋯⋯⋯⋯⋯⋯⋯⋯⋯⋯⋯⋯⋯⋯⋯⋯⋯⋯ 3
2 ⋯⋯⋯⋯⋯⋯⋯⋯⋯⋯⋯⋯⋯⋯⋯⋯⋯⋯⋯ 17
3 ⋯⋯⋯⋯⋯⋯⋯⋯⋯⋯⋯⋯⋯⋯⋯⋯⋯⋯⋯ 25
4 ⋯⋯⋯⋯⋯⋯⋯⋯⋯⋯⋯⋯⋯⋯⋯⋯⋯⋯⋯ 32
5 ⋯⋯⋯⋯⋯⋯⋯⋯⋯⋯⋯⋯⋯⋯⋯⋯⋯⋯⋯ 46
6 ⋯⋯⋯⋯⋯⋯⋯⋯⋯⋯⋯⋯⋯⋯⋯⋯⋯⋯⋯ 53
7 ⋯⋯⋯⋯⋯⋯⋯⋯⋯⋯⋯⋯⋯⋯⋯⋯⋯⋯⋯ 66
8 ⋯⋯⋯⋯⋯⋯⋯⋯⋯⋯⋯⋯⋯⋯⋯⋯⋯⋯⋯ 79
9 ⋯⋯⋯⋯⋯⋯⋯⋯⋯⋯⋯⋯⋯⋯⋯⋯⋯⋯⋯ 91
10 ⋯⋯⋯⋯⋯⋯⋯⋯⋯⋯⋯⋯⋯⋯⋯⋯⋯⋯ 106
11 ⋯⋯⋯⋯⋯⋯⋯⋯⋯⋯⋯⋯⋯⋯⋯⋯⋯⋯ 117

Part 2: Complications and Card Castles

12 ⋯⋯⋯⋯⋯⋯⋯⋯⋯⋯⋯⋯⋯⋯⋯⋯⋯⋯ 137
13 ⋯⋯⋯⋯⋯⋯⋯⋯⋯⋯⋯⋯⋯⋯⋯⋯⋯⋯ 143
14 ⋯⋯⋯⋯⋯⋯⋯⋯⋯⋯⋯⋯⋯⋯⋯⋯⋯⋯ 154
15 ⋯⋯⋯⋯⋯⋯⋯⋯⋯⋯⋯⋯⋯⋯⋯⋯⋯⋯ 161
16 ⋯⋯⋯⋯⋯⋯⋯⋯⋯⋯⋯⋯⋯⋯⋯⋯⋯⋯ 173

Contents

17 190

18 201

19 213

Part 3: The Battle of Mayview

20 229

21 238

22 245

23 254

24 261

25 267

26 277

27 283

28 313

Appendix

Timeline of *Strange Space Adventures* ···· 325

On Character Identities and Pronouns ···· 327

On Florivan Names ···· 329

On the Defense Fleet's Darter Squadrons ·· 330

The Song of the Darter Pilots ···· 333

The Darter Pilot's Anthem ···· 335

(Forward to Immortality) ···· 335

2nd DARTER SQUADRON
OTS
2nd DARTER SQUADRON
IOANE

The Garden in the Darkness

★ A Strange Space Novel ★

KATIE SILVERWINGS

Part 1: An Unscheduled Landing

IN THE OUTERMOST ASTEROID BELT OF THE STAR system known as Kapteyn, a dwarf planet in a wide orbit quietly circles its faraway host star, lonely save for a small collection of minor moons. The tiny red-toned dot of Kapteyn's Star itself is barely a faint glimmer from this distance, set among a multitude of other celestial lights.

Officially, this planetoid is registered as KOBP-8, although none of its inhabitants have ever bothered to call it that except when filing paperwork. The locals—when there *are* locals—know the place as Mayview, after the small but thriving outpost of the same name which had been built there to house them. As the most remote of the system's colonized worlds, it's long been the center of mining operations throughout the region and the last stop available to many a starship on its way out into deep space. In its heyday, Mayview had been home to almost five hundred long-term residents.

Now, the outpost is entering its seventh year of total abandonment.

With Kapteyn being the closest of the Sol Coalition's inhabited systems to the battlefronts of the ongoing conflict between the Novan Imperium and the Alliance of other Galactic Powers, all of the Outer Belt's residents evacuated to the system's inner planets almost immediately after humanity was drawn into the War.

At present, this near-forgotten outpost is the destination of a pair of darter pilots from the Sol Coalition Defense Fleet's starship SCV *Surnia*. Their mission for the day, officially, is to perform a general reconnaissance sweep of the area and then return to their rendezvous point to be picked up. Landing at Mayview itself wasn't part of their original flight plan, but has become a matter of rather urgent necessity.

As the two darters come into orbit of the planetoid, one of the pilots is trying desperately to persuade his radio to work—although whether pounding the radio control panel with his fist in an attempt to shake the relay crystals connected to it back into alignment is an *effective* means of persuasion is up for debate. The trail of leaking fuel and debris behind his darter is also a matter of some concern, but at the moment, keeping in contact with his comrade is of a higher priority.

"Say that again, Major?"

"*Looks like—lucky day—my old codes for—work! Give me five—clear us—*"

"I think I read you. Waggle your wings when you want me to follow you down."

"Gotcha—Just hang—minute."

"Who knows," the young pilot mutters to himself, flipping the microphone bar of his radio headset back up into the standby position, "maybe *one* thing will go right today."

He taps through one of his status panels and double-checks that his aft fire suppression system is still online. This is hardly the first time Pilot-Sergeant Julian Potts has found himself needing to land a crippled darter, after all—although usually there's a team on hand standing ready to put out the flames.

While Potts is waiting to hear back from the Major, a little alien roughly the size of a small squirrel climbs out of one of the inner pockets of his short ivory flight jacket and up onto his shoulder.

"Oh, hello, Mirawynd," Potts says, turning to look at them. "You done sulking now?"

The Florivan kitten in question makes a pointed bell-like squeak and pats Potts' pale, sandy-bearded cheek reassuringly with one of their four tiny hands. One of the others is busy scratching the itchy place between their upper shoulders where their soft coating of silver fur has begun shedding off to reveal bright blue skin with silver stripes, just as their large catlike ears have. Their long prehensile tail joins their feet and lower pair of hands in holding tight to Potts' collar so they don't go flying in the cockpit's microgravity. Their three golden eyes stare curiously out the polyglass canopy.

"Home?" they ask, looking back to their guardian with a small tilt of their head and flicking gesture of their ears. This is one of about twelve words the kitten knows how to say aside from their names for people—although Potts knows they *understand* a great many more than that.

"No, Wyndi, we're making a bit of a stop-over here, then we'll go back to *Surnia*. No hitchhiking for us today, though, I promise."

Wyndi squeaks at him in a tone which suggests they don't entirely believe that second part, and then goes back to staring out at the planetoid.

This is far from the first time Potts has gotten separated from his ship and squadron by some unexpected emergency. There are times he wonders if the galaxy has it out for him—not that he minds the adventures *too* much, if he's honest. He's always had a problem with getting bored when things were going too smoothly. Ever since he became little Mirawynd's guardian, though, he's seldom been bored for long.

Granted, he'd not *intended* to bring his ward along today. When he launched this morning, Potts thought they were safe in the care of the 2nd Squadron's beloved grouch of a darter maintenance technician.

He'd been wrong.

Wyndi had somehow escaped, tucked themself into the small storage compartment under the vacant copilot's seat in the rear of his darter, and fallen asleep—only to wake up from their nap and cheerfully announce their presence to Potts once he was already hours away from *Surnia*. The fact that the Florivan kitten's instinct for approaching danger and sense of objects in space around them had saved Potts and Major Ioane from an ambush by Novan scout-strikers at a nearby asteroid had *not* dissuaded him from giving them a proper scolding for stowing away in the first place, though.

For their part, now that majority of the action is over, Wyndi seems to have forgotten about being in trouble altogether. They're clearly more interested in looking out at the stars and the grey-green cratered orb of the planetoid.

"Sarge! Shiny!"

"What's shiny, Wyndi?" Potts looks up from his check of the readouts on the darter's damaged propulsion system.

"Shiny!" Wyndi points out at an area between several craters a few hundred kilometers away from the glowing green lines of the Mayview outpost's landing zones with both of their left hands. The tuft at the end of their fluffy prehensile tail tickles Potts' ear as it waves in time with the kitten's excited little non-word squeaks.

Potts' eyes follow the line of the kitten's pointing, but it takes a moment for him even to spot the landing zone lights through the layers of haze in the planet's atmosphere.

"Ah, I see it now." Potts chuckles and reaches up to bat Wyndi's tail away from his face. "That's our trail to line up with the hangar. Looks like they left the lights on for us."

Wyndi looks between him and the green lines, then makes an appreciative trilling sound. As Potts knows all too well, the kitten has an instinctive attraction towards lights and anything else that catches their eyes as "shiny". More often than not, Wyndi's curiosity about the things they find interesting is impossible for them to resist—and gets *him* into even more trouble than he'd wind up in on his own.

The radio crackles back to life.

"All right, Sarge, I've—hangar—open—land these birds."

"Confirmed, Major. Lead the way!" Potts gives the kitten's fuzzy little head a gentle pat. "Back in the pocket with you, Wyndi."

"Pocket?"

"Pocket. We're landing."

Wyndi squeaks reluctantly as they turn away from the view, but obeys and slips back into their usual place inside his jacket.

Potts is, once again, glad that he's been able to train Wyndi to stay safely tucked in their "pocket nest" and out of his way during intense maneuvers and landings. The last thing he needs today is to have his fuzzy little copilot thrown around and injured.

As soon as both darters have descended through the shimmering soap-bubble-like atmosphere containment field, a pair of thick steel-and-polyglass blast doors close over the rooftop entrance of Mayview's main cargo hangar. The hangar sits in a converted crater just outside one of the outpost's larger above-ground domes and has space to hold multiple cargo shuttles, but stands empty now save for stacks of dust-covered crates along the walls.

By the time Potts has finished his shut-down checks, the other pilot is already out of her darter and waiting for him. She climbs up onto the wing of his darter to meet him as his canopy opens.

"Welcome to Mayview, Sarge! Lucky for us I was right about the automatic systems still working. I was half afraid we'd land and not find any air." A relatively short, tawny-pale woman with straight black hair cut just below her chin, Major Ioane is the youngest of the three inseparable Pilot-Majors who make up the rest of Potts' unit. She's also—in Potts' eyes, at least—the one out of the three with the strangest sense of humor.

"You *could* have mentioned that, Major."

"I did!" Major Ioane grins at him. "I take it your radio cut out on that one? I could barely hear you at the end there."

"Must have." Potts chuckles reflexively.

"Short-range signal's never been the best out here," the Major continues, "but I *swear* it's usually not that bad."

"Did you get word to *Surnia* where we were heading, in the end?"

"No, I never did get my Relay connection or long-range transmitter back either after that hit I took." Major Ioane crosses her arms, sighing lightly. "If I'm remembering the flight plans right from the briefing this morning, the message I *tried* to send over my short-range after we dealt with the strikers should have reached them or one of the other wings by now... but who knows if the signal was strong enough to be heard—or if anyone was listening on the right frequency to pick it up."

"What does that mean for the two of us, Major?" Potts unconcernedly climbs up out of his cockpit to join her on the darter's wing. This is hardly the first time he and the Major have been off-course and out of contact, after all. The fact that they have most of two darters between them and somewhere with gravity and breathable air to hang out while they come up with a plan is something of a luxury, in his mind.

Major Ioane shrugs. "We might have to wait a few extra hours for them to realize we're not dead."

"Ah." Potts groans. "So it's *that* sort of a day."

"Seems like."

"It would have been nice to have the rest of the Musketeers with us earlier and not off training the 18th's fledglings…"

"Would have—pretty glad we didn't draw any of the fledges today *ourselves*, considering what happened—but there's no point sitting around talking about what might have been! Save that for when we're giving Colonel Bell our report." Major Ioane gestures down at the rear of Potts' darter. "Your tail's scorched worse than I thought, by the way. I'm surprised you made it down here in one piece."

"I'll take my miracles where I can, then." Potts slides down from the wing to assess the damage himself.

Major Ioane follows.

Wyndi slips back up out of Potts' jacket and onto their usual perch on his shoulder almost as soon as he's reached the ground. They look around curiously and then make an excited leap to the Major's shoulder when they see her, hugging her neck with all four arms. "Abi!"

"Well, now, if it isn't my favorite little good luck charm!" Major Ioane laughs and gives the kitten an affectionate scratch behind their ears. "Thank you for your help earlier, sweetheart."

Wyndi purrs happily in response and nuzzles into her hand. Their third eye turns back to Potts expectantly, as if they're waiting for him to chime in on the subject of what a good and helpful kitten they've been today. Wyndi might not talk all that much yet, but he's been flying with them long enough to know the meaning of most of their body language.

"Don't praise them *too* much, Major." Potts rolls his eyes in amusement. "Wyndi's still in trouble for stowing away in the first place and they know it."

The Florivan kitten pointedly looks up away from him to the Major with a small, sheepish squeak and takes their tail up in their lower pair of hands.

"Oh, don't worry, sweetheart!" Major Ioane gives Wyndi some more ear scratches as she starts walking towards her own darter. "You're not in trouble with *me*. Come on, Sarge will forget all about it by the time we get back with my repair kit."

Wyndi squeaks charmingly in reply. The kitten's long, fluffy tail swishes contentedly against the back of the Major's ivory flight jacket, obscuring the letters of her name where they're embroidered above the green fleur-de-lis and crossed swords of the 2nd Squadron.

"I wouldn't count on that!" Potts chuckles and turns his attention back to inspecting the damage the striker's attack did to his darter. It isn't pretty. Judging by what's left of his maneuvering engines and the missing section of the tail, he and Wyndi are fortunate to be alive.

"Y'know," Major Ioane calls to him from across the hangar a few minutes later, "if we do manage to get that bird of yours back in the air, Rudy's going to have a *fit* when he sees what you've done to her this time."

Potts can't help laughing. "Oh, naturally!" he calls back, "but if Rudy's cussing me out again, it means I got back alive. I'd call that a net win, wouldn't you?"

"I would! Point to the Musketeers indeed!" The Major is grinning as she returns and sets the small toolkit down on his darter's wing to unroll it. "Better you stay alive and flying, kid—after all this time, it'd be an *awful* pain to have to go and break in a new d'Artagnan again. And where'd I ever find one who can crash through solar sails as gracefully as you do?"

Potts shakes his head, trying to hold back a grin of his own. "You ever going to retire that joke, Major?"

"Now why would I go and do a thing like that?"

"Shiny?" Wyndi interrupts to ask, reaching down from Ioane's shoulder towards one of the tools in the unrolled case she's spread out on the wing.

"No, sweetheart, these aren't for you." Major Ioane gently nudges the kitten's four curious hands away. "But say! Do you have any of *Rudy's* tools stashed somewhere that you can bring me?"

Wyndi seems to consider the request for a few moments and then squeaks excitedly and leaps up into the open cockpit.

"I'm trying to train Wyndi *not* to be a fuzzy little magpie, Major," Potts protests, although not without a hint of a smile. "Try not to encourage them too much, will you?"

"Fair enough." Major Ioane chuckles and tucks a stray lock of hair back behind her ear. "At least hunting through their stash will keep Wyndi distracted for a bit—assuming we can fix this mess ourselves, I'd rather they're not in the middle of it all while we're working."

"Point taken."

A large chunk of the hull paneling over damaged maneuvering engines chooses this moment to fall off of the darter entirely. The loud *clang* of it hitting the floor reverberates through the hangar.

Potts grimaces. "Well."

"Well..." Major Ioane echoes.

"...So much for this being an easy fix." Potts sheepishly rubs at the back of his head.

"We'll have to scavenge parts from somewhere to patch it up—if you think we *can* patch it. I somehow doubt Wyndi's gone and stashed me any spare engines under the back seat with the rest of their 'treasures'... yet."

Potts has it on good authority that Florivan kittens *do* eventually grow out of the magpie stage, although no one's been clear on how long it takes for that to happen. The largest thing he's ever found in one of his little counterpart's hiding places and had to return thus far has been the gold-embroidered hat that *Surnia*'s Captain Brentwood wears as part of her dress uniform. Considering that he's had to return that multiple times, Potts is fortunate that the Captain thinks Wyndi's antics are endearing. The hat is an exception, though; usually the kitten's favorite things to borrow and stash away are tools and small component parts.

The two pilots stand there in silence for a minute or two longer, staring at the engine on the floor as if expecting it to magically return to its place in the darter's body. Somewhere from within the cockpit, Potts can hear the distinctive rustling and soft squeaking of Wyndi rearranging things again—they seem to have decided that the sound of the engine falling wasn't worth their interest.

"Well," Major Ioane says at last, "at the very least we need to make sure none of it is going to catch fire again." She gives Potts a teasing nudge. "You know how Rudy feels about you bringing him back cinders."

"I don't particularly enjoy trying to *fly* cinders, myself." Potts shakes his head, then nods in the direction of the Major's own darter. "How bad did that first striker get you, in the end?"

"Not as bad as I thought it had." Major Ioane shrugs. "A few scorch-marks here and there, and like I said, it shorted out my Relay connection and long-range transmitter—nothing too serious, really. I lost a third of my fuel charge with all the dancing I did to get the other fellow off your tail, though."

"Thanks for that, by the way. Do you have enough charge left to get home?"

Major Ioane folds her arms back over her chest again. "Not with as much of a safety margin as I'd like—especially if those weren't the only Novans lurking in this part of the belt."

"I see your point." Potts stares at the section of his darter's engines that are sitting on the ground for a few moments again. He's not fond of the idea of there being more Novans lurking in the area at all. "I suppose we can drain what's left of my reserves to top you up if we need to."

"*If* we need to." Major Ioane brightens and gives him a reassuring pat on the shoulder. "Looked like the recharge setup here's still intact, though! I'll get my bird hooked up while you take stock of your mess. If we can't pull off the repairs, the two of you will have to fly home with me anyway, charge or none." She takes a few steps away, then turns back with a thoughtful gesture to the door leading out of the hangar. "Might be worth us checking the rest of Mayview out too, as long as we're here and we're *technically* still on recon duty. I'm sure the Admiral would want word on whether this is in any shape to be a possible field base for the Fleet."

"I'm surprised it isn't one already."

"Oh, who knows, Sarge? Not really our department, all of that."

Just as Major Ioane is returning from connecting her darter to the outpost's recharging and refueling system, Wyndi reappears. They emerge from Potts' cockpit dragging a gold-handled laser saw as long as their entire body behind them.

"Abi!" the kitten calls to her, waving their tail excitedly. "Shiny?"

"Very shiny, sweetheart! We don't even carry one of these in the toolkits." The Major reaches up to accept the laser saw and allow Wyndi to scamper unencumbered and triumphant along her arm.

"They're getting bolder," says Potts. "I think that's the biggest tool they've squirreled away yet—Not that we're going to *need* it."

"You never know." Major Ioane clips the laser saw onto her belt. "We might run into a jammed door or something."

Potts shakes his head and then smiles at the Florivan kitten who's so expectantly staring at him from the Major's shoulder. "Fine, fine. Wyndi, thank you. We're going to go exploring now, though, so we don't need you to bring out any more tools. Okay?"

Wyndi jumps to his shoulder and sets about neatening up their fur, all four of their tiny blue hands carefully combing through the soft silver fluff. Their tail continues waving interestedly and their eyes stay mostly focused on his face.

"Now, you know the drill, Mirawynd." Potts takes on a firm tone, looking straight into the kitten's three curious golden eyes. "This is a new place, but we don't know if it's safe or not—so no running off, got it? You stay with me."

"Wyndi stay?" The kitten pauses their grooming routine long enough to twitch an ear at him.

"Yes." Potts affectionately pats them on the head. He has to admit, if only to himself, that the face Wyndi makes whenever they agree to try to behave is particularly cute. "Stay close."

Major Ioane chuckles. "Stars, Sarge—You say that like all they ever do is scamper off and get lost."

"*You've* never been the one having to track Wyndi through a ship's air ducts, Major."

T HE WALLS OF THE CORRIDOR LEADING FROM THE hangar to the outpost's central dome are covered in an incredibly overgrown mass of vines. The vegetation is so thick that soon the pilots come to a place where the vines have blocked the path ahead entirely.

"You know," Potts quips, tugging ineffectively at one of the larger vines, "I wasn't expecting to do any gardening today."

"Well, Sarge, no one's been here to prune these grapes in at *least* seven years... just be glad Wyndi 'borrowed' us something that can handle them." Major Ioane pulls out the laser saw with a laugh and sets to work clearing a path through the vines.

Wyndi chimes in from Potts' shoulder with an especially pleased series of little squeaks. Their tail swishes with enough matching emotion to brush against and tickle his ear.

"Now, don't you get smug on me, Mirawynd. You had *no* way of knowing we'd have a use for that." Potts pats the kitten's head anyway with an affectionate chuckle and looks back to the Major. "Do you think the rest of the complex is going to be this bad?"

"Oh, I doubt it." Major Ioane pauses for a moment, looking around the corridor. "I don't remember grapes on these walls the last time I was here, of course—but that was before I joined the Fleet."

"And that was *how* long ago, Major?" Potts grins.

"Oh, ten, maybe twelve years—but who's counting?" She laughs, plucking a grape and tossing it at him.

Wyndi snatches the grape out of the air with a cheerful squeak right before it can hit Potts in the forehead.

"Good catch, Wyndi! I thought for *sure* I'd get him that time."

Potts rolls his eyes. The Major has been playing that particular game with his little counterpart for so long that he doesn't even flinch anymore when she does it. He doesn't even remember now how it all started. "I'd wish you better luck next time, Major," he says dryly, "but I'm better off betting on Wyndi."

While the Major is giggling at that, Wyndi sniffs at the small purple-black fruit they're holding between their upper pair of hands. Once they've thoroughly inspected it, they pat Potts on the cheek with one of their grape-less lower hands.

"Snack?"

"Yes, Wyndi," Potts replies, "grapes are safe for you, and these look ripe enough to eat. Knowing you, you're probably hungry, too." He shakes his head lightly. "Of course, you *would* have gotten a proper lunch by now if you'd stayed with Rudy like you were supposed to."

The quasi-parental edge on his tone elicits a small squeak of acknowledgment from Wyndi, along with a light drooping of their ears and tail.

"And the two of *us* would have been in a different place entirely if they had," Major Ioane interjects. She slices off a good-sized bunch of grapes and offers it to the kitten. "Here you go, sweetheart. Sarge is just grumpy because he knows Rudy's going to lecture *him* instead of you now when we get home."

Wyndi squeaks happily as they accept the gift, any momentary feelings of guilt for having been disobedient clearly forgotten. They break off one of the grapes from the stem and hold it out to Potts with a questioning flick of their ears.

Potts takes the grape with a nod and sighs dramatically. "We're *both* going to get an earful, I'm sure—and not just from him." He pops the grape into his mouth and pats the kitten's head reassuringly. "But the Major's right, Wyndi. There's no need to worry about all of that at the moment."

Wyndi nuzzles his hand briefly, then contents themself with sitting on his shoulder and nibbling away at their grapes while he and Major Ioane deal with the vines.

Almost an hour later, the pilots finally cut through the last of the vines and emerge from the grape-filled corridor.

The large open space on the other side of the tangled vegetation is unexpectedly humid and just as overgrown. Plants of all sorts climb up the walls and across the ceilings of the atrium's lower encircling levels towards the central polyglass dome above. Years of fallen leaves and detritus have formed enough of a layer across the floor that new vines have begun to take root there. Many of the plants are in full bloom, while others bear a myriad of ripe fruits. The smell of flowers hangs thick in the air.

"Now that's what I'd call a *jungle*," Potts quips.

Wyndi, now riding on top of his head, makes a series of fascinated squeaks of agreement.

"It is at that…" Major Ioane shakes her head in amazement. "Mayview used to be called the 'Babylon of the Outer Belt' for the gardens here. I doubt the designers ever planned for everything to be left alone like this for so long, though. It's *incredible* just how much the plants have taken over."

"Well, at least we know the hydroponic systems are still working," says Potts, still marveling at the sight. "Maybe *too* well."

"Maybe—but that means we've got fresh air and most likely decent water around here! Considering how everything else has gone today, I'll count that as a point in our favor."

A swarm of tiny buzzing things flits towards the pilots on a path between the squash blossoms covering the lower walls on either side of them. Potts freezes as they fly past.

"*Pollen-bots*, Sarge." Major Ioane calmly sets a hand on his shoulder. "I'm sure they took all of the bees along when they evacuated."

Potts nods, relaxing. The Major is one of the few people in the galaxy aware enough of his little issue with insects to even notice him flinch. Around just about anyone else, he'd now be doing his best to appear as if nothing had bothered him in the first place. There's not much point doing that with Major Ioane—the two of them *met* in part because he was trying to get away from a bee.

One more pollen-bot zips past him. This one comes close enough to catch the attention of the Florivan kitten sitting on his head.

"Shiny!"

Before Potts can do anything to stop them, Wyndi leaps from their perch with a flourish of their long tufted tail. They land in the vines and scamper off as a streak of silver bouncing through the foliage.

"Mirawynd!" Potts calls, "Come back here! Leave those poor pollen-bots alone!"

Major Ioane laughs, giving him a pat on the shoulder. "You know, Sarge? I'm starting to see why they're not allowed in *Surnia*'s hydroponics bay unsupervised."

Potts lets out a dramatic sigh. "Someday, Wyndi is going to be old enough to be embarrassed about things like this..."

"You're looking forward to that, aren't you?"

"Oh... maybe a little." Potts smirks and makes his way out into the vast room, whistling loudly as he always does when he's trying to call his ward back from one of their little escapades.

The silver streak finally reappears several minutes later, leaping now from the vines which stretch down from the highest point of the great polyglass-domed ceiling's interior supports. Wyndi lets out a triumphant squeak as they capture the pollen-bot they've been chasing in mid-air—only to land with a splash into a large, lotus-covered pond in the center of the atrium a moment later.

Potts rushes over and splashes into the middle of the pond himself to scoop the flailing kitten out of the water.

"There you are! Easy, I've got you, it's okay. You *really* need to learn to look where you're jumping, Mirawynd," he tells them in a tone halfway between exasperated concern and amusement.

Wyndi continues coughing and spluttering, but clings tightly to his hands in a way that Potts takes as a sign that he got to them in time. He holds the soggy kitten close to his chest as he wades back towards the bank of the past-waist-deep pool. The cold water has already filled his boots, and he hardly wants to risk dropping them into it again.

"Granted, I didn't see this pond either under all the lily-pads—why's there even a pond here, Major? I thought you said this was the main hub of the complex."

"It is! That's why the designers got **creative** with the aquaponics setup." Leaning on the back of a bench next to the pond, Major Ioane gestures towards some rather large koi swimming nearby. "Far as I can remember, they've always kept decorative fish in this one to show off for visitors."

"You hear that, Wyndi? You might've been gobbled up by a *fancy* fish." Potts chuckles at the absurdity of it as he clambers back out of the pond.

Wyndi is still too busy clinging to him and coughing up the last of the water they've inhaled to respond. Once they can breathe comfortably again, they squeak softly and stare up sheepishly at him with all three golden eyes.

"Are they okay, Sarge?"

"Yeah." Potts breathes a small sigh of relief. "Just a bit wet—and I doubt they'll run off again for at least an hour. Right, Wyndi?"

"...Stay?" Wyndi climbs up to their usual spot on his shoulder.

"I'd appreciate it if you did, for once." Potts reaches up and gives them a bit of a reassuring scratch behind their soggy ears. "Next time the fish might get to you first."

Wyndi gives his cheek a damp nuzzle, then takes the opportunity to shake all the wetness they can out of their fur, spraying droplets of water all over the place. Seemingly satisfied, they drape themself over Potts' shoulder to let the rest dry.

Potts can't help laughing—he's too relieved that they're okay to scold them this time.

"I can't take the two of you anywhere without you finding trouble to get into, now, can I?" Major Ioane brushes the water off of her jacket with a chuckle. "Let's try to resist the call of the water for the rest of the day, okay?"

"Yes ma'am." Potts sits down on the bench and pulls his boots off, pouring the water out of each one in turn. "Don't suppose you remember where a washroom is in this place, Major? I wasn't exactly planning on going swimming today myself."

She looks around, then gestures towards a kiwi-vine draped archway on the far side of the domed space. "The public one's down there. Depending on how all the door codes were set up during the evacuation, though, I *may* be able to get us into my Dad's old suite if that's not enough for you."

"Public should be fine." Potts wrings the water out of his socks. "Mind watching Wyndi for a bit while I go dry off?"

"Sure." Major Ioane takes a seat on the bench beside him. She pulls a handkerchief out of one of the inner pockets of her flight jacket and then gently plucks Wyndi off of his shoulder. "Come on, sweetheart, let's see if I can't get your fur fluffed back up a bit while we wait for him."

Wyndi doesn't protest, although they make a small questioning squeak in Potts' direction.

"I'll be back in a bit," he promises, reaching over to ruffle his ward's damp ears briefly. "I'd take you with me, but I *know* how you feel about the sound speed-dryers make."

"Shout if you run into anything weird." Major Ioane is already busy lightly rubbing the kitten's damp silver fur with the corner of her handkerchief. Wyndi seems more than happy to allow themself to be groomed, contentedly purring and stretching out their various small limbs to provide her with easier access to their more soggy parts.

"*Weird*, Major?" Potts laughs, slinging his boots and wrung-out socks over his shoulder and starting barefoot towards the washroom. "I'm not sure I even know what that is anymore."

M IRAWYND HAS NOT YET SHED ENOUGH OF their soft silver kitten-fur to enjoy being made to take baths. They like water well enough while they're *in* it, as long as it's clean-smelling and suitably warm. They're even something of a good swimmer. All the same, they never like being put *into* the water and they rarely appreciate having to get back *out* of it.

Being *wet* after having been bathed is the worst part, in their mind, because it usually leads to being *cold*, which Mirawynd thoroughly dislikes. They do still have to submit to the soggy indignity of it, of course, whenever their human determines that they've gotten themself too dirty to simply be brushed and left to their own methods to clean themself. Thankfully, that doesn't happen more than once most weeks. Mirawynd is a rather tidy creature by nature; they're fully capable of keeping their fur clean, neatly arranged, and free of unpleasant odors.

Their human, by contrast, has yet to learn how to keep his hair from sticking up at odd angles even with Mirawynd around to help him. He seems to be having a bit more luck with his face-fur, at least, now that he's decided to let that grow.

Mirawynd usually allows their human to bathe them only after a long game of "steal the sponge and scamper around the lavatory at high speed evading capture." There have been occasions, though, where they've found their well-groomed fur tainted with annoyingly sticky or foul-smelling substances for one reason or another after one of their adventures and brought the sponge to him outright to request assistance.

Declared baths have a set procedure, once Mirawynd allows themself to be caught and put into the water: they let their human hold them under a stream of warm water and get their fur all soggy; their human does the work of gently scrubbing all of the grime out of their fur with the sponge and sweet citrus-smelling soap; they wriggle around in his hands while he rinses out all of the soap; they swim around in the nice hot water in the "rinse bath" for a while until it starts to be cold or their human loses interest in playing "fetch the water toys" with them; they swim around some *more* while their human tries to catch their wet and slippery self to get them out of the water; he catches them; they shake off most of the water onto *him*; he helps them dry off with a soft towel and the quieter sort of warm-air-blowing device.

The undeclared bath Mirawynd took today is perhaps the worst they've ever had. The water was *cold*, it smelled *icky*, and they found themself in it too abruptly to remember how to swim. On top of that, according to their human and Abi, there had been something in the water which would have possibly *eaten* them.

Their human had come just in time to rescue them. He always does, even though it's supposed to be Mirawynd's job to protect *him*. He usually needs more protecting than they do, anyway. It's no wonder their parent was so insistent that they stay with him and keep him safe. Mirawynd isn't entirely sure how he ever managed before they became his guardian.

While Abi had been able to help Mirawynd dry off, mostly, and the place where they are is warm enough that their remaining dampness isn't making them feel chilled, they were still put off enough by the whole experience to dive back into the warmth and comfort of their human's jacket just as soon as they could. His jacket pockets have been Mirawynd's home for almost as long as they can remember. They only have small dim memories of a time when they didn't have their human to snuggle with and protect.

When Mirawynd wakes from their nap some hours later, they immediately find that they *still* smell like the weird pond water. They're none too pleased by this and quickly come to the conclusion that they'll have to give in and request to be bathed properly once they're back home where the sponge and the citrus-soap and the water toys are. They much prefer that smell to the one they're wearing now.

Mirawynd emerges from the jacket with a small yawn and climbs back up to their usual perch on their human's shoulder. They find that while they were sleeping, he and Abi have moved to a different room in the jungle maze. This one is a big workshop-looking place underneath all of the plants. Mirawynd can even smell some faint traces of the shimmery non-conductive grease their friend Rudy uses to keep metal things that are supposed to be able to move from getting stuck in place.

Mirawynd brushes their cheek against their human's briefly to let him know that they're awake, since he seems too distracted by the large over-ripe orange fruit he's trying to free his foot from to greet them like he normally does when they first emerge from his jacket after a nap. They seem to have awakened at precisely the right time to witness him half-hopping and holding onto a nearby workbench to try and shake the thing off.

They look over to Abi with a questioning squeak. She seems to be holding back giggles.

"Did all his carrying on wake you up, sweetheart?" Abi asks, holding her arm out to them.

Mirawynd makes a noncommittal trilling sound and leaps to her arm. They much prefer their human's shoulder to anyone else's, but *not* when he's being such a comically unsteady perch. They climb up to Abi's shoulder and look back to their human.

"I wouldn't call it *carrying on*," he says, finally managing to pull his boot free of the offending fruit. The massive orange thing falls to the ground with a heavy *splut* and splits into several large fragments, revealing that its insides were originally hollow and full of slimy stringy stuff and seeds.

Mirawynd is intrigued, but doesn't investigate. The not-quite-moldy and almost-rotten smells wafting up from it are enough to make them not want to get closer. They have enough of a weird smell clinging to their fur as it is.

"Well, try to watch where you're walking from now on, Sarge—if you trip in here, I'm not sure I'll be able to find you under all of these pumpkin vines." Abi gives Mirawynd's ears a gentle scratch and shakes her head at their human. She's not doing well at keeping herself from laughing at his silliness.

"I *was* watching where I was going," their human says with a good-humored huff. He uses one of the large bristly leaves to wipe the rest of the fruit mess off of his boot. "You have to admit this whole 'indoor jungle' thing is starting to get ridiculous, Major. You said this was supposed to be a mechanic's workshop—why in the stars would there be *pumpkins* planted in here?"

"No idea why, Sarge. To be fair, it's not all pumpkins. I think that mess on the far walls are some kind of cucumber."

Mirawynd looks over in the direction she's pointing. The curtain of smaller, tangled vines cascading down from the walls is covered in long, narrow green fruits almost as big as themself.

"Cucumbers, kumquats, whatever." Their human takes a step forward, and only narrowly catches himself from tripping in the thick vines criss-crossing the floor. "It's all plants in the end, and there's too many of them."

"Well, at least there's plenty of fresh oxygen here thanks to this mess—and food, in the event things go horribly wrong today and we get stranded here for a while." Abi shakes her head at him again and begins carefully picking her way over towards one of the vine-covered walls.

"*Must* you tempt fate like that, Major?"

"It's not tempting fate if we're prepared for it!" Abi laughs, then pauses to consider the wall in front of her carefully. After a moment, she looks back to Mirawynd's human. "I'll admit, though, Sarge, it baffles me a bit too that there's been hydroponic equipment set up in this workshop at all. I certainly don't see a reason for it—high humidity and water and electronics are hardly a good mix."

"You're *sure* you remembered right which of these rooms was the maintenance tech's workshop?" He comes over to join her at the wall, carefully avoiding the rest of the large overripe fruits and vines on the ground.

"I know this is it. I spent the better part of my childhood sitting in here listening to Dad and Heb talking tech and shuttles." Abi clucks her tongue. "Heb would have a *fit* if they were here to see what's become of the place."

"Heb?" Mirawynd's human raises an eyebrow.

"Senior spacecraft maintenance technician Hebron—I've told you about them, Sarge. They're the one who taught me everything I know about modding flight gear. Even *more* of a prickly sort than Rudy is, if you can believe that. I still haven't met anyone who was a bigger stickler for neatness in the workspace."

"Now, if that's not a terrifying image, Major..." He shakes his head, stifling a laugh. "I don't get how someone like that would have let things get planted here at all—or why anyone *bothered* to plant things before they evacuated."

"No idea on that front, Sarge." She gestures at the cabinets hiding behind the curtain of vines on the wall. "Let's just see if they left some parts for us and worry about the rest later."

Mirawynd takes this opportunity to hop down off her shoulder so they can explore the room while the humans are busy cutting vines with the marvelous shiny thing they'd borrowed from Rudy this morning.

"Hey, now! Wyndi, try not to go too far!" calls their human. "Stay in this room. You hear me?"

Mirawynd pops back up out of the vines and waves to him with both of their left hands. "Wyndi stay!"

OME TIME LATER, MIRAWYND IS INVESTIGATING
the underneath of a table near the room's open
doorway. The table is covered in the same sort of bristly
vines and big leaves that the orange fruits have grown
from. The vines have formed a nice sort of cave out of the
underside of the table, too. Underneath all of the vines on
the floor of the table-cave, Mirawynd finds a forgotten and
partially-buried shiny thing. It's the slim-handled tool sort
of shiny thing, like the ones their friend Rudy carries in
his vest pockets.

Mirawynd likes shiny things, particularly ones like
their friend's. Since no one seems to be around that this
one belongs to, they assume no one will mind if the shiny
thing becomes *theirs*.

It takes a while, but soon they've freed their new favorite shiny thing from the vines. Normally, Mirawynd would take it back to their nest or one of their other shiny-stashing places. At the moment, however, the nest they share with their human is somewhere far away and the shiny-stashing place in his darter isn't an option either because they promised to stay in the room.

Instead, Mirawynd decides that they'll take their new shiny thing to show him and Abi. Both of them have all sorts of nice pockets for stashing shiny things in. If they put their shiny thing in his pocket for safekeeping, they can take it back to put in their nest when the adventure is over. This thought pleases Mirawynd. They wave their tail excitedly. They can show *Rudy* their shiny thing too, when they all get home, and then he'll tell them what its name is.

As Mirawynd starts to slip back out from the vine cave carrying their treasure, they see a pair of legs come to stand beside the table. The legs don't belong to their human, though, or to Abi—the pants aren't the right sort of pocket-covered ivory color, for one thing, and the feet are wearing the wrong kind of shoes.

They poke their head out and take a better look at the person. Mirawynd is a bit perplexed by what they see. The person *is* human, as far as Mirawynd can tell from the shape and the sounds they make, but the fabric of the clothes and face-covering hood they're wearing makes their whole body shimmer and try to blend in with the plants and the rest of the room. Still, though, Mirawynd's three keen golden eyes can see the new human distinctly. They can even make out a little bit of the face hiding underneath the hood.

Mirawynd looks over to where their human and Abi are still trying to get into all of the cabinets on the wall. They have the distinct impression that neither one has noticed the new human entering. The new human, in turn, seems to be standing very still and watching the two of them.

Since the new human isn't paying any attention to Mirawynd themself, they slip out of their vine cave and come a little closer to the back of the new human's legs. A cautious sniff of the new human's ankles tells them that underneath the shimmery clothes, the new human smells like flowers and *greenness* along with the usual 'human smell'—and a bit like Abi and Monica-the-Navigator, their Entile Indigo's human, too. Mirawynd likes the smell, and they can *almost* smell something else in it that's familiar, but they'd have to get closer to know for sure.

Mirawynd knows it's not polite to scamper up to the shoulder of a person they've not been introduced to yet, even if they have a good impression that the person is friendly. Their human has made it *very* clear recently that Mirawynd is supposed to ask him first if they can cuddle with people from outside their family, or ride on their shoulders, or inspect their pockets, or borrow their shiny things, *before* they try do any of those things. They're not quite sure *why* he wants them to do this, since their instincts for knowing whether a person is a potential friend or not are *far* better than his. All the same, they do recognize that they're supposed to listen to their human.

Mirawynd decides, then, that they should let their human know that there's another person here so they can be introduced—and *then* they can inspect the new human and see if there are any pockets in the shimmery outfit worth their interest!

With their new shiny thing gripped securely in their tail, Mirawynd quietly scampers through the vines. Once they reach their human, they deftly climb up onto his shoulder. They slip their new shiny thing into his pocket first for safekeeping, then tap politely on his cheek to catch his attention.

"What is it Wyndi? Did you get tired of exploring?"

"Sarge! Friend!" Mirawynd waves their tail excitedly. This is the best word they know how to say for the occasion, although what they mean is something a bit more complex.

He doesn't seem to understand. Their human can be painfully oblivious at times. "Yes, we're friends... did you just put something in my pocket?"

"Shiny!" Mirawynd explains, and then they tug on his ear gently and point towards the new human standing in the doorway. "Friend!"

"What the—stop that, Wyndi—what do you mean, 'friend'? There's no one here but—" Mirawynd's human turns around abruptly and stops mid-sentence, tapping Abi on the shoulder and nodding in the direction of the doorway. He slowly raises his hands above his head.

Abi turns, then slowly raises her hands as well. "Well, hello there... friend... don't mind us, we're just passing through."

"Friend!" Mirawynd mimics the gesture with all four of their hands and makes a few laughing squeaks. This is a new sort of a game to play when meeting potential friends, and they're not sure what the point of it is, but they like it.

"Wyndi," their human hisses softly, "how many times do I have to tell you? People who point neural pulse stunners at us are *not* our friends."

Mirawynd takes a closer look at the new human. They are, in fact, holding some sort of long multi-pronged shiny thing. The new human also doesn't seem amused by the commentary at all, although the hood of their shimmery outfit covers most of their expression.

Mirawynd doesn't understand. Usually, people who make their human tense up like he has and point things at him are of the sorts whom *they* naturally dislike. This one certainly isn't of the monster variety that makes their fur stand up, either. Besides, their human never even notices when he's met one of those until Mirawynd starts being fierce at them to warn him. They don't feel any instinctive need to be fierce at the new human at all.

"Try any tricks," says the new human in a muffled, distorted voice, "and I'll have ye out cold in an instant." They gesture with the shiny thing they're holding. The pronged tips of it glow green as it begins making a high-pitched electronic hum.

"No tricks," Abi agrees, nodding lightly but otherwise staying still.

"Now," says the new human, gesturing with their humming, green-glowing device again, "who the blazes are ye? And what're ye doing *here*?"

"We're darter pilots from the Defense Fleet's SCV *Surnia*. My Sergeant here's had a bit of engine trouble that we're trying to sort out so we can get back to our squadron." Abi nudges Mirawynd's human with her elbow, but keeps her hands up and her voice as calm and cheerful as ever. "We didn't know anyone was still living here."

"Well, *I* live here—and I ain't one what takes kindly to trespassers."

"We're hardly trespassing," Mirawynd's human comments dryly. "But while we're on the subject, do we get to ask who you are?"

"Settle down, Sarge," says Abi under her breath, nudging him again. "This isn't the time to do your impression of Rudy."

"It's a perfectly reasonable question to ask, Major," he protests, forcing a laugh. "Besides, if we *were* going to get stunned, our 'friend' here would have done it before we turned around."

"If you keep insisting on antagonizing folks," Abi hisses, still sounding more amused than not, "we're going to end up stunned and hog-tied again anyway."

"That doesn't happen every—"

"—I *will* stun ye if ye try anything, so don't think ye little argument is going to catch me off-guard." The new human doesn't seem to be amused by Mirawynd's pilots at all.

"You'll have to forgive my Sergeant, friend," says Abi. "He's having a bit of a rough day."

"I only asked—

"—Wait," the new human interrupts again. They tilt their head to one side curiously, staring at Mirawynd's human. "I *know* ye..."

Mirawynd's pilots share a look, then Abi gives a light shrug as a signal to wait and see what happens. Mirawynd tilts their head to match the new human, curious themself about the abrupt change in voice tones.

"*Julian*?" The new human asks after a long silence, with a distinctly shocked and disbelieving tone now. "Can it really be *ye* under that scraggly mess of a beard?"

"That would be my given name, yes—although I wouldn't call my beard *scraggly*—are we supposed to know each other?" Mirawynd's human sounds equally skeptical.

"If ye be my Julian—" The new human abruptly takes a step forward, pointing the glowing end of the shiny thing they're holding directly at Mirawynd's human's chest. Their tone sharpens. "—Or is it ye've finally found the way into *my* head, too?"

Mirawynd's human looks over to Abi, who shrugs lightly once again. He looks back to the new human and squints. "Your voice rings a bell, friend—well, I know a Millefleur Moon Three accent when I hear it, at least—but I can't rightly recognize your face when it's all covered up."

"Oh, *that's* ye game today, is it? Here, ye tricky devil—it'll be the last ye see before I put ye to sleep like the others." The new human pulls their hood back with one hand, revealing a pale, freckled face with bright green eyes and a tied-back mass of long red curls. The expression on the face is stern and determined.

"*Reba*?" Mirawynd has never seen their human's eyes go so wide as they do now. "It can't be—but you're—what in the *stars* are you doing here? I—I thought—"

"—Say something so I know ye ain't another pair of Novans come hunting first." The green eyes narrow with a sparkling sharpness.

Mirawynd's human groans dramatically and lowers his arms, crossing them over his chest. "Reba Kiely, of all the—the last time you looked at me like that, you were in a nice *safe* residency at Teegarden's Shipyards Medical Center, chewing me out for having the gall to get hurt crashing through a solar sail on my first run with the Musketeers while they were deciding whether they wanted me for their fourth or not. You called me an idiotic—something?" He glances over to Abi. "Major, you were there. Do you remember?"

"Oh!" Abi chuckles, looking between him and the new human. "How could I forget, since I was sitting there waiting for her to get around to treating *me* once she was done with you? 'Idiotic self-destructive nincompoop,' wasn't it? And then Penny and Anna teased you for *ages* that they'd tattle to dear Dr. Kiely any time you so much as stubbed your toe in the hangar."

"Yeah, that's what it was!" Mirawynd's human grins. "Is that enough for you, Reba, or do I have to start bringing up embarrassing stuff from when we were kids? I don't think I've ever told the Major the story about your *salamanders...*"

"Nay, Julian, I believe ye." The new human sighs and deactivates the green glow of the shiny thing, clipping it onto her belt.

Mirawynd's human smiles and approaches her.

She pulls him into a tight embrace.

Mirawynd squeaks and hops up onto their human's head to get out of the way of the hugging. They're pleased that they seem to have been right about the new human being nice—judging from what they understood of the conversation, this "Reba" person is just a friend of their human's whom they'd never met before. They pat curiously at one of her stray curls. It has a *very* pleasing texture: not so tightly curled as their friend Penny's bouncy white hair is, but soft and loose and brightly copper-red.

"Not that I'm sad to see you again, Reba," says their human, seeming reluctant to let go, "but seriously, why are you here? *How* are you here? I know I'm the worst in the galaxy at keeping up with people, especially with the way the last few years have gone… but they told me you were *dead*—"

"—I *ain't.*"

"I can see that!" Mirawynd's human laughs, hugging her tighter. "Stars," he whispers, "I thought I'd lost you forever."

"Last I'd heard, Julian," Reba replies, laughing in a way that sounds happy and sad all at the same time, "*ye* were still lost y'self."

"Well…"

"Lost is an understatement," Abi interjects. "Luckily, the Prelvee returned him to us in the end. Forgive me for interrupting the reunion, Dr. Kiely, but how long *have* you been here?"

"We've been stranded for almost four years now. We thought *Psiloscops* would come back for us, but…" Reba finally lets go of Mirawynd's human, shaking her head sadly. "Well, nobody came looking for us in all that time what were actually human. We'd almost given up on ever being found."

"Come back for you?" Abi asks.

"Aye. *Psiloscops* dropped our shuttle off on its way to a rendezvous with some convoy or another what were leaving the system and needed supplies transferred. Our team were coming to see if it were worth making a proper field hospital out of this place, but they'd planned to drop by on their way back to Kapteyn b and check on us."

"And *Psiloscops* was destroyed with all hands less than a night's jumps out from here." Abi comes over and leans on the nearest vine-covered table. "They must have been far enough away from Mayview that no one realized there were survivors to look for. Plus, the Outer Belt has been a no-fly zone ever since except for the transit corridor—which is too far away from here for anyone to have stopped by on accident before now." She sighs, shaking her head in the same way Reba had. "I'm sorry you were overlooked like this, Dr. Kiely. It shouldn't have happened."

Reba nods vaguely in acknowledgment. "Bittersweet, knowing we'd been right to guess everyone thought us dead—or didn't know we were missing."

Mirawynd's human pulls her back into the hug. "If I'd known there was a chance…"

"Ye'd have come looking sooner." Reba rests her head on his shoulder. "I know."

A silence descends upon the room. Mirawynd doesn't quite understand why. They *do* understand that their human is too busy hugging his apparently-lost-and-now-found friend to remember that he's *supposed* to be introducing them to her.

"Friend?" asks Mirawynd, breaking the confusing silence. Their tail waves excitedly as they lean down from their human's head to get a better look.

"Yes, Wyndi, you were right." Their human smiles softly. "Reba's a friend."

"Friend!"

Reba lets go now, giving him a sideways glance. "Ye have a pet what *talks*, now, Julian?"

"Wyndi's not a *pet*, Reba. I'm their guardian. There's a difference."

"Who in their right mind would go and make *ye* anyone's guardian?" She raises her eyebrows, resting both hands on her hips. "Ye can barely keep *y'self* out of trouble."

"Long story."

Reba looks up to Mirawynd.

Mirawynd looks back down to her with a cheerful squeak of greeting.

She looks at them a little longer, then shakes her head. "Ye can tell me about the wee beastie later, then. What *are* ye doing here, if this ain't a rescue?" Her eyes narrow for a moment as they turn back to Mirawynd's human. "*Tell* me ye ain't gone and crashed again."

"Oh, no, it's like the Major says." Mirawynd's human sheepishly rubs at the back of his head. "Just a bit of engine trouble..."

"...In the sense that his engines were shot out by a Novan striker," Abi finishes for him, stifling a laugh. "But really, Dr. Kiely, do you expect anything else from the man?"

"Not hardly." Reba takes Mirawynd's human by the hand. "Come on; I need to introduce ye both to Nyx before they think something's happened to me and flood this place with anesthesia gas."

"Nyx?"

Reba laughs. "Ye think I could keep all this up without a properly mad botanist?"

"You're not alone here, then?" asks Abi.

"Nay, thank the stars. But I'd rather explain to ye with Nyx there to help so ye only have to hear the story once."

"Lead on, then," says Mirawynd's human. "Maybe I'll be able to keep the vines from grabbing me if I have someone to follow."

"How many times has he tripped already since ye've been here?" Reba chuckles and shoots a knowing look over to Abi.

"Y'know, Dr. Kiely, I've stopped counting?"

"Now, don't the two of you start picking on me..."

Since Reba is leading their human along through the vines now and doesn't seem to be planning to let go of his hand, Mirawynd decides it's as good an opportunity as any to inspect their new friend more closely. They slip down to his shoulder and tap on his cheek with one of their upper hands to catch his attention.

"Friend?" Mirawynd asks again when he looks over to them, making a point of wiggling in the way they always do before making a leap. They don't have enough words to make such requests more straightforwardly yet, but he usually understands their meaning anyway.

"*Reba*," he tells them, in the tone he uses for trying to teach them words. "And I'll ask her."

"Ask me what?"

Mirawynd's human laughs and reaches up with his free hand to pat them on the head. "The 'wee beastie' here wants to know if they can ride on your shoulder."

"What?" Reba looks over to Mirawynd. "Why'd they want to do that?"

"They get excited about new people." He laughs again. "Mostly I think they're just curious because they can tell that I'm friends with you."

"Ah."

Mirawynd squeaks politely at her, taking this as a yes, then makes the leap to her shoulder. They swish their tail excitedly as they begin to inspect her hair more closely. It's very soft, and smells even more like sweet herbs and human-ness than her ankles had. There's still another smell there underneath that they can't quite place. It's familiar, like *family* somehow, but they need to investigate further.

They're only on her shoulder for a moment, though, before they're interrupted.

"Hey! Wyndi, now cut that out. She didn't say you *could*—" Mirawynd's human reaches up and plucks them back off despite their squeaks of protest and attempts to wriggle out of his hands. "—Sorry, Reba, I'm still trying to teach them to be polite."

"Friend!" Mirawynd protests again, doing their best to wriggle out of his hands. They look over to Reba with the saddest expression they can muster. They really don't understand why their human is making such a fuss—they did *ask* before they jumped this time.

"Ye seem to be missing a few lessons, Julian." Reba shakes her head, lightly smoothing her hair back from where Mirawynd had been inspecting it. "What sort of a critter did ye say they be?"

"They're not a *creature*, Reba—even if they do act like it sometimes." He lightly begins to stroke Mirawynd's ears to encourage them to settle down. "Wyndi here's Florivan. Just a bit of a young one, that's all."

"Florivan?" Reba looks at Mirawynd for another moment, then chuckles. "I should have guessed that, now that I look at ye. Ye just be a fuzzy wee miniature..."

Mirawynd tilts their head to one side at her. They wriggle enough in their human's hands to be able to hold their upper pair of arms out towards her. "Re-ba friend?"

She nods. "As long as ye don't go tying knots in my hair. Hand them here, Julian, maybe *I* can teach ye little friend some better manners than ye have."

Mirawynd is quite pleased by this, and contents themself with sitting on Reba's shoulder while the walk to wherever it is Reba is taking them continues. Their human does his best to tell the story about how he came to be Mirawynd's companion along the way—although as always, he seems to have forgotten the part about Mirawynd's parent telling *them* to protect *him*.

PILOT-MAJOR ABIGAIL IOANE HAD CALLED THE Mayview complex home for most of her childhood and adolescence. She'd once known every corridor and room in the place by heart, even the "secret" places which were supposedly off-limits to anyone without the highest staff clearances.

Now, following Dr. Kiely deep into the complex's underground heart, she barely recognizes the place.

The smell of greenness, even, has fully taken over the smell of "home" that her memory is seeking, along with the varying smells of flowers and over-ripe fruits. The path itself is somewhat familiar, but all of the landmarks are changed or obscured by the overgrowth of flowering plants of every kind. Many of the doorways memory tells her *should* be there are hidden altogether, and more than one corridor filled with plant matter so much as to seem impassible.

For the first time she can remember since she was a very small child, Ioane genuinely feels *lost* in the place. She doesn't know how much of that is the fault of the passage of time, though, and how much of it is that of the overwhelming growth of plants.

Dr. Kiely seems to know precisely where she's going as she leads the way down through the corridors. She never stumbles on the vines—although since she's still leading Sarge by the hand, she has to stop to help him up more than once—and she slips through seeming dead ends as if it should be obvious that a path lies beyond the curtains of dense foliage.

Ioane walks behind the two reunited childhood friends, trying keep track of where they're going and how she might retrace the path if she needed to. She's puzzled by Dr. Kiely's presence here, even with the partial explanation. If nothing else, *Wyndi's* reaction to the woman is a good indication that it is, in fact, Dr. Kiely herself and not some bizarre new Novan trick. The kitten isn't good at being *subtle* when Sarge is in danger.

With that in mind and no reason to have more than her usual level of cautious alertness underneath the surface, Ioane is content to follow along and wait for the rest of the explanation. It's a pleasant change that one of the misadventures she and her Wing-Sergeant so often find themselves on has come with finding a friend they'd thought dead—and amusing to no end watching the young man literally tripping over himself because of that.

She's seen Sarge flustered before, but never quite to this extent.

"I remember this place being a bit of a maze," Ioane says finally, dusting herself off after having squeezed through the latest vine-choked doorway. "But with the plants cutting so many of the paths off like they do it's more like a labyrinth. I keep losing track of where we should be— we're down near the main geothermal pumping station now, though, aren't we?"

"We've done our best to *make* a labyrinth out of it," Dr. Kiely replies. "But ye be right. We ain't far from home now."

"Why in the stars are you living down in the basement when there's perfectly good living quarters up above?" Sarge wipes beads of perspiration from his brow.

"Warmer, safer... we have our reasons."

"I don't remember you being this cryptic, Reba."

"I've had reason to learn. Besides, ye'll be hearing the whole story soon enough."

"You've been saying that for an hour now." Sarge teasingly nudges Dr. Kiely's arm. "Just how much further is this lair of yours?"

"Ye still haven't learned to be patient, have ye?" Dr. Kiely laughs brightly. She stops and leans against a wall near a seeming dead end.

"I'm not so good at that myself," Ioane interjects. She looks around at the vine and flower-covered walls of the corridor, trying to align what she's seeing with her memories. "Am I right to think we're there?"

Dr. Kiely nods, then pushes a thick curtain of jasmine vines aside to reveal a door. She taps a hidden keypad behind the hydroponic growtubes holding the roots of the jasmine vines along the wall, then beckons for them to follow her. "Nyx!" Ioane hears her call as soon as she's through the door, "I'm back and I brought someone to meet ye!"

Ioane follows her sergeant in, the curtain of vines falling back across the opening behind her. The room inside is spacious, warm, and filled with well-maintained flowering tropical plants. Unlike the rest of the outpost, the floors are neatly cleared and none of the vegetation seems to have been allowed—or perhaps *encouraged*, Ioane now wonders—to grow out of control. Monitor screens showing different areas of the outpost have been installed along one of the walls in some semblance of a technological control center. Assorted equipment scavenged from other parts of the outpost is set up elsewhere amongst the plants, including a basic meal-preparation setup and some sort of makeshift medical station.

A Florivan in a casual ruby-toned tunic and matching loose-fitting trousers comes over from behind a hanging screen of additional jasmine vines which partitions off the innermost portion of the room. Unlike Wyndi, they're a fully grown adult: human-sized with smooth silver-striped inky-blue skin and neatly half-braided silver hair on their head instead of the all-over coating of fur. Ioane can't tell precisely how old they are, but she has the impression that they're young, somehow. Curiously, both of the Florivan's right arms are missing; they bear significant scarring along the same side of their face and neck.

The Florivan greets Dr. Kiely with a relieved hug, wrapping their silver-tufted tail around her in place of the missing arms. They're roughly the same height as her, if the fullness of the large catlike ears atop their head is counted.

"I was beginning to worry, Reba," says the Florivan, softly. "It usually doesn't take you so long to get back from the upper levels." Like all members of their species, their voice is lightly accented and carries wind-chime like after-tones.

"*Usually*, I ain't got a man in tow what can't go ten meters without tripping." She glances back to Sarge with a smirk as she says this. He rolls his eyes in response.

"I see your point." The Florivan's lower two eyes turn his direction as well, although their third one stays focused on Reba's face. "So, our visitors turned out to be friendly after all? I can see that you're right about them being human."

"Oh, better than that, Nyx!" Dr. Kiely laughs brightly and makes a wide sweeping gesture to Sarge. "This be my Julian, come by accident to rescue us!"

"*The* Julian?" The Florivan—Nyx, apparently—laughs. "The one you always talk about? I almost can't believe it."

"The very same! Along with Major Ioane from his squadron and—" Dr. Kiely pauses, taking on a teasingly exasperated tone. "And where's ye wee beastie gone now, Julian? They're just as bad as *ye* are for getting lost."

"I'm not *that* bad, am I?" Sarge whistles towards the vine curtain. "I swear they were on my shoulder a second ago."

"You are, Sarge—don't try to deny it." Ioane shakes her head. "Heaven help the poor captain who gets *you* for a Navigator."

Nyx flicks their ears curiously. "I thought Reba said you were a pilot?"

"Well, I am, but—"

Wyndi pops out of the vines as a bouncing silver streak. They chatter and squeak excitedly as they bypass all of the humans and scamper up onto Nyx's shoulder.

"Why, hello there, little one!" Nyx makes a bell-like trilling sound as they accept the kitten's enthusiastic greeting cuddles. "You're *awfully* young to have chosen your Navigator already, aren't you?" They turn their third eye to Sarge too, now. "An orphan?"

"Yes." Sarge nods solemnly. "Their parent was the jumper for a civilian cargo ship called *Equinox* that the Novans destroyed a few years back—Iolite Mereday, if you knew them, from Elder Marine's household. I... couldn't do anything for them, when I found them, but they gave their kitten to me to look after."

"I see... I'm afraid I didn't know them, but the loss is felt all the same." Nyx nods, their ears drooping momentarily. After a short silence, they look back to the kitten who's perched on their folded upper arm and snuggling against them. "What do you call this little one?"

"Their given name's Mirawynd." Sarge smiles. "We're thinking Cerulean for their public name—That's not official yet, though; I'm supposed to be presenting them to your Elders in a few months when *Surnia* makes port at Luyten's Star again."

"Wyndi!" says the kitten in question, purring happily. They nuzzle Nyx's neck for emphasis. "*Friend.*"

"Wyndi, then, if that's what you prefer, little cousin." Nyx chuckles, lightly stroking Wyndi's head and ears with their lower hand. They gesture with their tail towards the corner of the room where a sitting area has been assembled, complete with a small couch and an arm chair. "Come, I'll make us all some tea and we can share our stories."

Ioane follows them.

"Guests first!" Dr. Kiely takes Sarge's arm again to lead him over to the sitting area. "Ye'll have the shorter one, I'm sure, and I've already heard the half of it."

"Fair enough." He chuckles. "Well, we set out from *Surnia* this morning on a routine patrol…"

MIRAWYND CONTENTS THEMSELF WITH snuggling in the lap of their newly-discovered cousin while their human and Abi explain how and why the three of them came to the garden place. They aren't sure quite how Nyx is related to them, but they *know* this person is family somehow from the way they smell and feel to be around. Mirawynd also recognizes now that Nyx is the source of the family smell that their human's friend Reba has. They have the impression that Nyx protects her just like they protect their human. Mirawynd can't help but wonder if that means Reba is *special*, since in their experience only the best and warmest sorts of humans get to have someone like them as a guardian. If they knew the right words, they'd ask their cousin about that.

At the moment, they're simply enjoying the fact that Nyx seems to know *exactly* how to properly scratch the itchy places on their shoulders and ears where their fur is missing. Mirawynd always appreciates having someone to snuggle with and help them with their itchy spots. They're almost enticed to fall asleep from the warmth and attention, but for now they're keeping their ears pricked towards the story Abi is telling and their third eye open to make sure their human doesn't wander off without them again.

"—And that's about the size of it," they hear Abi conclude. "Our priority once we landed was to see if we could patch Sarge's darter enough that he'd be able to fly back, and take mine if we couldn't." She gestures vaguely with her teacup. "Seems I'll have to rethink that plan, now. If we can get one of our long-range or Relay radios working first, we'll be able to contact *Surnia* to come pick all of us up."

"I'm not sure how much luck you'll have with that, Major, even if you do make the repairs," says Nyx. "We've tried since we got here to call for help, but the signals can't get through the jamming field."

"Jamming field?" Abi exchanges a look with Mirawynd's human. "That'd explain a few things... you're saying the Novans set one up here?"

"Either somewhere on the far side of the planetoid or orbiting close by." Reba shrugs. "We ain't been able to figure out where for sure, but we've been told it's there."

"You've been *told*?" Abi asks.

"Aye." Reba exchanges a long look with Nyx and then sighs. "I... expect ye be wanting to know who told us?"

"And quite a few other things, Dr. Kiely." Abi sets down her teacup and lightly crosses her arms. "For example, why it seems to just be the two of you here? From what little you told us earlier, I thought you'd been part of a larger team—or are the rest all out gardening?"

Mirawynd isn't used to Abi using her version of their Aunt Jenny's "unamused person in charge" tone so much. Usually, she saves that for special occasions, like when their human has done something terribly stupid and dangerous and needs someone to point it out to him. It's confusing to hear her talking that way now, since as far as Mirawynd can tell, their human *isn't* in danger at the moment.

"There were eight of us," says Nyx. There's a sadness in their tone that wasn't there before. They turn all three eyes down to Mirawynd, as if avoiding the gaze of the humans. "Reba and I are all that's left."

Mirawynd doesn't understand the conversation entirely, but they do pick up on their cousin's change in mood. They make a point of nuzzling closer into the one of Nyx's hands that's petting them and purring more loudly—the purr, after all, is the sound of affection and reassurance.

"Shuttle accident?" Mirawynd's human asks.

"Novans." Reba sighs sadly. "*Psiloscops* dropped our shuttle off about a day's journey from here... The ship had just jumped away from us, and Nyx here were still setting the Drive up in the shuttle's cargo bay to bring us the rest of the way when the Novans came out of the black and attacked us—and us being clearly marked as a non-combatant vessel, at that."

"We've learned over the years that the Novans don't seem to care whether the ships they attack actually belong to the Defense Fleet or not." Mirawynd's human shakes his head. "But I thought *Psiloscops* was a Fleet ship?"

"It were," says Reba, "but our team had a civilian shuttle of our own to use."

Abi raises an eyebrow. "Oh?"

"Because of me," Nyx explains. "I'm not... well, I hadn't *officially* decided if I wanted to volunteer for the Fleet at the time. Even though I was borrowing one of the Fleet's Nav trainees to get us here, I couldn't be running the Drive on a Fleet vessel."

"That makes some sense," Abi replies.

"I'd worked out here at Mayview for a few months after I was released from my apprenticeship—up until the evacuation orders came out—and then I'd stayed on with the gardeners at Horizon Prime Station after that," Nyx continues. "When Dr. Monroe put together the assessment team, he asked if I'd be willing to come back with him as a civilian consultant, since the hydroponics setup here is integral to the outpost's life support systems and no one else who was familiar with it was available... and having *me* with them would give the team the option of leaving earlier than planned if they needed to."

Abi nods lightly. "Having you and your Navigator around to run a shuttle with the Quantum Space Drive for the team would make things easier, yes. So you got ambushed after *Psiloscops* left... then what?"

"They nearly destroyed us." Nyx absently continues to pet Mirawynd's ears with their lone upper hand as they talk. "One of the shots that hit us started a fire in the cargo bay I was sealed in to run the Drive from... I was injured, but I managed to get us into the Strange and stay conscious long enough to make the jump here—and that's the last thing I remember."

Mirawynd makes a point of squeaking softly through the bell-like rumble of their purr and nuzzling their cousin's hand again. The sad, faraway tone of Nyx's voice is, to their mind, a very clear sign of someone who needs comforting.

Nyx makes a soft trilling sound of acknowledgment back to them while Reba picks up the story.

"Dr. Monroe and I had our hands full with saving Nyx's life," she says, "so I didn't pay much attention to anything else when we first landed the shuttle. We were busy in the outpost's infirmary operating on them for *hours*. I ain't sure of the specifics of what went on when the rest of the team found the two Novans what were already here, or for a while after that. I weren't able to leave Nyx long enough to meet them until the third or fourth day after we arrived."

"There were Novans *here*?" Mirawynd's human's eyes widen.

"Aye—Not that we even knew that's what they were, since nobody'd ever seen one in person before and they were disguised as humans. They said they'd gotten left behind in the evacuation." Reba stares down into her teacup. "No one suspected—the others were too *smitten* with them to question their story, if ye know what I mean."

"I've... met... a Novan or two." Mirawynd's human awkwardly rubs the back of his neck. "I know what you mean."

"Ye *have*?"

"He *dated* one a while back." Abi shakes her head, holding back a laugh. "And only lived to tell the tale because Wyndi's overprotective of him—and I wasn't affected by her and helped them stage an intervention."

"*Julian*. Really?" Reba rolls her eyes dramatically. "It *would* be ye that a spy went after..."

"Well... We're not telling that story right now, are we?" Mirawynd's human asks in his most sheepishly hopeful tone. "I'd rather hear the rest of yours first."

"I'm sure ye would—but don't think I'll forget to pester ye for all the embarrassing details of it later." Reba gives him a good-humored nudge.

"*I'll* be glad to tell you all about it if he leaves anything out, Dr. Kiely." Abi picks her teacup back up and takes a small sip. "I did think there was something off about that one from the start, you know—aside from Wyndi hissing and carrying on whenever they saw her, I mean. Most everyone else didn't even notice it. If the Novans you met here were disguised the same way, it's no wonder your team was fooled."

Mirawynd looks up to her with a questioning squeak at the mention of their name. From what little they've been paying attention to of the conversation, they think she must be talking about one of the hungry monsters made of pinkness and teeth that they've had to protect their human from. They only ever hiss at predators, after all.

Nyx looks up curiously to Abi now. "You're like Reba, then, Major? Somewhat immune to whatever it is the Novans use to charm folks?"

"As much as a human can be," says Abi. "That's what we learned after a few of the Fleet's jumpers helped me catch Sarge's Novan girlfriend, at least. Turns out humans like me who don't experience romantic or sexual attraction in the first place are harder for them to fool. I can't see through their disguises like Florivans can, of course, but they can't mesmerize me all the same."

"That... does explain a lot." Reba sighs softly and folds her hands together in her lap. "I be pretty solidly demi-attractional, meself, and I were the only human on the team what weren't affected by the ones here—though that may be more because I had me hands full keeping this one alive."

"For which I am grateful." Nyx stops petting Mirawynd and reaches over to set a hand on Reba's folded-together ones for a moment.

Since Reba is sitting on the small couch between Nyx and Mirawynd's human and she seems to be the same sort of upset that their cousin has been since all of them started talking, Mirawynd takes it upon themself to scoot over into her lap now and pat one of her hands. When she looks down to them, they make a comforting squeak and nuzzle her hand.

"What's this?" Reba lets out a small, awkward laugh. "I thought ye were keeping Nyx company."

Mirawynd looks up to their cousin with a swish of their tail and makes the same sort of squeak again, hoping that *they* will be able to understand. They don't have the right words themself.

Nyx smiles at them and pats them on the head briefly before looking back up to Reba. "Wyndi is concerned about you because of the undertones in your voice and wants to know if you need cuddles for reassurance that you're safe now. Kittens are perceptive like that. Their instincts say that cuddles fix everything."

"Ye never grow out of that instinct, do ye?"

"Not really." Nyx shrugs.

Reba hesitates, then gives Mirawynd a gentle pat on the head. "I'm fine, Wyndi, dear, but ye can sit with me if ye want all the same."

Mirawynd takes this to mean that she *does*, in fact, want to be snuggled with. They nuzzle her hand again and then make a point of curling up in her lap like a soft silver ball. They're not particularly tired at the moment, but their usual napping position seems appropriate and comfortable. They're most content with how warm Reba's lap is, too.

"So," Abi asks, "what happened, then, with the rest of your team?"

"The devils learned enough to have done with us." One of Reba's hands starts absently stroking Mirawynd's fur as she talks. "I didn't see for meself what they did to the others, only the remains..." She trails off for a moment, a near-imperceptible shudder running through her body. "If I hadn't moved Nyx to one of the garden rooms while they were recovering, we'd both be prisoners of the Novan Empire now instead of sitting here having tea with ye."

"I'm not sure I follow, Reba," Mirawynd's human says.

"At the time, the room where the locals had grown their most tropical sorts of plants were the warmest place here," she explains. "We'd gotten Nyx stable, but they were still in torpor to heal—ye probably know how bad getting chilled is for folks what are barely warmblooded in the first place?"

"I'm aware..." Mirawynd's human looks over to them and briefly reaches over to scratch their ears. They purr a little louder in response. "But if the Novans killed the others, why would they want to take the two of you prisoner?"

"According to them?" Reba shakes her head. "They had a 'capture at all costs' order out for Florivans, since the Fleet can't get anywhere without them running the Drive... and had an interest in studying *me* to find out why I could resist their tricks."

Mirawynd's human and Abi share a look and a nod of understanding.

"That lines up with what we've seen," says Abi. "So, how'd y'all manage to escape, then?"

"*Jasminum sambac.*" Nyx gestures towards the fragrant white-flowered vines hanging on the inner part of the room.

"What?" Abi sounds utterly confused.

"The two of them cornered me while I were checking on Nyx," Reba explains. "Then, right in the middle of their 'ye be prisoners, come quietly or ye'll suffer' speech, the one got all giggly and the other started *ranting* about how this place were driving them crazy and it were just as well they'd be able to use us as an excuse not to have to be the ones to hack out all of the plants—at which point, since they weren't paying attention and I keep a neural pulse stunner in me work bag anyway..." Reba shrugs, but Mirawynd feels her hand quiver where it's resting on their head. "Well, long story short, I've got the both of them down the hall in cryostasis, all wrapped up and set with farm-rigged physioscanners to gather information about their biology on the off chance what someone friendly ever showed up to rescue us."

"Along with a number of their comrades who've come looking for them," Nyx adds. "Once I came out of torpor, we were able to confirm that the pollen and fragrance of most Earth-origin plants have intoxicating or psychoactive effects on Novans. Every now and again another one shows up to investigate this place..." They pause, glancing over to Reba. "...And winds up joining Reba's collection. We're fortunate that so far we've had room to store them all."

"That explains the jungle, then—and why you were so suspicious of us." Mirawynd's human rubs at his beard. He sounds very pleased with himself for coming to this conclusion.

Nyx nods, hesitating. "I'll be forever grateful that Mayview's botany team had decided to leave everything running when we evacuated." Their eyes turn downwards for a moment. "I've rearranged all the plantings and encouraged them to overgrow and slow down anyone who comes to bother us. We haven't been able to do anything about the communications blackout, though, since their jammer's not where we can get to it... and they made a point of destroying what was left of our shuttle before they came after Reba."

"Which explains why the two of you weren't able to leave once you'd recovered enough to be able to run the Drive and jump back somewhere with people," Abi comments thoughtfully.

"It does at that," Nyx says. That particularly sad tone is back in the edge of their voice, although Mirawynd doesn't understand why.

"Well," says Abi, returning to her usual cheerful self, "my darter should be fully charged by now—I can deal with that jamming station once we sort out where it is. We'll get the two of you back to civilization before you know it!"

"I'll be grateful for that." Reba continues lightly stroking Mirawynd's fur. "I can still hardly believe ye've come... it feels like we've been alone here for *ages*."

"I'm glad we're the ones to find you, Reba." Mirawynd's human wraps his arm around her shoulders. "I'm just sorry you had to wait so long to be rescued."

Reba leans into him with a sigh. "It'll be nice to be back from the dead."

Mirawynd looks up to the two humans now and makes a questioning trill. Their human has said that Reba is his friend. All the same, he's not usually so quick to be touch-forward with other humans—at least, not with ones who don't end up being a *problem* sooner or later. After a moment to think it over and consider his behavior in the past, Mirawynd scampers up to the back of the couch and then along their human's arm and up onto his head, squeaking rapidly down at him the whole time.

It's not that they don't like Reba, but Mirawynd *certainly* doesn't appreciate people who make their human act weirder than usual and leave them to share Abi's nest instead of his at night. They don't understand *why* that happens, but they're keenly aware that it does—and that they don't like the prospect of leaving him alone for very long, much less overnight. He usually gets into trouble when they're not there to protect him.

"Wyndi!" Their human tries to bat their pointedly swishing tail out of his face. "Why do you always do this—"

"—*Mine.*" Mirawynd locks eyes with Reba, as if issuing a challenge. Their tail swishes pointedly to match. Really, they just want her to understand that their human is under their protection and they're not willing to share his attention with just *anyone.*

"Is he now?" Reba asks, almost laughing under the seriousness of her tone. "Nyx, dear, how do I tell the wee beastie he were mine *first*?"

"They're old enough that they probably understand you, but I doubt they'll care." Nyx stifles a giggle. "Kittens tend to get a bit *protective* of their guardians."

Abi laughs outright. "Protective is an understatement. How many times have they saved your life now, Sarge?"

"Including this morning?" Mirawynd's human rubs at his beard thoughtfully for a moment, then shrugs. "Enough that I've stopped counting."

"Well, then, it seems I owe them for taking such good care of ye." Reba smiles and offers her hand to Mirawynd. "Ye said we be *friends*, Wyndi, remember? I promise I ain't taking the silly man away from ye."

Mirawynd considers this for a moment, then squeaks contentedly. "Re-ba *friend*." They climb back down from their human's head and scamper over to Reba's shoulder so they can hug her neck. They've decided that they might be open to keeping her. She is quite a warm human, after all.

While Reba is learning the finer points of how Mirawynd likes their ears to be scratched, Abi stands and looks to Nyx.

"Well, that's settled. So about that jamming station..."

NYX YRITAL DOUBLE-CHECKS THE SET OF STRAPS holding them securely to the rear seat of Major Ioane's darter. They're not an anxious person by nature, but they'd heard enough about the Defense Fleet's darter pilots and the crafts they fly while they were still working at Horizon Prime Station to be a touch apprehensive. Reba, too, has told them more than a few stories from her residency about the sort of wounds she'd had to treat among these pilots.

Still, somehow, despite everything they'd been told, Nyx has found themself agreeing to fly with the Major. They're still not entirely sure *why* they said yes, but one way or another, it's happened.

Major Ioane flips the switch to lower the polyglass canopy of her darter and seal it into place. The thick, translucent bubble of it completely encloses the two of them and marks its airtight sealing with a soft hiss and several clicks. She turns around to look back at the nervous Florivan sitting in the copilot's seat behind her. "You got the seat restraints secured okay, Nyx?"

"I did, yes." Nyx checks them again, just for good measure. Thankfully, they seem to still be secure. "Have I *mentioned* that I've never flown in one of these contraptions before?"

The Major laughs in a way that makes her dark eyes sparkle and turns back around to double-check all of her flight preparation displays. "Twice now, I think! No worries, you're safe as can be—*Sarge* is the one who forgets to account for gravity when he lands, not me, you know."

"That's... good to know." Being sure that they're fully strapped into the copilot's seat gives Nyx only a small boost to their sense of security, but it does help. At least they know they won't go floating up at an inopportune moment.

"Besides! We'll be back in an hour or so—less, even, if we manage to find this jamming station or whatever it is soon."

"Again, I'm not sure how much help I'll be..." Nyx hesitantly begins to say. "Or why you invited me along..."

"Well! I have a Florivan friend or three, you know, and I've worked with them enough to know there's a pretty good chance you *can* help—" Major Ioane pauses mid-sentence to clear a preflight checklist and send her code to open the hangar's doors. Nyx can see the pilot's face and part of her displays reflected in the polyglass of the canopy above her. She's still all cheerful excitement, if her expression is any indication. "—Anyway, your eyes can pick out things mine can't, for sure, and you've got that... oh, 'sense of stuff in space' whats-it. If my sensors can't spot the thing through all of the interference out there, *you* might still be able to get an impression of where to look."

"And here I thought I was just coming along to keep you company and give Reba a chance to be around someone who *isn't* me for a change." Nyx finds themself smiling as they absently readjust the folds of their empty right sleeves. They're not sure why, but the Major is beginning to remind them of their parent's Navigator. They decide it must be all the cheerful practicality—although there's a notable difference in the distinct lack of horrible puns from this human so far.

"Well... I'd say it might be a small added bonus that neither of us has to sit around being awkward with the recently-reunited childhood sweethearts? They get to catch up, we get to sort out this jamming station... Two birds and all that." Major Ioane chuckles softly, making a gesture towards their friends. "I figure Wyndi's more than capable of keeping the two of them out of trouble for an hour."

Nyx genuinely laughs at that. "Considering what Reba's told me about your Sergeant, I'm not surprised you think a *kitten* is more likely to stay out of trouble."

"Remind me when we get back to make him tell you the full story about how he *found* Wyndi—that's Sarge's trouble-magnet streak in a nutshell if anything is." Major Ioane shakes her head, then pulls down the bar on her flight headset's microphone. "All right, aside from my long-range radio and relay connections, everything's checking clear. We're ready for takeoff, 'Mayview Control'. I'll keep in touch."

"*We'll be standing by,*" Nyx hears Potts call back over the short-range radio. He waves from the wing of his own damaged darter, where he and Reba are sitting. The small silver fluff of a Florivan kitten on his shoulder waves too.

"Good, Sarge—stay out of trouble."

"*Don't I always?*"

The Major laughs instead of answering and engages her darter's anti-gravity takeoff gear. The little spacecraft rises up slowly through the shimmering atmosphere containment bubble and the open hangar doors. The doors slide neatly shut again almost as soon as the darter has cleared them.

"Launch successful, Mayview Control," she says as she turns the darter towards the planetoid's upper atmosphere and her maneuvering engines kick in with a roar. "I'll check in like we scheduled."

"*Confirmed, Major—to immortality!*" The younger pilot's voice is overlaid with static now.

"Forward to immortality!" Major Ioane echoes cheerfully, then flips up the microphone bar on her headset. "And now we get down to business."

"Do you think your short-range radio is going to be enough for this?" Nyx asks. They're distinctly concerned about the possibility of losing contact altogether.

"It worked well enough when we were landing earlier." She shrugs lightly. "As long as I can get those hangar doors to open for me again when we're ready to land, we'll be fine. Besides, Sarge will be able to figure out how to open them manually if he needs to. He's clever like that."

"Ah."

The darter continues to rise further and further from Mayview, gaining speed all the while. Soon, they've completely cleared the atmosphere and pulled into a low orbit. Nyx looks out at the planetoid below them and the expanse of black and stars all around. They lightly set their upper hand against the cool polyglass bubble of the darter's canopy. It's been so long since they were properly out in space that the sight of it all takes their breath away.

"It *is* nice seeing this from above again..." they say after a few moments, looking back towards the Major's reflection in the canopy. "The view of the stars from Mayview is good, but with the haze layers from the atmosphere, it's just not the same."

"Glad you're up in the sky again?"

Nyx finds themself smiling. "Glad I came with you."

After making another round of checks to be sure all of the darter's systems are functioning as expected, Major Ioane cracks her knuckles and glances back to Nyx. "So," she asks, "did your 'guests' give you *any* clues as to where this jamming station is, or whether it's more than one?"

"From what Reba heard when the one was ranting, all we really know is that there *is* one here. We've..." Nyx hesitates. "Well, I'm sure you can understand us not really wanting to run the risk of waking any of them to ask..."

"I can, yes." Major Ioane nods, then chuckles softly to herself. "For what it's worth? I doubt you would have learned much from them even if you did. In my experience, Novans don't interrogate well to begin with."

"I'd... imagine not." Nyx isn't quite sure they *want* to ask what her experience with that is at the moment. They gesture out towards the stars vaguely. "My guess is still that we're looking for a satellite of some kind."

"We'll do a sweep of the surface too just to be sure, but I'd agree. If it was going to be on the surface, the best place I can think of to put something like that is up at the top of one of Mayview's observation towers—and you said you and Reba checked there?"

"We've checked the whole complex twice." Nyx nods, even though they know the Major isn't looking at them now. "I've done my best to watch for satellites passing over the main dome over the years... I'm afraid I'm not as skilled with keeping track of such things as some, but I'm sure there's at least four or five objects up here in orbit that aren't natural."

"Well, that's a start." Major Ioane flips a few analog switches on her control panels. "Plan is, we do our orbital sweep first. Keep an eye or two down on the surface as we go, though. If we're lucky, anything that *is* down there is on the surface instead of underground so we'll stand a chance of finding it."

"Works for me." Nyx is glad the Major knows what she's doing. They've managed over the years with Reba to keep things running and stay reasonably safe, but they were never trained for things like this. It's more of a relief than they could have imagined to have the two pilots now to help them.

"Oh! Do let me know if you start feeling spacesick or anything," Major Ioane adds after a minute or two. "Darter flight takes a bit of adjusting to for most folks—not that I'm planning to do anything *fancy* or go at full speed at the moment, but still."

"I'll keep that in mind." Nyx nods, turning their gaze out at the planetoid again. They've never been the sort to get spacesick at all—at least, not in the same way humans do—but they appreciate the warning. "I should be fine, Major. It's been *years* since I was in microgravity at all, but I'm comfortable enough at the moment."

The Major is silent for a while, and then chuckles. "You're probably better suited to the way this bird handles than *I* am, now that I think of it. I've taken Celadon out on a jaunt or two before to show them what darters are like and such—if I remember right, they said it was 'exhilarating, and about the closest thing a human could come up with to match the experience of being caught in a rough part of Quantum Space.'"

"I take it you were showing them the *full* capabilities?"

Major Ioane turns back to them with a grin. "I was."

"I think I can see what they meant, then." Nyx can see a touch of the exhilarating aspect already, with how swiftly the small craft is moving. Their tail waves curiously as they consider that they're not the first Florivan she's flown with. "This Celadon is a friend of yours, then? Your ship's jumper or something?"

"No, that's Indigo—also a friend, but far less willing to get into a darter with *anyone*. Celadon's with *Aegolius*. Their Navigator is involved with my squadron's mechanic, and they've been cross-training Sarge for Nav ever since Wyndi took custody of him... so we've all gotten to be pretty good friends." Major Ioane pauses, shaking her head with a self-deprecating chuckle. "I'm forgetting my manners, Nyx, aren't I? It's probably more proper I call them 'Elder' around you."

"Ah! *That* Celadon." Nyx can't help laughing. In hindsight, they should probably have guessed who she was talking about more quickly. Who else but the Fleet's Elder, Celadon Toreval? They're the same person who's notorious for persuading the rest of the Florivan Council of Elders to allow them and their followers to "defect" from their neutral and pacifist people so the Defense Fleet could have jumpers to run their ships' Quantum Space Drives.

"I take it you know them?"

"We've only met once that I remember, but my Nida's friends with them—and I *certainly* know their reputation. Elder Celadon being willing to get into a scary sort of flying machine like this with you more than once doesn't surprise me at all."

"I wouldn't call the bird *scary*..." Ioane chuckles as she pauses to adjust her trajectory. "...Although you wouldn't be the first who has. The girls and I were around back at the beginning of all of this to show them off for the Alliance diplomats—I'm sure you've heard how they thought humans were *nuts* as a species for even dreaming up a craft like this?"

"Vaguely? I think Reba mentioned it once when she was trying to explain what her residency was like." Nyx shrugs. Most of the stories Reba has told them from when she was in medical school are inevitably about her best friend the aspiring darter pilot getting himself injured during training.

"It was a surprise to all of *us*, of course," Major Ioane continues, "that neither of these two big 'ancient galactic powers' who were taking us on as a junior ally had ever considered using live-piloted craft to counter the Novan strikers in the first place."

Nyx remembers now what Reba always says in her stories: humanity's allies are advanced enough to have less personally dangerous ways of defending themselves like drones and functional ranged weaponry… and have more of a proper sense of self-preservation as a whole than any human darter pilot is born with. Having remembered that, Nyx also finds themself reminded of the sturdy but *tenuous* nature of the craft they're strapped into and the delight their new acquaintance who is flying said craft seems to take in her work. It's not an entirely comforting set of thoughts.

"Anyway! We had a few T'irsh-fel observers who were volunteered by their Admiralty to fly with each of our wings of test pilots for some of the demonstrations—since even a Prelvee *male* is a bit too big to comfortably fit into the seat you're in, and the Alliance needed to know what we were capable of for strategic purposes." The Major glances back at Nyx with that same grin again. "You should be happy to hear that I hold the distinction for being the only pilot who didn't have their observer pass out from terror at some point during all of that."

"Do I *want* to ask why yours didn't?" Nyx finds themself raising all three eyebrows.

Major Ioane shrugs, still grinning as she turns back to her controls. "Jury's still out on that, Nyx—best guess is that it worked out better because my observer was the closest thing the T'irsh-fel have to a thrill-seeker. Well, that and the fact that I was the only one of us 'demonstrator hosts' who wasn't creeped out by having a telepathic copilot and consented to let her fully link up and experience the mock-combat maneuvers against her Admiralty's drones from my perspective."

"I can see how that would help..." Nyx is about to say something else, then pauses, their ears swiveling around as they try to focus on the tonal sensations of the planetoid and its moons and everything else between them and the familiar feelings of the distant stars. They close their eyes. "I think I've gotten my sense of the stars oriented now, Major. Do your sensors show any satellites around us?"

"Yeah, two so far. Closest's off to starboard and planetary north—about 900 meters. We'll circle around and check that one first."

"Good." Nyx nods. "That's in line with what I thought was there."

"Say, as long as you're going to be my backup proximity scanner anyway," Major Ioane begins while she's readjusting her flight path, "if you happen to notice anything moving... well, *fast* and trying to line up with our tail, let me know *before* they're lined up, will you?"

Nyx is immediately alarmed by the implication. "You have a concern about Novan craft appearing?"

"Nyx, I *always* have a concern about strikers appearing on my tail—that's why I'm still alive! And since we ran into some in the neighborhood earlier and you've said they have a history of showing up around here..."

"...And you're planning to destroy their signal jammer, wherever it is..."

"Yes, and that! But generally, it doesn't hurt to be careful—and I *know* you'll be able to feel them, unless you think Wyndi only can because they're a kitten."

"Kittens *do* have strong instincts for knowing when they're in danger... but no, you're right, I should be able to warn you." Nyx grimaces lightly, staring back out towards the stars now. "Let's hope it doesn't come to that."

"Agreed."

Several minutes pass in silence while Major Ioane slows and maneuvers her darter to bring its speed and trajectory to match the nearby satellite. Soon, she's gliding right alongside it.

"Come in, Mayview Control," she calls over the radio.

"*—trol here. —ahead, Major.*" Potts' voice is still overlaid with static enough to have words drop out of the signal.

"We've got our first satellite." The Major taps through one of her keypads. "I'm sending you the orbit coordinates now to check against the outpost's database."

"*—coordinates confir—just a—to check.*"

"Standing by." She flips up her microphone bar and turns around halfway to look between Nyx and the geometric array of antennas and computer modules making up the satellite. "What do you think?"

"It looks... standard? I guess?" Nyx shrugs, not knowing what else to say. "I'm a *botanist*, Major. This sort of thing is a bit beyond my training. It's Thalassa you'd want for identifying a satellite just by looking at it, not me."

"Thalassa?"

"My littermate—they're the sort of engineer who's keen on things like that." Nyx gestures vaguely at the satellite.

The thought occurs to them for the first time that they may actually be able to *see* their littermate again soon, and the rest of their family. Thinking about that brings back all sorts of kittenhood memories. They find themself smiling softly even as their eyes lightly mist over from the complex mix of emotions. "They had little scale models of all sorts of satellites and space stations hanging in our cabin when we were apprentices, even."

"Let me guess," asks Major Ioane, clearly stifling a giggle, "and you had plants?"

"Naturally!" Nyx can't help grinning now. "Thalassa's yet to let me live down the time one of their smaller models got 'eaten' when its hanging string broke, too."

"Eaten?" Major Ioane turns her gaze to them again, raising an eyebrow.

"I had a particularly *large* pitcher plant growing in a pot underneath it at the time."

Major Ioane shakes her head, holding back laughter. "Of course you did. Well, if you like carnivorous plants, then I can't wait to introduce you to Penny—"

"—*Come in.*"

The Major is still chuckling as she pulls her headset microphone back into sending position. "Go ahead, Mayview Control."

"*Your satellite—firmed geosyn—cleared.*"

"You're breaking up a bit; this one's supposed to be here? Please confirm."

"*It's good—confirm. Don't go and—ock out the—ing to fix.*"

"I get it, Sarge, thanks. Stand by while we find the next one."

"*—Control stan—by.*"

Major Ioane goes back to her proximity readouts. "Looks like we've got a standard communications satellite of some kind here... so it *shouldn't* be the thing we're looking for. You have any thought where the next closest one is?"

"Hmm..." Nyx closes their eyes and falls silent for several minutes. "Possibly something above us and around... fifty kilometers or so to planetary south."

"Let's see... bearing 79 degrees?"

"About that, yes—forgive me, Major, it's been a while since I had to coordinate locations like this..."

"You're doing fine, Nyx. I'd probably be shaky trying to remember how to convert things into hex points if we were doing this the other way around."

The cheerful sincerity in her tone sets Nyx at ease. It's been a long time since they've been around humans aside from Reba, but they're glad that the people who've accidentally come to rescue them are nice. They can see themself easily becoming friends with this one, too, if given the chance.

"Ah! Got it on the radar now, right where you said!" Major Ioane says, "Hang tight, Nyx, I'll have us there in two shakes."

M ORE THAN HALF AN HOUR AND THREE MORE innocuous satellites later, Nyx and Major Ioane are still circling the planetoid in search of the Novan jamming station. They fill the space in between the satellites with genial conversation about Mayview itself and the acquaintances the two of them have in common from living there before the War. They're both quite amused to find that they had come within weeks of meeting no less than twice.

Then, as they're making their thirty-first orbit, Nyx's keen eyes catch a glimmer of light on the planetoid's surface through the layers of atmospheric haze.

"Say, Major? I think we might have something." They lean forward in their seat restraints to tap on her shoulder and gesture out the window in an appropriate direction. "Does the map you got from Mayview's database show anything down there near those craters? Oh... something like two or three hundred kilometers to the west of the landing lines."

"Nothing I remember, for sure..." Major Ioane takes a few moments to swing around and slow down to take a closer look and pulls up the approximate coordinates on her darter's guidance control system. "Ah! No, not unless it's something that was built after this map was compiled— which isn't likely if it was official. According to the map, that area's nothing but craters and emptiness."

"Well..." Nyx taps one of the four digits of their upper hand on the polyglass of the darter's canopy for emphasis. "To *my* eyes, there's some sort of odd shine at the center of that group of smaller craters. I know we were looking for a satellite... but could this be it?"

"I can't see it myself from this distance, but it might be!" Major Ioane switches over to her radio while she's changing course. "Mayview Control, come in if you can hear me! I think we may have found something."

"*—Say again?*" they hear over the radio, "*—static's—lot worse—barely—*"

"I said I think we found it, Sarge." The Major laughs. "And if you're getting more short-range interference, that might be a clue we're heading the right direction. Stand by."

Major Ioane takes her darter back down towards the planetoid's surface, flying in slow circles above the group of craters Nyx had indicated. "Scanner's clouded with interference too," she tells them, "It's not showing up on my radar at all, whatever it is."

"There!" Nyx points ahead of them towards the ground. "*That's* the shine I saw, at the center of those three boulders. Can you see it now?"

Ioane squints and circles around again, descending and slowing until the darter is hovering barely fifty meters above the planetoid's dusty gray soils. "It's... Ah! There's a glimmer or something, I think, if I stare at it long enough. Right between the boulders, like a heat-shimmer?"

"That's it." The silver tuft at the end of Nyx's tail dances excitedly. "To my eyes, that shimmer you're seeing is a large pointy object with something of an oil-slick *glow* to it."

"How pointy?"

"From this distance..." It takes Nyx a moment to come up with an appropriate analogy. "You know how Head Botanist Falstaff always insisted on growing kiwano melon vines somewhere in the outpost's gardens, even though the fruits have a tendency to burst when they're overripe?"

"Yeah—I got into so much trouble as a kid for leaving one of those little spike-balls under the pilot's seat in my Dad's shuttle long enough that it did that." Major Ioane stifles a laugh, then turns her tone of voice to something more serious. "So, that's what it looks like?"

"Yes, but about three times the size of this 'bird' of yours, if not a bit more."

"That's *got* to be it, then." Major Ioane takes the darter down within ten meters of the planetoid's surface and slowly circles the trio of boulders from a distance. "Okay, Nyx, I can see the edge of the shimmer a bit clearer now if I squint, but it looks like the sensors are still convinced we're looking at an empty patch of dirt. I'd say this is as close as I'm willing to take us in just yet. We're just outside pulse laser range, at the moment."

"It *is* there, Major." Nyx pauses, twitching an ear concernedly. "You think it might have weapons?"

"If the Novans put it here? I wouldn't be the least bit surprised." Major Ioane chuckles. "I know us darter pilots have a *reputation*... but it's the voice of healthy caution that keeps us alive."

"Ah. And your 'healthy caution voice' is telling you... what exactly?"

The Major gestures out in the general direction of the object she can't see. "That it's more a matter of how *well* the melon is armed than whether it is or not."

"...Ah."

"Now," she continues, "If it's just pulse lasers like they put on their strikers? I can deal with that! I dance through those all the time—but if it's set up to take a big chunk out of the planet when it's destroyed? That's a bit more of an issue."

"...I can see how it would be." Nyx begins absently straightening the silver tuft at the tip of their tail with their lower hand to keep it from twitching and showing how much of their earlier nervousness that thought has brought back. They know Major Ioane can't see the twitching, but they still feel a need to keep it contained. "What do we do about it, then?"

"Well, even if they say they can't see it, I've got all of my scanners and cameras focused that direction... and I have *you* here to describe what it actually looks like. I figure we compile as much information as we can, and then head back to Mayview to sort out a melon-removal plan."

"Nothing is ever simple in your work, is it?" Nyx does their best to hold back a nervous sigh.

"Not usually. To tell you the truth, Nyx, I get wary when things seem that way—it's usually the lead-in to an ambush."

"Ah..." Nyx can't decide what they think about how calm she seems about all of this. "What are the chances of you running into two of those in one day?"

Major Ioane laughs in that same bright, carefree way that seems to be her trademark and looks back to Nyx briefly with a knowing wink. "Trust me when I say you *don't* want to run the odds on that. Just focus on telling me about our friend the melon and let me do the strategic worrying, okay?"

"I see..." Nyx hesitates, then nods. Something in this human's voice makes them feel like they're safe with her, regardless of what's going on. They're not sure quite *why*, but it does. "Well, like I said, it looks a bit like a massive kiwano. The conical spikes are about the same size, proportionally, and randomly distributed across the surface. Each spike has what looks like a set of antennas poking out of it."

"Check. And it's at the center of those three boulders?"

"It is." Nyx shifts their position in the seat's straps to get a better view through the darter's polyglass canopy. "It looks like it might be suspended *from* the boulders, somehow? There's a gap underneath it, at least, and I can't be entirely sure from this distance, but I think I can see some sort of pillars or rods connecting the base to the boulders."

"Hm... well, that'll make targeting easier, at least."

"Aside from the spikes, the surface is smooth, and—" Suddenly, Nyx breaks off mid-sentence, swiveling their ears and turning in their seat to look out from the other side of the darter towards its tail. Something in their sense of the stars and space around them has *changed*, and they don't like it.

"What is it, Nyx?"

Nyx closes their lower two eyes and grows still, although their ears and tail are still twitching with nervous agitation and their third eye is fixed on the pilot's reflection in the darter canopy. "Major, you said to warn you if I felt anything small and fast-moving heading towards us?"

"Which direction? My proximity scanner is still jammed from the melon."

"Behind and above—just came out of orbit and turned our way."

Major Ioane nods and subtly changes her flight path to begin climbing from the surface while still making the same circles. "Thanks. Any idea how many?"

"More than one... I'd almost say from different directions—" Nyx opens their eyes long enough to twist around in their seat and look out in the appropriate direction again. "—But at least one that's diving towards your tail!"

"You can see it?"

"Yes!"

"It's yellow?"

"How did you know?"

"Just a guess!" Major Ioane forces a laugh as she pulls the darter up higher and increases its speed. "Hang on, Nyx, this is going to get a bit rough!"

Both of Nyx's hands tightly grip the armrest of the seat they're strapped into. Their tail curls around one of the support bars underneath it for good measure. They're not entirely sure if holding on will do much good if something happens, but it does allow them to ground themself and keep their rising panic inside.

Almost as soon as she's clear of the concealed object's vicinity, Major Ioane dives back down towards a wide crater in the planetoid's surface. She deftly twists her darter around in the process so that at the last possible moment, instead of crashing into the powdery grey rock of the crater's base, the darter glides effortlessly upside-down along it. With barely two meters of clearance from the surface, she skims along the contour of the crater at increasing speed all the way back up in a loop.

The pursuing Novan striker is in front of her when she reaches the top of the loop, just coming into the darter's range of attack. Two quick bursts from her main laser cannons, and the striker is spiraling down into the crater, a debris trail following it made of the fragments of one of its side engines. In the base of the crater a few moments later, a plume of debris and dust flashes up into the planetoid's thin atmosphere with a brief jet of fire.

Major Ioane continues her trajectory out of the layers of haze towards a high orbit and away from the suspected jamming station. "They come in packs, Nyx!" she calls behind her without turning to look. "Where are the other two?"

"Ah! Above us, bearing around... 145 degrees by fourteen?" Nyx returns to keeping their lower two eyes closed and the tufted tip of their tail securely gripped within the fingers of their lower hand. Their upper hand's fingers rest against their left temple to help them focus on absorbing all of the information their sense of space around them can possibly provide.

Major Ioane swiftly changes course, spinning the darter back so its canopy is facing out into space. "Aha! There they are!"

One of the strikers ahead of her breaks off just before the bursts of her laser canons hit their mark. The second one takes the brunt of the attack, crippled in a brief flash of fire and fast-moving debris spreading along its previous course and falling towards the planetoid's surface.

With the skillful motion of a dolphin swimming through a school of fish, the Major zips around the debris trail and out further from the planetoid. Her darter's external energy shield shimmers with auroras as the smaller bits of fast-moving particulate debris strike it and the shock wave from the brief explosion makes contact.

Having evaded Major Ioane's initial attack, the second Novan striker now goes on the offensive. It fires its pulse lasers, only to have her twist her wings at the last moment and avoid being hit. The two small craft continue to dance back and forth in acrobatic spirals and bursts of light as they trade shots, all the while staying high above the orbits of the scattered satellites.

In the back of their mind, frightened as they are, Nyx can't help but be amazed at Major Ioane's skills. To them, it seems almost as if the darter is an extension of her body—and her highly-tuned reflexes, they realize, are the only thing preventing the two of them from meeting the same fate as the striker whose debris she's still dodging periodically. This is not a pleasant realization in the slightest, but they force themself to focus on her deft hand with the small craft's controls rather than the danger they're in.

Just as it seems the Novan is gaining the upper hand and Major Ioane's status display is beginning to flash a "nearing low charge" warning light, Nyx feels something change in the area of space they're flying through.

"Major!" they call, "There's something else—"

Before Nyx can even finish their sentence, two powerful bursts of laser canon fire from different directions hit the Novan striker at precisely the right spots to destroy it outright. Major Ioane pulls up from the resulting explosion and billowing sphere of debris just in time to avoid being struck, save for one large fragment which clips the tip of her darter's left wing.

The Major laughs and twists her darter back into a steady posture and more leisurely speed as soon as she's clear of all of the debris. She taps a button on one of her console displays and pulls down the microphone bar on her headset. "About time y'all showed up!"

"—*Don't we—ow up?*" says one brightly accented voice over her short-range radio underneath the static.

"—*ought you'd—an assist—Abigail*!" calls a second voice, laughing.

Two more darters pull into formation on either side of Major Ioane's, matching her perfectly for course and speed.

Nyx is equal parts relieved and puzzled by this development, but more than anything they're still trying to keep all of their panic inside. They close all three of their eyes and slowly run the tuft of their tail through their fingers to straighten out the fluff of it and try to let the rhythm of the motion be a focus for calming themself. They tune their ear to the Major's voice, letting the pleasant tones of that overpower the memories of the last time they were in such immediate danger and wash away the sounds of flames.

"I'm grateful you weren't any later," they hear Major Ioane say to the voices on her radio, her tone of voice suggesting that all is well now. "Listen, girls, signal's not the best here and my radio's worse. Follow me down to Mayview and Sarge and I will explain everything."

"—*clear!*" calls the first voice.

"—*ith you—the way!*" the second chimes in.

"Now that's what I like to hear!" Major Ioane changes her course to head back down towards the outpost.

"...Friends of yours, I take it?" Nyx asks at last, finally able to relax a bit, although still with their eyes closed.

"The best of them!" The Major graces them with one of her signature 'all's well with the world' sort of laughs. "I knew they'd come looking for us eventually. They always do."

"That's a good kind of friends to have, Major." Nyx opens their third eye now and glances out the canopy at the two darters that have come into formation on either side of Major Ioane's. They can't see either pilot through the reflective coating on the outside of the canopy bubbles, but they're reassured somehow to know that each contains a friend of the Major's who will be able to help resolve the situation they've all found themselves in.

"They really are." Ioane's tone is soft, clearly denoting a deep fondness for the pilots in question. After a moment, she glances back over her shoulder. "You holding up okay back there?"

Nyx hesitates, still absently straightening the tuft of their tail and keeping most of their mind focused on making sure nothing else drops out of the black to attack them without notice. "I... will be able to re-center myself properly once we're on the ground again."

"Fair enough." Major Ioane smiles at them, but as she turns back to her displays she betrays a note of concern underneath her characteristic cheerfulness. "For what it's worth, Nyx, you're a good copilot. I owe you one for spotting those strikers early—and another for bringing you up into the mess in the first place."

"As long as we land in one piece and we will all be leaving together?" Nyx forces a chuckle. "I'd say we're even, Major."

"Okay, then. We're even." Her giggles at that are genuine and *warm* in a surprisingly comforting way. "Oh, Nyx?"

"Yes, Major?"

"I've been meaning to say," Major Ioane tells them in that warm, cheerful tone that reminds them so much of their parent's Navigator, "you can call me Abigail. You survived flying with me. That makes us *friends*!"

"Thank you." Nyx finds themself smiling back at her reflection in the darter's canopy. "Well, then, Abigail, my friend... do you think you can get us back on the ground *gently*? I'm not spacesick yet, but this is the closest I've ever come to it."

Abigail's reflection gives them a giggling salute. "One gossamer landing, coming right up!"

MIRAWYND IS PLAYING ONE OF THEIR FAVORITE games with their human and their new friend Reba: "run around the hangar and retrieve the shiny thing so one of the humans will throw it again!"

The shiny thing in play is a bit of crinkly golden foil rolled up into a ball. It makes the *best* sort of a sound when Mirawynd pounces on it, too. They're not sure where Reba found the foil, but they've been most pleased to chase after it.

When Mirawynd finishes extracting their prize from the box it's fallen behind on the far side of the hangar, they pause to shake the dust out of their fur before scampering back over to their human's darter. He and Reba are still sitting on the craft's wing, right where Mirawynd left them.

The bigger game at the moment is "wait for Abi and Nyx to come back," so the three of them have been playing in the hangar for a long time now. Mirawynd has done all of the scampering parts of the game themself—from what they can tell, their human and Reba are more interested in sitting on the wing and talking about things that aren't particularly interesting.

Mirawynd has also determined that Reba must be like them and get cold easily, since their human seems very keen on letting her sit close to him and has his arm around her shoulders to keep her warm. They can understand that, though; their human is *very* good at being warm and comforting. Since Reba is their friend now, they don't mind letting her borrow him like this for a while. It's nice having someone to watch him so he doesn't wander off while they're playing and get himself into trouble.

Mirawynd climbs up the side of their human's darter and onto the wing, carefully carrying their shiny foil ball in their lower pair of hands. They bounce into Reba's lap and offer the ball up to her with a cheerfully triumphant squeak.

"Aye, Wyndi, dear, I see ye found it!" Reba giggles lightly as she takes the ball from them. "And here I thought it were lost forever this time."

"Shiny!" Mirawynd agrees. "Again?"

"*Again*? I'd think ye'd be tired of playing fetch by now..." Reba tosses the ball back and forth between her hands.

Mirawynd watches its path intently, waving their tail in time with the motion and crinkling sounds of the ball.

They have learned that their new friend is better at ball-throwing than their human is. *Reba* can make the shiny thing fly all the way over to the other side of the hangar, if she wants to.

"You'd be surprised how long Wyndi's attention span is," Mirawynd's human remarks, *"especially* when something they consider 'shiny' is involved."

"Considering we've been at this for an hour now, Julian? I ain't all that surprised."

"Again?" asks Mirawynd, tapping one of their upper hands on Reba's elbow.

Reba catches the ball in one hand and pats them on the head with the other. "Fine, but it's *Julian's* turn to throw it for ye." She sets the ball in his hand. "See if ye can get it further than the end of the wing this time?"

"You know," their human replies with a laugh, re-crinkling the ball, "If you come up with another game to play with them, Wyndi'll change tacks pretty quick—" He pauses, pulling down the microphone bar on his headset and holding up a hand to let Mirawynd and Reba know they need to be quiet again. "Mayview Control here. Say again, Major? I didn't catch all of that over the static."

"*—Control.—friends—coming in!*" says Abi's garbled voice over his headset.

Mirawynd perks their ears up at the sound and bounces up to their human's shoulder to listen.

"If that means you're preparing to land, Major, then yes, go ahead."

Almost as soon as he says this, Mirawynd hears the sound of the big doors in the ceiling slipping open to reveal the shimmery field between inside and outside.

Within a few minutes of the doors being fully open, first Abi's darter and then two more land in the hangar.

"Ye *were* expecting company, weren't ye?" Reba asks, hesitant as she stands up and dusts herself off.

"We hoped so," Mirawynd's human replies. He waves broadly to the pilots of the three darters.

Abi is the first to get out. She stretches as she climbs onto her darter's wing and then reaches in to help Nyx out of the copilot's seat.

Mirawynd leaves their shiny ball with their human and excitedly scampers over to say hello to Abi and their cousin. By the time they've made it up onto the wing of Abi's darter, Nyx has mostly climbed out. Mirawynd squeaks a cheerful greeting and hops up into their cousin's lower hand to offer a welcome-back hug.

"Ah, hello, little one." Nyx raises them up and gives them a proper snuggle in return. "How did you know I needed some fuzzy reassurance after that flight?"

Mirawynd purrs happily and then makes a brief leap over to Abi's shoulder to give her a hug as well—and so they'll be out of the way while she helps their cousin climb down from the darter's wing, since Nyx only has hands on one side to steady themself and Abi only has the two to begin with to help them.

"See, Nyx?" asks Abi, once they're all on the ground, "what did I tell you? Safe and sound, and none the worse for wear!"

"Aside from that bit on the tip of your other wing that's missing?" Nyx gives Abi a knowing look of amusement.

"Well... That's hardly a scratch, as far as I care."

"I'm not sure I ever want to see what you consider 'damage', then, Abigail."

Abi chuckles warmly. "Take a good look at Sarge's darter later—that's more of the sort of thing we start worrying about. Now, come on." She offers them her arm. "I'll introduce you to my wing-sisters—they'll be happy to meet you, I'm sure."

Abi and Nyx join Mirawynd's human and Reba in the middle of the hangar. Mirawynd obligingly hops back to their usual place on their human's shoulder, now that they've properly greeted their friends. They look over to the other two darters curiously.

"Friends?" they ask, tapping on their human's cheek. Their tail waves expectantly. People who appear in darters are *usually* friends, after all.

"Who else?" he replies, reaching up to ruffle their ears.

Almost as soon as their human says this, the canopy of one of the two new darters opens and the pilot within hops out. She's the deeply tan sort of a human, with her hair neatly braided up and hidden beneath a carefully folded and pinned ivory headscarf. Mirawynd immediately squeaks in joy and scampers over to meet her. She hops down from her darter's wing with her usual flourish.

"Anna!" Mirawynd leaps up onto her shoulder and gives her neck a hug, nuzzling into the soft cloth of her headscarf for a moment. The familiar scent of rose-and-cedar soap is a welcome relief from the pond smell that's still clinging to their fur. This is, after all, another one of *their* pilots—and they've been wondering where she was all day.

"Hey, Wyndi! You know, we were *looking* for you earlier..." Anna laughs and gives their ears a gentle scratch while she walks over to the wing of the last darter. Its canopy has just risen. "Need any help with your copilot, Penny?"

Mirawynd squeaks excitedly, unable to stop their tail from swishing to match. Penny is their other pilot, and like Anna and Abi counts as "family" in their mind because she's been flying with their human for longer than Mirawynd can remember. Penny's the one who always lets them share the crispy edges of her waffles at breakfast time. They're happy to have most of their family all in the same place like they're supposed to be again.

"No," Penny calls back, "I think I can manage—just need to give him a minute or two to believe that we're on the ground." She climbs out onto her darter's wing and runs a pale, fingerless-gloved hand through her tight white curls to untangle them from her headset and pull them back into her usual pair of low, poofy ponytails. As usual, she's wearing the fancy tinted wraparound glasses that protect her pale, sensitive eyes from the lights of the world and help her see clearly.

By this time, everyone else has come over to join them at the side of Penny's darter.

"What's this about you having a copilot, Major?" Mirawynd's human asks.

"Well, now!" Penny sits down and dangles her legs over the side of the wing. "We weren't about to believe it when we got back to *Surnia* with the fledges and they told us that the two of you were last heard from under attack and had been presumed dead."

"Dead already?" Abi laughs. "We've only been missing for a few hours this time!"

"Monterrey and Saunders found nothing but debris when they went to answer your distress call, and enough of it was darter-trace-ish to convince them," Anna explains with a shrug. "Not enough to convince *us*, of course, but it's not their fault for being the sort to follow protocols."

"Ah, *that* explains it." Abi shakes her head.

"So naturally," Penny continues, "when Colonel Bell's wing finally got picked up, she cleared us to come check the only place Abigail'd have come if y'all *weren't* dead but couldn't get back to the rendezvous point for some reason. And we had the hunch that at least one of you had to have taken a bad enough hit to need to land somewhere and probably couldn't get back off the ground..." Penny trails off with a knowing grin and a vague gesture at her darter's cockpit.

"Sounds reasonable to me, but what's that got to do with—" Abi's eyes widen and she bursts out laughing. "Oh, *seriously*, girls? Tell me you didn't."

"We did!" Anna laughs, similarly grinning. "After all, anything that kept the two of you grounded enough to need a rescue would certainly be beyond *our* skill to repair if we managed to find you."

Mirawynd's human tilts his head with a confused expression. "What in the stars have you two gone and done this time?"

Mirawynd's ears catch a familiar sort of a groan coming from within Penny's darter. Ever the willing follower of their own curiosity, they scamper up onto the wing to investigate.

"What, Wyndi, don't *I* get a hello from you?" Penny teases as they pass by her.

Mirawynd pauses to scurry over along the wing and give Penny a brief hug so she doesn't feel left out before curiosity compels them to continue up the side of the darter and into the cockpit. They are surprised, but *most* pleased, to find that their pilots have brought their second-favorite human along for the adventure.

At the moment, he's sitting hunched over with his restraint straps undone and has one pinkish-pale hand set over his eyes. His shoulder-length golden-brown hair has escaped from its hair-tie and fallen into his face again. As usual, he's wearing the emerald green trousers and matching loose-fitting shirt that he always keeps partway unbuttoned and with the long sleeves rolled up past his elbows, along with the many-pocketed ivory work vest which is marked on the back with the same shiny design Mirawynd's pilots wear.

Mirawynd makes a soft trilling squeak of greeting and hops down onto the man's shoulder as gently as they can, since he seems to not be feeling well.

"Oh, now you show back up." He lets out a weak groan, not turning to look at them. "I searched the whole bloody *ship* for you, kitten. Where've you been hiding?"

Mirawynd waves their tail sheepishly and gives their friend a light pat on the hand and the most apologetic squeak they can muster. They hadn't *intended* to leave him all alone today, after all. They'd just left for a moment to rearrange their stash of shiny things before their human left on his patrol. Falling asleep in the cozy spot under the darter's rear seat had been an accident.

His other hand reaches up to gently pat them on the head. Mirawynd takes this as a gesture that he's forgiven them for the accidental abandonment.

"Come on, Rudy," Penny says, leaning on her elbows on the edge of the open cockpit. "We're on the ground now, and there's even a bit of *natural* gravity here! You can't tell me you'd rather stay in my bird all afternoon."

"I never should have let you talk me into getting *in* the bloody bird, Albright," Rudy mutters. "You fly like a drunken hummingbird with a death wish—you know that?"

"Aww..." Penny takes on her most innocent tone and lightly reaches out to nudge his shoulder. "I kept the acrobatics to a minimum like I promised, though, didn't I?"

"If that's what you call a *minimum*," Rudy replies, finally taking his hand off his eyes to shoot her a weakly barbed look, "it's no wonder I keep having to replace your bloody stabilizer coils."

Down on the hangar floor, Mirawynd can hear their human laughing. "I almost can't believe it. They really got *you* into a bird this time?" he calls up, sounding like he's standing right beside the wing now.

"Under *protest*," Rudy bellows back, haltingly doing his best to stand and climb out of the cockpit without falling or dislodging Mirawynd from his shoulder. "And on your account, no less, seeing as how if one of you had gone and gotten shot up or crashed again, it'd *have* to be you."

"I *might* have had a bit of 'engine trouble'," Mirawynd's human admits, offering a hand up to help the unsteady mechanic down from the wing.

"He's getting better, Rudy," calls Abi, chuckling. "He was only a *little* bit on fire when he landed this time!"

Rudy glances over to the side of the hangar where Mirawynd's human has left his damaged darter and the parts of it that have fallen off and are sitting on the floor now. "I don't know what I hate more, ladies—the fact that you coerced me into coming along on this fool's errand… or the fact that the bloody fool himself actually *did* need me to fix his mess again." He wobbles significantly as he tries to shoo all of the helpful hands away and stand on his own.

"All these years and ye still haven't gotten past ye space-sickness, have ye?" Reba asks through a stifled giggle.

"I've just spent the last *four hours* cooped up in that death trap with wings, and—" Rudy suddenly startles and looks Reba over with a questioning tilt of his head, as if he doesn't believe what he's seeing. "—And what the bloody stars are *you* doing here, Kiely? Last I heard, you were…" he trails off, looking between Abi and Mirawynd's human now for an explanation.

The only response he gets is a matched pair of cheerful shrugs.

"Dead?" Reba finishes for him.

"Yeah…" Rudy looks back to her now, wobbling slightly and reaching up to rub at his temple. "*That.*"

"If I be a ghost, mister Rudolph," says Reba, offering Rudy her arm with a wry grin, "I still be one with a good stock of remedies for vertigo—if ye don't mind a bit of a walk through our ghostly garden to get to them."

Rudy shakes his head, and once again seems to pale afterwards, but takes her offered arm. "I don't know why

I expected that this day would get *less* weird once we got here."

"Re-ba friend!" Mirawynd gives his cheek another reassuring nuzzle.

"An old friend, yes," Rudy tells them. After a moment, his eyes flicker over to Nyx. "Have we met?"

"We haven't," Nyx tells him with an amused swish of their tail. "Although, if you're the same mechanic Abigail was telling me about while we were flying, I believe I'm familiar with your household."

"If these ladies had a second mechanic, *I* wouldn't have been the one to come along, that's for sure." Rudy groans, digging around in one of his work vest's pockets for something with the hand that isn't clinging to Reba's arm for stability. "And since when are you the gossip, Ioane? I thought you left that to your sisters."

"Technically," Abi says, holding back a giggle, "we were gossiping about your husband's counterpart. *You* just happened to come up in the conversation by association."

"Ah. I should have guessed..." Rudy fishes a spare hair-tie out of his pocket and shakily hands it up to Mirawynd. "Is Dons a relative of yours, then?"

Mirawynd squeaks happily and gives his cheek another nuzzle before they set about gathering his hair back up and practicing the side braids their Entile Celadon taught them to make the last time their ships were in the same place. Helping Rudy get his hair to stay out of his face is one of their entile's favorite games. He really must not be feeling well if he's *asking* for Mirawynd to do something about it rather than making a show of being reluctant to let them practice.

"About four lines distant," Nyx tells him. "I've met them once, but I know them more by reputation than anything."

"They do have quite the reputation, don't they?" Rudy offers Nyx his free hand now, although it's still not-so-subtly shaking. "Elias Rudolph—if we're being formal, you can tack on 'of Elder Celadon's household' to that, but I understand the Council's Eldest also has a claim of some kind on me."

"Mine," Mirawynd adds, looking up to their cousin from the strands of hair they're busy untangling and waving their tail happily.

"Ah. Right. And Wyndi here does too."

"Nyx Yrital of Elder Caeruleus' line—the Eldest is my entile." Nyx takes his hand between their upper and lower one with a broad, cheerful smile. "I'd offer you a hug, cousin, but something tells me you wouldn't appreciate that at the moment?"

"Maybe after the ground stops trying to move under my feet."

Nyx's third eye glances over to Abi. "I'm not surprised it is, considering what I just went through myself."

"Oh, I don't know, Nyx," Abi quips, "I'd still say you make a pretty good copilot! Now, before we go off to pick kiwano melons and talk strategy, I have two more introductions for you: my wing-sisters, Pilot-Majors Anna Toussaint and Penny Albright." She gestures to each of them in turn. "Couldn't ask for a better rescue party."

"Welcome to Mayview," Nyx says, nodding their head softly. "We're grateful for your help."

"Aye." Reba pats Rudy's hand where it's still resting on her arm. "Now, assuming he cooperates, I'll be taking me patient here back to our nest so he can recover from whatever it is ye've gone and done to him. Come find me when ye be ready to show them me Novan-cicle collection, Nyx."

"Novan-cicles?" Penny asks, raising her eyebrows.

"It's a long story..." Nyx begins.

Mirawynd stays on Rudy's shoulder as Reba leads him off down the grape-vine-draped corridor, since they're not done braiding his hair yet and still feel guilty about leaving him behind this morning.

"So, Kiley, old friend," says Rudy. He's still leaning on Reba's arm for stability as he walks and doing his best not to trip on any of the vines, since his feet are already giving him problems. "What's a nice ghostly doctor like you been up to... *wherever* here is?"

"Oh, ye know how we ghosts be, Mister Rudolph." Reba laughs. "Haunting folks and gardening, mostly. And yeself?"

"Putting your boyfriend's bloody darter back together a thousand times, mostly."

"He ain't my boyfriend *yet*." Reba rolls her eyes amusedly for punctuation. "But thank ye for looking after him, all the same."

"I promised you I would, didn't I?" Rudy smirks at her, albeit still with the dulled-down voice he's been using since he got out of Penny's darter. "Granted, Wyndi here's pretty good at keeping him in line, when the both of them aren't off finding trouble to get into."

"So he tells me."

Mirawynd finishes the two hair-holding braids now and secures them together with the hair-tie. They tap on Rudy's cheek to let him know.

"Thanks, Wyndi." He reaches up with his free hand to pat them on the head, then stops walking as they come to the archway into the big dome area with the pond, taking hold of the edge of the arched doorway.

Reba stops walking too, looking up to him with concern in her eyes. "Ye *can* sit down if ye need to."

"I'll be fine—just... got a little light-headed again, that's all." He blinks a few times and lets go of the wall to rub at his temples. "Bloody mad pilots and their bloody acrobatics..."

Mirawynd gives his paler-than-usual cheek a small nuzzle and begins making their most reassuring purr. They're not sure why their friend isn't feeling well, but they do want to help.

"I did notice ye were forcing yeself to stay upright back there out of stubbornness." Reba raises an eyebrow. "Why in the stars did ye go and let them talk ye into coming along? I seem to recall we first met because ye needed to be sorted out so ye could at least tolerate being in a *shuttlecraft* for more than twenty minutes."

"Eh... mechanic's duty to his pilots and all that—and not wanting to have to fix one of Sarge's bloody patch-up jobs again." After another deep breath, Rudy slowly pats her hand as a signal that he's okay for walking again.

"Oh, is that all? Just ye sense of duty getting the better of ye?" Reba asks, leading him through the tangled maze of plants once more.

"Well…" Rudy lets out a weak chuckle, still leaning on her arm. "The fact that it's *Aegolius* that's dropping by in a few days to pick us all up didn't hurt."

"Not the ship ye came from?"

"Captain Brentwood couldn't break off from her patrol course any more than she already had because she had some other big rendezvous to make, so *Surnia*'s already out of darter range by now. The madwomen called in a favor or three to make arrangements." Rudy rubs at his temples again, but halfway smiles now. "Can't say I mind the temporary reassignment."

"Ah." Reba gets a teasing shimmer in the corner of her eye. "Julian told me ye went and married an *officer*. That'll be his ship, I take it?"

"It is. Of course he's told you…" Rudy sighs lightly, although whether to try to clear his head or out of exasperation, Mirawynd can't tell. "Sarge is even more of a bloody gossip than the *rest* of the Musketeers are."

"Well, now, Mister Rudolph! I've only rejoined the ranks of the living this morning." Reba laughs, pausing to let him lean on a different wall near some fragrant purple and white flowered vines for a while and rest. "I'd say I be entitled to a few years worth of missed gossip."

Rudy nods, although it seems to Mirawynd that he immediately wishes he hadn't, since the motion makes the color drain out of his face again. "Tell you what, Kiley," he says, once he's able to talk again, "you get me somewhere where the world *isn't* wobbling, and I'll fill you in on the entire Fleet's worth of gossip."

"Deal."

★

POTTS AND THE OTHER THREE PILOTS OF THE 2ND Darter Squadron are gathered around a small table that's been set up in the middle of Mayview's main hangar. For the last fifteen minutes, they've been watching Nyx build what would, on first glance, seem to be an abstract sculpture out of an oblong spike-covered yellow fruit and bits of wire. Each of the pilots also has one of the same sort of fruits to snack on as they watch, cut in half to expose the bright green pulp-coated seeds contained within. Potts himself is pleased to enjoy having a snack at all for once without curious little kitten hands getting in his way. He makes a mental note to thank Reba later for taking Wyndi with her when she took Rudy down to her lair.

"Now," says Nyx, cutting three lengths of plant-support wire from the coil they'd retrieved when they took the pilots to pick the fruits they needed, "This isn't *quite* the right relative thickness for the scale, but it should work to show you what I'm talking about." They take care in straightening out the wire by running it along the edge of the table.

"Considering that the recordings I tried to take were a bust, Nyx," says Major Ioane, "I'm just glad you can show us what you saw at all."

"*I* still can't believe we're fighting oversized melons now," Major Toussaint chuckles, gesturing with her spoon.

"Pity we have to destroy the thing, almost." Major Albright shakes her head. "I'm sure there's *someone* up the line who'd be keen to take it apart."

Nyx pauses from jabbing the wires into the base of the large kiwano melon they're holding in their lower hand. "From what I saw of it and what the Novans who've come here have been like, I... well, I somehow *doubt* that it was designed to be taken apart safely."

"They have a point there," says Major Ioane, reaching down into Nyx's basket to pass them the three small potatoes they'd stopped to dig out of a hydrogel pot on the way back. "Besides, you said there were strikers left behind in the secondary hangar, didn't you?"

"Six of them, yes—hold those steady for me, will you, Abigail?" Nyx's tail waves with a subtle agitation while they secure the other end of each of their melon-supporting wires into one of the potatoes Ioane is holding. "Reba and I haven't dared try to touch them, aside from sort of... nudging them into the holding bays as carefully as we could so any future visitors wouldn't notice them."

"Huh." Potts looks up from his melon thoughtfully. "I forgot you'd mentioned that."

"You were a bit *distracted* at the time, Sarge." Major Ioane gives him a nudge.

Potts rolls his eyes at her, but doesn't say anything. He can't exactly deny it, after all. Between Wyndi's usual kitten-antics and Reba's *being alive*, it's been something of a distracting afternoon.

"In any case," Major Ioane continues, "the folks back at I&R will have to make do with the strikers—we can't exactly contact the Admiral at the moment to ask if she wants to risk leaving the melon intact."

"True," says Major Albright. "Or even warn her that there's Novan activity in this region at all—*stars* but it seems there's a lot of that going on around here."

"Does a bit to resolve that little mystery of how 'Jane' made it all the way to Kapteyn b, though." Major Toussaint shakes her head lightly. "Or rather, why she seems to have been the only *one* who got through."

"Can we *not* bring her up?" Potts sheepishly runs a hand through the back of his hair. "It was embarrassing enough trying to explain that earlier..."

"I'll be your excuse for avoiding the subject, then," says Nyx, winking their third eye at him. They carefully set their arrangement of melon and potatoes on the table and adjust the position of the thinner wires they'd already stabbed around the edges of each of the melon's cone-shaped spikes. "This is the best model I can make you—mind that the spikes aren't *quite* arranged like this, but this was the kiwano that came closest..."

"It's good enough to give us an idea, Nyx," says Major Ioane, lightly setting a reassuring hand on the Florivan's shoulder for a moment. "Now, which way is north on this table?"

"Ah, the same way north is in here?" Nyx gestures in the appropriate direction with their tail. "I went ahead and lined it up. The nearest craters go... about here and here." They pause to lay out some large leaves they'd taken from the grape vines in the corridor in the correct spots.

Potts has to give them credit for creativity. Most folks he's met would have settled for trying to draw out some sort of rough diagram instead of going to so much trouble to make a model.

"And you said this thing is three times the size of a darter?" asks Major Albright, taking on a particularly serious tone on the edge of her crisp martian accent. She's officially the lead Musketeer, but she doesn't tend to use her officer voice like this outside of tight situations and strategy meetings.

"At least." Nyx nods. "I've cut the 'antennas' to about the right length proportionally. I didn't see anything like doors or access panels, unless the shimmer of whatever's keeping it hidden from your eyes was hiding those too... or we weren't able to get close enough. The surface just seemed *smooth* except where the antennas attach to the spikes."

Major Toussaint gestures at the wires holding the melon up from the potatoes with her spoon. "I'd wager that's going to be our weak point, then. No clue why they'd need it suspended above the planetoid's surface, though."

"Hm." Major Albright looks over the model again. "And you didn't find anything else like this on the surface or up in orbit, Abigail?"

"No." Major Ioane absently drums her fingers on the edge of the table. "I catch your drift, though. It might be worth doing another sweep of the surface once we're all charged back up to make sure we only have the one melon to worry about."

"I'm willing to help you however I can," says Nyx, sighing lightly. "Although forgive me if I'm a bit… hesitant… to do that under fire again."

"We can't promise you absolute safety," Major Toussaint tells them with her most reassuring smile, "but it won't just be you and Abigail up there next time—Penny and I will be right there at your wings in case anything happens."

Nyx nods slowly. "I… appreciate that, Major Toussaint." Their tail continues lightly waving in a somewhat nervous fashion. "When did you want to do this?"

"That's the spirit!" Major Albright stands and stretches. "Not 'til Rudy's had a chance to look over Abigail's bird, at least—since we have him here, we might as well make sure everything's still in order after that hit you took."

"That gives us a few hours to wait, then, at least, knowing how he is about flying at all," Potts comments. He's flown with the man before—an ordeal for both of them, for sure, and that was only for twenty minutes or so transferring between ships. He's not surprised at all that

Rudy seemed to be staying upright through sheer force of will when Reba led him out. "Do we have the time?"

"We do," Major Toussaint tells him. "*Aegolius* won't be within jumping range for a few days, much less within flight."

Potts raises an eyebrow. "What'd they expect you to do if you got here and didn't find us or a place to land? Sit around in your birds in orbit and *wait*?"

Major Albright laughs. "Something like that! Or, since we had no way of knowing about the signal jammer, we were supposed to call in over the relays so they could sort out a rendezvous point for us within better range. Nothing too extreme, really, considering some of the stunts you've pulled."

Potts, once again, has to settle for rolling his eyes. She has too valid of a point for him to be able to properly argue against the remark.

Nyx looks up at Major Albright with a curious flick of their left ear. "Why do I get the impression that you *didn't* tell cousin Elias about that part of your plan?"

"We didn't," says Major Toussaint. "There's some things that aren't worth worrying people about, you know."

"He'd never have agreed to come along if you'd told him, I'm sure." Potts adds, chuckling. He gestures to the melon sculpture on the table. "Glad you brought him, though—if there's *any* chance of that thing being packed with some sort of bomb, I'd rather not be grounded when it goes off."

Major Albright nods. "We'll have to wait 'til we can get your bird safely up in orbit before we take the melon out. I don't spare much sentiment for the Novans you say Dr.

Kiely has on ice, but I'm not about to gamble on leaving any of *us* behind to ride out potential earthquakes."

"I wonder..." Major Toussaint holds up her hands to make a small window between her fingers and stares thoughtfully at the nearest impaled potato through it. "Remind me what the natural gravity here is outside the outpost, Abigail?"

"Point zero-six, give or take. Why? You have a scheme in mind already?"

"Well..." Major Toussaint grins. "We're wanting to avoid potentially taking a chunk out of this lovely home 'planet' of yours when the melon most likely blows up in our face, right?"

The other Majors share a look, then nod.

"So, we get it up higher off the surface to blow it up— that should help soften things, wouldn't you say?"

"And how do we do that, Major?" Potts can't help but admit he's somewhat lost with where she's taking this. Major Toussaint is the 2nd Squadron's best strategist, but she tends to leap ahead of his own reasoning quickly enough to leave him confused.

"We blast the potatoes first—not the *supports*, mind, the potatoes themselves."

"You mean the boulders?" Potts asks, raising an eyebrow.

"Yes, Sarge, come on, you're usually quicker than this." Major Toussaint smirks at him and retrieves her spoon, gesturing at the base of the nearest potato with the bowl end of it. "Now, if we time it right, even if the melon's anchor bars actually go further into the ground... we can take out these and let the shock wave from them vaporizing push the melon up higher from the surface—I'll have to run the numbers on it, but that *should* get it close to escape velocity. Then, if it doesn't blow up on its own, we can take it out before it comes back down."

Major Albright grins. "This is why I like you, Anna! Never met a target yet you couldn't sort out how to turn into a nice friendly cloud of mathematical debris."

"Agreed," says Major Ioane. She looks to Nyx. "We can pull it off, but if the melon's camouflage doesn't drop when we hit the boulders, we'll be relying on you to tell me where to direct our fire."

"I understand." Nyx's tail is waving more slowly now.

"Thank you." Major Ioane lightly sets a hand on their shoulder again. "I know the day's been a bit overwhelming, but try to leave the worrying to us?"

Nyx looks at her for a long moment, then nods silently.

Having had more than his fill of strategy for the evening, Potts takes the opportunity to stand and stretch. He cracks his knuckles. "Well! Now that the plan's out of the way, we just have one more problem."

"What's that, Sarge?" asks Major Albright.

Potts lets out a bit of a laugh. "It's getting what… close to midnight by now as far as *Surnia*'s concerned? And we've *all* had a long day of it." He looks to Major Ioane and Nyx. "Some of us longer than others. If we're going to be here for a few days, we might as well sort out somewhere for everyone to bunk down and get some rest."

Major Toussaint reaches over to give him a teasing nudge. "And here *I'm* supposed to be the practical one."

"I do have my moments, Major," Potts teases back, returning the nudge.

"We have access to my old quarters, if you want," says Nyx, absently readjusting the sleeves over the stubs of their right shoulders. "We've just been using them for storing some of the gear we brought with us... and I'm sure Reba can get you into one of the guest suites on the upper habitation level if you need more room. We've not really had reason to unlock most of the private areas since we've been alone here."

Major Ioane tilts her head to them curiously. "All of Mayview's old access codes still work, right? Not just the flight clearance ones for the doors up there?" She gestures vaguely towards the hangar's roof.

"They do, although you shouldn't need to worry about that. Dr. Monroe used his old codes to put Reba into the system as 'official outpost assisting physician' before he died... so Mayview's systems now recognize her as the chief medical officer." Nyx's ears and tail droop for a moment as they say this. "Any place my staff code doesn't work, *she* can get in on a medical emergency override."

Major Ioane nods. "Well, then, I can get us girls into my Dad's old suite for sure—assuming you don't have too much of the jungle blocking the way, that is."

"Where was it?"

"Level three on the East minor dome, number 28." Major Ioane makes a small gesture in a particular direction, as if that will mean something when the five of them are still standing in the middle of the hangar. Granted, to a Florivan like Nyx with knowledge of the outpost and their species' inherent sense of direction, it probably does. "Not that far from the trail that leads down to your lair, if I'm remembering right?"

Nyx closes their eyes for a moment, then smiles at her. "Not far at all. I have some rather tangled runner beans there, but I believe I can lead you through them without having to resort to cutting a path."

Major Ioane stands and stretches much as Potts had, chipper as ever. "Lead the way, then, Nyx! Come on, girls, there's room there for the three of us, and *I* for one could use a chance to freshen up." She turns to Potts. "We can put you and Rudy in the suite next door, Sarge—from what I remember, that's a two-bedroom."

Potts stifles a yawn he's been holding in for quite some time as they all follow Nyx into the corridor. "If there's a bunk and a place to properly wash the pond water smell off, I'll take it."

"Pond water?" asks Major Albright, laughing. "What in the stars did you fall into this time, Sarge?"

"It wasn't my idea," Potts protests. "*Wyndi's* the one who fell in—ack, which reminds me, I probably need to give *them* a bath, too, now that we're staying here for the night instead of going back to *Surnia*..." He's not looking forward to having to wrangle his little copilot tonight, that's for sure. If there's one thing he's learned about Wyndi since he met them, it's that they seem *determined* to make bath time a challenge for him.

Nyx looks back over their shoulder. "Would you like me to take care of that for you, Julian?"

"If you're offering?" Potts' laugh comes out as half of another unbidden yawn. "I'll warn you, though, Wyndi can be a bit of a *handful*..."

"I was a kitten myself, once, you know," Nyx replies. "I think I can handle them."

The pilots exchange a look.

"You know," says Major Toussaint, giggling, "our little mascot has something of a reputation for making folks *regret* saying things like that..."

M IRAWYND, TRUE TO FORM, DOES NOT WANT TO get out of the nice warm water once their cousin is done helping them rid themself of the icky pond smell that's been clinging to their fur all day. Instead, they splash over to the other side of the basin and retrieve the floating piece of plant sponge they've been playing with.

They swim their prize back over to the side where Nyx is waiting and offer it up hopefully. "Again?"

Their cousin makes a mildly exasperated trilling sound back at them, but accepts the soggy fibrous thing. "You know, Mirawynd, if you don't come out of the water before it gets cold, you're going to get *chilled…*"

"Again!" Mirawynd's excitedly waving tail splashes a bit of water up towards Nyx's face by accident.

Nyx shakes their head as they reach up with their upper hand to wipe the water away. "Okay, one more time... and then you're getting dried off whether you agree to it or not."

Mirawynd squeaks back something that is not *precisely* an agreement and swims over to the far side of the basin to wait for the game to begin. It's a new game that they've invented today to play with their cousin, but it's already one of their favorites. They can't wait to show it to their human the next time he decides to give them a bath.

"Ready?" Nyx holds up the plant-sponge in their upper hand and squeezes the water out of it.

Mirawynd nods excitedly and splashes with their tail again.

"All right..." Nyx pantomimes tossing the plant-sponge into the air twice. On the third time, they let go so it flies up high above the center of the basin. "Catch!"

Mirawynd dives down into the shallow water and then pushes up so they jump out of it just in time to catch the plant-sponge between all four of their hands. They fall back down with a big *splash*, showering their cousin in lukewarm rinse water.

Nyx applauds them anyway, snapping the fingers of both hands and then making an exaggerated gesture towards Mirawynd—who is now triumphantly holding the sponge up above their head to show off that they have, in fact, caught it.

"Behold, the galaxy's greatest luffa-catcher!" says Nyx, halfway laughing.

Mirawynd squeaks happily and then swims over to bring the plant-sponge back to them. "Again?"

"What, again?" Nyx reaches out with their upper hand to give Mirawynd's ears a gentle rub.

Mirawynd purrs lightly at the touch and holds up their toy. "Again!"

Before Mirawynd can think to swim away, both of Nyx's hands have closed around them and swiftly lifted them out of the water. They wriggle to try and slip free, dropping the plant-sponge onto the floor beside the basin in order to have use of all four arms to try and peel the gentle but persistent fingers away. It lands with a soggy thud.

"I think that's quite enough splashing for today, Mirawynd," says Nyx, seeming determined not to let go. "Julian *warned* me what to expect from you, you know."

Mirawynd stops wriggling for a moment to look up into their cousin's eyes with the most pitiful expression they can muster. They're not sure Nyx understands that resisting capture is an integral part of all stages of their bath time routine.

"Now, now, don't give me that face." Nyx smiles softly and loosens their upper hand's grip enough to pet Mirawynd's soggy head some more. "I *know* you like being dry and clean better than wet and cold."

Mirawynd nuzzles their hand and relaxes—then uses the next moment to slip free of their cousin's grasp altogether with a triumphant squeak. They quickly bounce up over Nyx's shoulder and down onto the floor to scamper out of the washroom and into the bigger part of Nyx and Reba's nest room, leaving a trail of small splashy puddles behind them.

The room is mostly dark right now, but that doesn't matter so much to Mirawynd. Their three keen golden eyes can see clearly in what little light is there.

"Mirawynd!" their cousin calls in a whisper that's half laughing and half exasperated admonishment. "Come back here before you wake anyone up and let me dry you off, at least!"

Mirawynd pauses for a moment to shake off as much of the water as they can and then continues scampering around so Nyx can have fun chasing and looking for them. Nyx seems to be trying to chase them as silently and slowly as possible, although Mirawynd doesn't understand why. Usually, when they play this game, the person trying to catch them with the towel makes an appropriate amount of fuss to show that they're having fun too.

After a few minutes, Mirawynd starts to get cold even though the room is mostly nice and warm because their fur is still soggy. Chilly, but not quite ready to let their cousin catch them, they slip under the couch in the little sitting area. They see Nyx's quiet feet walk past and through the curtain of vines at the door.

Mirawynd giggles. Nyx seems not to have realized that *they* didn't leave the room at all. They're still chilly and wet, but they can't resist a good game of hide and seek.

A few moments later, a hand dangles down from above. It wiggles its five distinctly pinkish-pale human fingers at them in a way that makes the slim gold band on the fourth finger catch the tiny bit of light in the room and sparkle. Ever drawn to shiny things and *warmth*, Mirawynd scoots over to the fingers and taps them with one of their own upper hands.

The hand moves around until it finds Mirawynd's head so it can ruffle their ears, then withdraws from the hiding space beneath the couch and beckons them upward.

Mirawynd follows, hopping up onto the couch and then more gently onto the chest of the human who's been sleeping on it. They greet him with their softest and most charming squeak.

"I *thought* I heard a little silver rascal under there." Rudy lightly strokes their ears again. "Ugh. And a wet rascal at that, I see. You've gone and escaped from the bath again, have you?"

Mirawynd makes a sheepish expression and takes hold of their soggy tail in their lower hands. They squeak softly as an acknowledgment.

"Well," says Rudy, feigning annoyance, "go on, then. Go get your towel so I can dry you off. You can snuggle with me until Nyx comes back to collect you."

"Pocket?" Mirawynd asks, reaching down with one of their upper hands to lift one side of his vest. Rudy *does* have very nice warm pockets for sleeping in. That's part of why they like him so much.

"Only *after* you're dry."

It only takes Mirawynd a brief bit of scampering and dragging to bring one of the big towels from the washroom and climb back up onto the couch where their second-favorite human has been ever since Reba brought him down from the hangar. They present the towel to him with a triumphant squeak, waving their tail in a way that sends small droplets of water flying around them.

Rudy obliges by wrapping the towel around their small slightly-chilled body and rubbing their fur to get the last of the water out and fluff it back up—although he doesn't make any attempt to sit up any more than he has to. "If Dons' kittens are anything like *you*, Wyndi," he tells them in a quiet, conspiratorial whisper, "we're all going to have our hands full from the moment they open their eyes."

Mirawynd contents themself with being dried and snuggled and curls up contentedly on his chest under the towel so that only their head is peeking out. They yawn softly, their purr loud enough now to almost drown out the sound. Part of the reason they like Rudy so much is because he's always a good source of warmth and his voice is *almost* as comforting as their human's. They can't help but feel safe when they're with him.

Mirawynd has nearly fallen asleep when they hear Nyx return. They swivel one ear in the direction of the door at the sound of the soft footsteps.

"Don't worry," Rudy calls softly to their cousin. "Wyndi went and tired themself out before they could leave the room."

"Ah." Nyx sighs and comes over to the sitting area. "I'm sorry they disturbed your rest, cousin Elias."

"I was awake." Rudy chuckles softly. "And believe it or not, they do this when Sarge bathes them too, if he forgets to lock the door to our lavatory first."

"Julian *didn't* tell me that part." They hear the sound of Nyx settling down into one of the chairs opposite the couch. "I don't know how he ever manages to get them clean... I've never met a kitten who was so enthusiastic about being difficult to bathe."

"Wyndi's a bit of a bloody handful when they want to be, yeah—unless Li's around. They're almost *eerily* well-behaved for him. He doesn't even have to try to mimic Dons' kitten-you-are-going-to-behave-now tone, either." Rudy continues lightly stroking Mirawynd's ears as he talks. "Dons tells me every kitten he's ever met has been like that with him, though... not that I blame them."

"Kittens are drawn to people their instincts say are warm and safe or somehow family," Nyx comments with an amused tone. "I'm not surprised, somehow, that Elder Celadon's Navigator is the sort to draw them. He's a Beacon, after all."

"You said you'd met Dons—was that recently enough that you've met Li too?"

"Once, about oh... a year or so before we left Horizon Prime?" A light teasing sparkle manifests in Nyx's voice. "Assuming that he's the same nice young man with the dark hair and the bright voice who was with them then? Grows orchids for a hobby?"

"That'd be him. Best Navigator in the Fleet, too, as far as anyone's ever told me." Rudy chuckles. "I'm sure they'll both be glad to see you again when *Aegolius* gets here."

"I'm looking forward to it..." Nyx trails off with a barely suppressed sigh.

Mirawynd opens one of their eyes and looks over, concerned for their cousin but sleepy enough that they don't particularly want to leave the nice warm human whose chest they're so comfortably snuggled up against.

"Hmm," Rudy says after a few moments of silence. "Been a bloody *long* day, hasn't it?"

"It has," Nyx agrees. They start to stand up. "Forgive me, cousin Elias. *I'm* the one disturbing your rest now—"

"—You aren't. I take night shift often enough I'm nocturnal by default." Mirawynd feels him lightly shrug. "Just laying about here in the dark hoping the bloody vertigo will go away before morning, that's all."

"Ah."

"If you want to leave Wyndi with me and go get some sleep yourself, go ahead," Rudy says, still in the same soft voice he's been using since Nyx reappeared. "Kiely's probably wondering where you are, if any of her's awake still."

"I might." Nyx hesitates, then settles back down into their chair. They fold their legs up underneath them, curling their tail up into their lap where their lower hand can reach the tuft at the tip of it. "At the moment, I'm... well, still trying to calm my thoughts enough that I *could* sleep, to be honest."

"I get that. Is it the thing with the strikers earlier, or...?"

"Mostly. I... never expected to find myself in a situation like that." Nyx sighs softly. "Even less than I ever expected to wake up in a situation like this in the first place."

"Kiely did fill me in earlier about what happened to the two of you." Rudy absently continues stroking Mirawynd's fur. "She mentioned you weren't one of the Fleet's volunteers?"

Mirawynd purrs louder, both because they feel like it and because they want their cousin to hear the sound and feel comforted too, considering the tone of voice they've been using. They're glad they have Rudy here to talk to Nyx for them; he's very good at being comforting when he wants to be, even if he can't purr.

"I'm not... I was only able to join the team because it was a joint civilian aid and Fleet auxiliary venture." Nyx hesitates again. "Ensign York wasn't even my... well, *Psiloscops'* Captain had assigned him to watch over me because he was the only Nav certified crew member available. He was a very nice person, but I..." They make a vague gesture with their lower hand before absently beginning to run their tail-fluff through its fingertips over and over again. "I still hadn't decided whether I wanted to keep him for my Navigator or if I wanted to stay on *here* as a civilian staff member with the hospital we were hoping to set up when... everything happened."

"Mm. And now with this 'accidental rescue' bit and having to be in the bloody middle of things, you're back to being uncertain about *that* decision on top of everything else from the last four years that's been dredged up for you today?" Rudy's hand moves away from Mirawynd's head just long enough to make little quotation gestures for emphasis.

"...To a certain extent, yes. The decision about whether I could properly volunteer for the Fleet if I wanted to has been made for me, though." Just the barest hint of a sigh escapes as Nyx says this.

"Oh?"

Nyx's upper hand gestures at their right ear. "The scarring isn't quite as obvious because of the way I keep my hair... but there was enough damage that I've lost most of my hearing in this one. I don't know if I could get an earpiece to work in it properly again, and I'd *have* to use the other one to listen to the Strange if I was going to run jumps and actually get anywhere."

"Which wouldn't leave you much margin for being able to hear your Navigator giving points or be able to anchor to their voice so you didn't get lost." Rudy nods. "I know just enough about things from hanging out with Li and Dons to see where you're going with this."

"Yes..." Nyx sighs more audibly this time. "I don't have much to offer as a jumper, even if it *does* seem that Abigail has found an alternative use for me... although I'll admit I'm still not sure how I feel about being carried around to spot things your sensors can't if it means being out in the middle of a battlefield."

"I see what you mean. Wouldn't blame you one bit for wanting to stay out of the bloody darters, myself." Rudy gets quiet and thoughtful for a while before he replies. "Well, Nyx, I can't say I'd have any more advice for you than you'd have for yourself—if you asked me for any— but if you're anything like Dons? This is the part where I'm supposed to remind you that you *do* need to try to sleep instead of staying up for days on end with the weight of the galaxy on your chest."

Nyx chuckles halfheartedly. "That... sounds like something my Nida would say."

"It's something I've picked up from Li's playbook, actually, but I wouldn't be surprised if he'd been given the line by one Elder or another."

Mirawynd gets an itch along the edges of the bare patch on their shoulders and uncurls themself with a yawn to try to scratch at it. Their sleepy eyes turn to Rudy with a soft, requesting sort of a squeak.

"Ah, and here I thought you were asleep." He obliges with gentle scratches, since he can reach the itchy bit more easily than Mirawynd themself can.

"I should probably return them to Julian soon," says Nyx. "I'm sure he's wondering by now if they've managed to accidentally drown me."

"From what I can see of you in this light? I'd think they almost did." Rudy shakes his head with a light chuckle. "Sarge won't worry—he knows they're safe with us, and the man sleeps like a rock when you can ever get him to settle down long enough. He probably wouldn't even notice you'd slipped in to deliver them until morning anyway."

"Ah." Nyx stifles a yawn. "I'll take your word for that." After a moment, they come over and bend down beside the couch, lightly ruffling Mirawynd's ears. "I'll leave it up to you, then, Mirawynd—do you want to go upstairs to watch over your guardian's dreams tonight, or are you staying here with us?"

Mirawynd looks up to their cousin with a questioning squeak. They had been under the impression that their human would be coming *back* to the nice warm nest to join them after he washed off his own pond smells. In fact, they'd assumed he was already *in* the nice nest they'd found when they explored behind the curtains dividing the room earlier, and that they'd be able to go snuggle with him whenever they wanted.

An old fear surfaces in their mind; one that's almost as old as Mirawynd themself. It's the fear that says they have to find their human *now* before he's gone forever like the parent and littermates they only barely remember and they're all alone—the fear that says that monsters like to try to take their human *away* if they leave him alone for too long. The fact that their cousin and their second-favorite human are there with them now barely registers. All that matters to Mirawynd is that they find their human.

They scamper off before Nyx or Rudy can say anything to stop them, first in the direction of the nest where they were *so* sure their human was supposed to be tonight. They dart under the edge of the vine curtains and hop up into the soft bed to search the blankets for him. There's *warmth* there in the blankets for sure.

Mirawynd seeks out the warmth, tunneling through the blanket layers until they find first a leg and then the rest of a human—who is *not* their human at all, they discover, and seems to be all alone sleeping in the nest. They let out an alarmed squeak when they realize they were wrong about him being safely where they expected him.

Before Mirawynd can scurry off into the labyrinth of vines to find him, the human under the blanket catches them up in her hands. She starts lightly petting their head, forcing their instinct for growing still and relaxing in response to that to take over in spite of their urgent need to rescue their human from whatever trouble he's surely gotten into while they weren't watching him.

"Easy, now, ye wee fuzzy thing." Reba yawns as she sits up in the nest and holds them so they're looking right into her eyes. "What's got ye all wound up?"

Mirawynd tries to explain to her that they need her to let go and stop petting them so they can go find their human, but it comes out as a series of somewhat pitiful and distressed squeaks because they don't have the words.

"I'm sorry, Reba." Nyx appears at the side of the nest and taps the side lamp with the tip of their tail to turn it on. "They're looking for Julian. They'd just settled down from their bath, and I don't think they understood that he wasn't going to be sleeping here with us until I asked if they wanted to be taken to him."

Reba looks back to Mirawynd with a raised eyebrow. "Ye been listening to too much gossip, kitten."

"To be fair, Kiley," they hear Rudy's voice call from the couch, "they know *Nyx* shares that nest with you, which makes it 'family territory'... and Sarge and I have yet to get out of being bunkmates, even if we do have a bit more space on *Surnia* than we did back at the bloody shipyards. With us all here, do you really think Wyndi's fuzzy little brain could expect him to be sleeping anywhere else?"

"He has a point," says Nyx, sitting down on the edge of the nest.

"I see he has." Reba lets out something halfway between a laugh and a yawn and gives the itchy patch between Mirawynd's upper shoulder blades a light scratch. "Well, Wyndi, dear, our man ain't here, but I know for a *fact* he be somewhere safe—and I can take ye to him if ye promise to settle down and not run off along the way."

Mirawynd gives her hand a small nuzzle of thanks. They sit and wait in the nest of blankets with their cousin while Reba pulls on another layer of clothes over her sleepwear so she's more suitably dressed for the trek through the vines, then ride on her shoulder all the way to the room their human has inexplicably chosen for sleeping in.

Reba knocks on the door five or six times before she gives up and uses the keypad beside the door to open it herself. "Julian?" she calls from the doorway of the darkened apartment without entering. "Are ye awake?"

Mirawynd hops down from Reba's shoulder and scampers through the set of rooms until they find the one where their human's boots are sitting in the floor beside the nest. The lights turn on just as they're inspecting the warm lump underneath the thin blanket, confirming for them that it *is* their human. He's sound asleep and the edges of him feel like dreams—not nice ones, though, so Mirawynd takes it upon themself to scamper up to his head and tap his ear until he wakes up and bats them away.

"Mm, Wyndi, quit that..." he murmurs, still sounding more asleep than not.

"Sarge!" Wyndi squeaks, nuzzling his bearded cheek now. They're very pleased to see that he's safe and uninjured.

"It's not morning yet, is it?" He rubs at his eyes with one hand and gives Mirawynd's fur an absent stroke with the other.

"It ain't," Reba says, leaning on the door frame with her arms crossed. "Still, since Wyndi decided to wake *me* up, I figured ye needed to wake up too."

For reasons Mirawynd doesn't understand, the sound of her voice is enough to shock their human into actual wakefulness and make him grab around blindly for the shirt he'd set aside like he usually does when he goes to sleep. Supposing this must be a new game, they hop down from the bunk briefly to retrieve the shirt for him from the floor. They're not sure why he wants it back, though, since it's gone all cold and it still smells like pond water.

Mirawynd's human pats them on the head in thanks when they present it to him. "Ah—sorry, Reba, were they pestering you?" His voice is muffled by the shirt he's still scrambling to pull on. "I thought they'd decided to stay with Nyx—"

"—Don't ye go falling out of ye bunk on my account, Julian. I only came to return ye counterpart, and freshly laundered at that." Reba giggles. "And they *had* settled down... right up until they found out *ye* weren't in easy reach."

Mirawynd's human relaxes a bit. "Wyndi does have a bit of a thing about us being separated when they're not expecting it. They're usually calmer about it when I leave them with Rudy, though."

Mirawynd takes the opportunity to nuzzle against their human's neck some more, just to make sure he's okay and actually there. He reaches up to reassuringly stroke their fur in return.

Reba shrugs, still leaning on the doorway. "Ye be in a place they don't know, Julian—and from what I'm told, Wyndi has their hands full keeping ye out of danger when they're *with* ye."

Their human laughs awkwardly. "Do I *want* to know which stories Rudy's been telling you?"

"Enough to have filled in the gaps of some of the ones *ye* told me, but not all of them." Reba stifles a yawn. "And my curiosity for the rest ain't enough to keep me from my bed. If the two of ye are sorted now, I'll be off back to my lair."

"If..." Mirawynd's human hesitates, looking down to their own contented set of golden eyes instead of up at Reba now. "Well. I'd say we are. Thanks for bringing them, Reba."

"What else were I supposed to do with the sad little beastie what woke me up?" She comes over to give Mirawynd's ears a goodnight ruffle. "See, now, Wyndi? He's safe and sound and ye don't have to worry anymore."

Mirawynd purrs softly and nuzzles her hand with a squeak of gratitude. Reba is quickly taking a place on their list of most favorite humans.

"And as for *ye*, Julian?" Reba gets a teasing sort of a sparkle in the corners of her eyes for a moment and then playfully ruffles his hair too. "Goodnight. Thanks again for coming to rescue us—I'll turn out the lights as I go."

With that, she's gone. Mirawynd's human stares in the direction of the door for a minute or two before sighing. He sheds his pond-water shirt again and settles back down under the blanket into his temporary nest. Mirawynd doesn't quite understand why he wouldn't want to go with Reba back down to the nice warm room where the *family* nest is, but they're somewhat used to their human being odd about his sleeping arrangements.

He's quiet in the darkness for a while before he shifts from his usual sleeping position with Mirawynd curled up contentedly on the pillow in the nice cozy spot between his neck and shoulder to look at them. "Well, Wyndi... you've met my dearest friend, now—and she's *alive*. What do you think of her?"

Wyndi yawns sleepily and reaches out to give him a reassuring pat. Their hand winds up patting his nose, since it happened to be closest within reach. "Mine."

"Heh." Their human smiles broadly and gives them one last scratch behind the ears before relaxing and drifting off to sleep. "I hoped you'd say that."

★

Part 2: Complications and Card Castles

LONG AFTER THE THREE PILOT-MAJORS AND their somewhat reluctant "civilian melon spotter" have left to perform their survey of the planetoid's surface, Rudy is still hard at work trying to put Potts' darter back together. The young pilot *himself* is once again playing the role of the "Mayview Flight Control" radio operator, and attempting to be helpful in the meantime.

As usual, the majority of Potts' helpfulness is in the vein of staying out of the way and occasionally fetching tools or holding one of the larger or heavier pieces of his darter's fallen engines in place so Rudy can reattach it. Potts might be a skilled pilot, and capable of making basic repairs on his own if he needs to, but the specifics of the craft he flies and a majority of the mechanical details of how it functions are beyond his knowledge. Darter pilots, after all, are seldom expected to survive long enough to need to know how to repair their own engines if something goes wrong enough for them not to be able to return to their mother ship and whatever skilled mechanic is responsible for keeping them flying. This fact has never bothered Potts all that much; he's always too busy with the wonderful business of *flying* to worry about the dangers of it.

"No." Rudy rolls his eyes and hands back the tool Potts has just brought him. "That one's the point-five mil rivet setter—I asked for the point-six."

"They look exactly the same—"

"—The number's written on the end of the bloody handle, Sarge." Rudy taps the tool to point it out. "And they're packed in the case in sequence, unless you've gone and jumbled them up again."

Potts shakes his head and goes back over to the tool bag to rummage through it again in search of the slim black case holding his best friend's set of micro-rivet tools. The man's *particular* about things, that's for sure. The handles all look alike, as far as Potts is concerned.

"You know," Rudy teases with a gruff chuckle, "I should have sent *you* out on errands with Kiely instead. Wyndi's better at picking the right tools on the first go."

"Yes. Well..." Potts returns with what he thinks is the correct rivet setter and passes it to his friend with a smirk. "At least *I* don't go stashing your tools under people's back seats when you hand them back to me."

"Oh, is that where they're keeping the stash now?"

"I think so—haven't bothered trying to clean it out yet. We're pretty sure that's where they had your laser saw, at least."

Rudy laughs, going back to work reattaching one of the smaller outer parts of the darter's rear engine housing. "I still can't believe Wyndi's gotten big enough to carry that bloody thing off."

"*I* still can't believe we ended up having to use it." Potts crosses his arms, chuckling. "Remind me when they get here that I need to ask Celadon if kittens are supposed to be able to predict the future like that?"

"It's probably just Wyndi. They've had to grow an extra sense of how to keep your arse out of the fire to survive, you know. I don't *think* that comes standard with Florivans."

Potts is about to respond with an equal amount of sarcasm, but a sound over his radio headset catches his attention. He holds up a hand and pulls down the microphone bar. "Mayview Control here—Say again, Major?"

"*Well, we've—a bit—new weirdness...*" Major Albright begins, her voice heavily overlaid with static.

When Potts finally finishes parsing everything the Major has to relay to him and flips his microphone bar back up, he does so with a sigh and a shake of his head. He turns back to Rudy. "Care to hear the latest little potential snag in our 'get out of Dodge alive and in one piece' plan?"

"Why am I not surprised?" Rudy rolls his eyes. "Are we talking 'bloody inconvenient' or 'worst case scenario just dropped by for tea,' here?"

"What are you considering 'worst case'?"

"Either the whole bloody Novan armada shows up—" Rudy pauses to seal the last of the rivets in the section he's been working on. "—Or I have to get back into one of the birds with you fools. Can't decide which is worse."

"Ah. Well... not either of those things *yet*." Potts leans back against the side of his darter, staring upwards at the closed hangar doors.

"I don't like the sound of that 'yet,' Sarge. What is it, then?"

"Good news—as far as I could understand Major Albright through the static—is that there's only the *one* melon down here on the planetoid, and the plan to get rid of it should work." Potts runs a hand absently through his hair, which does nothing to smooth out the un-combed mess of it. "Bad news... is that Nyx thought they spotted a similar sort of a shine on the innermost moon. So now, since the Majors have enough charge left to do it, they're going to check there and the other six minor moons to make sure nothing else has been missed."

Rudy shakes his head. "Of *course* they are." He goes over to his tool-bag and starts rummaging through it and switching out which of his tools are slipped into the pockets of his green-trimmed ivory uniform vest.

"It's just one thing after another, isn't it?"

"Seems that way..." Rudy pauses, taking on a peculiar expression and looking between his tool bag and the closed hangar doors above them for a few moments.

"What now?" Potts has seen his friend get that look before, and it's never a good omen.

"Just a notion." Rudy shakes his head and goes back to digging through his tool bag. "Do me a favor, Sarge?

Call back and see if someone can spare a minute to cycle through com frequencies with you while they're orbiting each of those moons."

"What? Why?" Potts makes a confused gesture at the headset he's wearing. "You already tuned all their short-range transmitters with the complex's flight control channel to clear up our signal before they left."

"I did. I need to check the frequencies the interference is strongest on again."

"But *why*?"

"The gals started getting long-range and relay radio interference about halfway between here and that spot where you and Ioane got ambushed yesterday—lost both once we got close, as far as I remember—and I wouldn't be surprised if that was when we came near the outermost moon's orbit." Rudy goes back over to the darter and climbs up onto the wing, unsealing an access panel on the small craft's left side beneath the cockpit. "If the melon's strong enough to do *that*, we shouldn't have even the short-range working as well as we do at this distance. Not if it works like any bloody signal-jammer I've ever heard of, at least."

"So... what, then?" Potts looks at his friend with a hesitant curiosity. He's well aware that Rudy knows his stuff when it comes to coms tech and the like even more than with all the things that go into keeping the darters flying. The man had been one of the people *installing* that sort of thing on the Fleet's starships when the two of them met.

"I'd wager we're looking at a bloody resonance network, is what, and one that's gone unnoticed for *years*—and with how many strikers showed up in the area yesterday? It's got something worth hiding that goes beyond the scouts that Kiely's been collecting."

"That's..." Potts' eyes widen as the implications sink in. "*Stars*, I hope you're wrong."

"So do I, Sarge." Rudy shakes his head and then looks back down into the open access panel. "Now get back on the line and tell the gals I need one of them to cycle com frequencies with you once they're orbiting that first moon—and then get up here and help me with this. I've got an idea."

"Right." Potts flips his microphone bar down. "Mayview Control calling Musketeers..."

"Have ye found it yet, Wyndi, dear?"

"Shiny!" Mirawynd calls back. Their small voice echoes brightly within the metallic cavern they're exploring and out into the room where Reba is waiting.

Reba's playing a game of "fetch the tools and repair parts" with them, but she's too big to get through the space between the pile of heavy crates and the cabinet doors. She'd only managed to get the outer-bottom corner of the left door bent open enough for Mirawynd's small silver-furred self to slip inside, and then to break the latch on the door to give them more room to get the shiny things out. Mirawynd has been hunting through the otherwise inaccessible space on their own ever since.

Soon, Mirawynd emerges, triumphantly dragging one end of a rather long piece of thick optical cable behind them. They offer the end up to Reba with a cheerful wave of their tail.

"Good job!" She laughs and starts rolling up the cable into a coil. "Ye know, Wyndi, dear, I didn't quite believe Mister Rudolph what ye would know what all the things on his list meant if I needed help finding them... but it seems ye understand more of what goes on than anyone suspects."

Mirawynd tilts their head to one side curiously. They're not sure why their humans make such a big fuss when they're helpful. They've been helping Rudy keep his tools in order for most of their life, after all. Even if they can't *say* the words yet, Mirawynd knows the names of all of his shiny things. The only hard part of the game today has been *finding* the things and getting them out of the small spaces where the humans who lived here before Reba and Nyx had hidden them.

Mirawynd settles for making a charming squeak of acknowledgment for the compliment. They brush as much of the dust out of their fur as they can before scampering up to Reba's shoulder. Once there, they tap politely on her cheek. "Drink?"

"Aye, just let me get this in the bag. Considering ye looked like a wee dust-bunny when ye came out, I ain't surprised ye need one." Reba tucks the roll of optical cable into the backpack she's been putting their treasures in and pulls out a water bottle that's a bit bigger than Mirawynd themself and a small cup. She pours a bit of water into the cup and offers it to them before taking a sip from the bottle herself and putting it away.

Mirawynd gives her a squeak of gratitude and drinks. They save a little of the water in the bottom of the cup to dip their upper hands in so they can try to wash the last of the dust off of their face. They're not *too* dirty yet—certainly not enough to require bathing, in their opinion—but they don't like having dust clinging to their eyes and nose at all.

"Let's see," says Reba, pulling out her pocket-com, "that's just about everything on the list. We're just missing a spool of 'optic micro-circuitry solder wire'... and lunch, but that's on my list, not Mister Rudolph's." She smiles and holds the little picture up on the holoscreen to show Mirawynd. "Don't suppose you saw any of this in that cabinet?"

"Shiny!" Mirawynd nods enthusiastically and offers her back their now-empty cup.

"It's a good thing ye came with me, ye know?" Reba tells them, patting their head before she takes the cup. "Aside from the fact I couldn't get into the cabinets... Even with the pictures, I ain't got more than a vague idea what half of this stuff *is*. Now, if we needed medical supplies? That's another story... and trust me, I'm glad we haven't any need to get into my stash of those just yet."

Mirawynd gives her a small comforting pat on the cheek in return. They're used to having to help Rudy in part because *they* can tell shiny things and tools apart and are good at fetching things—and their human isn't. He's very good at coming home with interesting broken things on his darter for them to help Rudy fix when he goes out flying, though!

They're quite sure Reba is good at a lot of things herself, even if she does need help with shiny-thing-collecting.

Mirawynd scampers back through the space between the crates and the cabinet wall and into the hole where the cabinet door is bent open. Only a tiny bit of light can seep in, but their three golden eyes are just as keen in near darkness as they are in the light. It takes them a while to shimmy up through the small space between the door and the shelves and climb all the way to the top of the cabinet where they remember seeing their prize when they were searching for the previous thing on their list. When they get there, they knock on the cabinet door to get Reba's attention.

"Ye okay in there, Wyndi?" her voice calls to them, muffled lightly through the door.

"Shiny!" Mirawynd squeaks back cheerfully. There are three spools shaped like the one they need sitting on the shelf in front of them. All they need to do now is to get them down to Reba so she can read the labels and make sure it's the *correct* sort of spool.

"Ah! Ye found it already, then? Good, bring it on out so we can be done with this."

Mirawynd replies with a trilling affirmative squeak. They're ready to be done exploring dusty cupboards and cabinets for a while too.

They carefully brush the tall piles of dust off of the top of the spools with the fluff of their tail before picking each spool up and rolling it over to the space between the shelf and the door. The spools are just *barely* too big to slip down the gap easily.

Mirawynd stops for a moment to think through the puzzle, then sets each of the spools into position on its edge along the gap before climbing back down and out to ask Reba for assistance.

"I thought ye said ye found it?" she asks when they emerge and scamper up the pile of crates to the cabinet door handles.

Mirawynd looks back at her and jiggles the door handle of the other side of the cabinet where the latch is still working. "Reba help?"

"Ah, I think I can." Reba pulls her pry-bar out of the loop on her belt and climbs into a position where she can wedge it under the edge of the door. "Ye just need this side open now?"

Mirawynd nods and scampers up out of the way.

In moments, Reba's broken the latch holding the right door closed. When it flies open the small amount the crates allow it to, three clunking sounds echo from within, one after the other.

Mirawynd claps excitedly with both pairs of hands and gives Reba a rather dusty hug before heading back down into the cabinet to retrieve the three spools. Just as they'd expected, their treasures are waiting for them on the floor of the cabinet where they can easily be rolled over to the hole in the corner and slipped out.

"Well, now," says Reba, laughing as Mirawynd brings her the third spool, "we only had the one of these on the list... but I doubt Mister Rudolph will turn down spares. Anything else useful in there you want to take with us?"

Mirawynd dusts themself off a little while they think. There had, after all, been quite a lot of shiny things inside the cabinet. Most of the *very* interesting ones were too big to fit through the wider space Reba's made for them to get things in and out, though, or too heavy for Mirawynd to *push*, much less get down to the bottom shelf safely. Aside from the dust, they think the cabinet is an excellent place to stash shiny things for future use, so they can leave most of it there for now.

After a few moments, Mirawynd swishes their tail excitedly and scampers back into the cabinet. There'd been a particularly interesting-looking box on one of the shelves that they hadn't taken the time to try to get unsealed. An experimental pull on the box's handle tells them it's *just* light enough that they can manage, and it's the right width to fit through the gap between the door and shelves.

Several minutes of slow and careful balancing and climbing later, and Mirawynd has their box on the cabinet floor and all ready to push through the hole in the corner. They quickly realize, though, that the hole isn't quite big enough. They squeeze back out and wave to Reba, squeaking excitedly.

"What in the *stars* have ye found now?" she asks, wedging herself as far as she can down between the crates and the wall so she can bend the corner up into a wider hole.

Mirawynd shrugs, sending off plumes of dust from the excited anticipatory swishing of their tail. They don't know what's *in* the box; only that the box was *interesting* and had the sorts of picture-symbols on the label that are usually on Rudy's cases of fragile shiny things that he doesn't let their pilots touch. They consider that enough to make it worth bringing the box back.

In the end, Reba has to help them pull the box out because there's still not much room for it to pass through the hole and between the crates and the wall. When they do have it out, she looks the box over.

"Wyndi, dear, I know ye mean well," she says, wiping the dust off of the label on the front of the box, "but I ain't sure this were worth the hassle. It's just some sort of spare parts for a starship's Nav intercoms, from what this says—and we ain't got one of those to worry about just yet."

"Shiny!" Mirawynd swishes their tail again and climbs up to her shoulder. They start to try to express in squeaks how interesting the box is even though they're not sure what sort of shiny things are in it yet, but they're interrupted by their own sneezing.

"I'll take ye word for it," Reba says, slipping the box into her backpack. She pulls out a handkerchief and hands it to them. "Here, I think that's enough dust for ye for today."

Mirawynd sneezes again even after they've blown most of the dust out of their nose and rubs at their face and ears while she's getting them another drink of water. The box had stirred up a *lot* of dust while they were trying to retrieve it.

Reba helps them wipe the dust off their face and out of their ears with a moistened corner of the handkerchief. She runs the damp cloth over the rest of their fur too, to settle down what's left of the dust. "Better?"

Mirawynd nods.

"Good." She smiles and gives their ears a gentle rubbing. "Now, how about we go find some lunch before we go and take these treasures of yours back to mister Rudolph?"

While Reba treks back through the garden corridors to the place where she and Nyx keep their supplies, Mirawynd contents themself with sitting on her shoulder and carefully grooming the last bits of dust out of their fur. It takes a lot of combing with all four of their hands just to get the fluff on their tail sorted out.

"Ye know, Wyndi, dear," Reba says, pausing to cut some bunches of grapes off of one of the walls of vines on the way, "as much as I'll be glad to be back among people… I think I might miss this place just a touch."

Mirawynd responds with a curious squeak. Like the rest of their little human family, it seems that Reba is the sort who wants to keep a running conversation with them, even though they don't have many words to talk with yet. They don't mind, of course—they like being talked to, even when they don't quite understand everything. To them, this is just another sign that she's someone they want to keep.

"Well." Reba pauses to stash her knife back in its sheath on her belt and tuck the grape bunches into her backpack. "I ain't missing the 'visitors', no… and I'll be glad not to be living in the middle of the worst of the memories anymore. But in a way, this were almost… *home*."

Mirawynd stops grooming the fur on their lower-right arm long enough to give her a reassuring nuzzle. They don't really know how else to respond.

Reba lets out a sigh and pats their head gently. "I don't know if ye'd understand, wee fuzzy thing that ye are, but thank ye." She starts walking again. It's a few minutes before she says anything else. "I were like *ye* once, ye know? That's how I met ye silly guardian, even."

Mirawynd tilts their head curiously and makes a soft questioning squeak to match. They know this tone of voice: it's the one people who want to tell them stories always use. Mirawynd likes when people tell them stories.

"Aye," says Reba. "This ain't the first time he's come blundering in to rescue me..." she trails off, shaking her head lightly. "I were barely ten the first time, when the quakes started at Moon Three. I were one of the lucky ones, but I still lost everything... Julian's the same age, but he and Edwin were there helping evacuate us survivors because their uncle were one of the intra-moon shuttle pilots who'd answered the emergency call." Reba pauses. "Have ye met Edwin yet? I've a hunch he'd like ye."

Mirawynd thinks about it for a moment, trying to connect the name with one of the people their human has introduced them to over the years. They scratch at the itchy bare spot between their upper shoulder blades while they think.

"Julian's older *brother*," Reba clarifies. "The one what plays with bugs for a living."

Mirawynd's tail swishes excitedly. "Uncle Eddie!" They've only met the man who looks just like their human—but taller and much less scruffy—over the relay video calls their human has with him sometimes, but they do like him. Calling him their uncle is part of the game their human plays at teasing Uncle Eddie about being "old." Mirawynd is reasonably certain he *isn't*, but they play along anyway.

"Right." Reba giggles. "That's the one." She reaches her food supply stash and continues telling the story while she's packing neatly wrapped things into what little space is left in the backpack. "So there I were, trapped in what were left of me bedroom because the quakes had brought most of that side of the settlement down on top of us, staring up at this big hole in the debris what I were too small and scared to be able to climb up and escape through. I were in there for days, too... and just when I were sure I'd never be found, this *boy* falls down in there with me and goes and breaks his arm in the falling."

"Sarge?" Mirawynd asks, swishing their tail knowingly.

"Ye know him too well." Reba giggles again. "But aye, it were him. And I'll never forget it, Wyndi—first thing he said to me, even being in pain like that... were to ask if I wanted to come back to Teegarden-Millefleur with him once Edwin caught up and figured out how to get us out of the hole." She shakes her head. "His were the first arm what I ever tied a sling on, too."

Mirawynd looks up to her with a curious flick of their ears. They hadn't quite put together before now that their human and Reba had been kittens together, but it does make sense. Reba being there to take care of him also explains, in a way, how someone as bad at staying out of trouble and uninjured as their human is had managed to survive his own kittenhood.

"I know it were little more than wishful thinking, but what I held onto for the longest time, when I were all alone waiting for Nyx to come out of torpor—and even after, all these years—were that my Julian were still alive out there somewhere, and if anyone could find me, *somehow...* he would." She absently reaches up to give Mirawynd's fur a gentle stroke or two now. "I don't know what to think, really, now that he has."

Mirawynd purrs softly and nuzzles into her hand. She's using the same tone of voice now that their human did when he asked them what they thought of her—although also colored with some of that same sadness that she and Nyx always seem to have hanging around them.

Reba shoulders the full backpack and heads back up towards the hangar. "Do *ye* believe in coincidences, Wyndi? Nyx always tells me there ain't such things, as far as Florivans care."

Mirawynd makes a small questioning squeak in response, and then shrugs. They're not entirely sure what a "coincidence" is supposed to be, if they're honest. The word, in their experience, is usually one that's used when their pilots or their Entile Celadon are joking about things they don't understand.

"Nay," says Reba, laughing, "I had a feeling ye didn't."

PILOT-MAJOR IOANE PULLS HER DARTER UP OUT OF the small moon's orbit and into formation behind the darters of her wing-sisters. She double-checks that all of her gauges are still showing the right numbers, then turns around to grin at her reluctant Florivan copilot. "Five moons down, one to go... quite the melon patch you've got here, Nyx!"

"If they were *my* sort of melons, we could resolve this with the simple application of an appropriate herbicide." Nyx gives her just the smallest hint of a teasing smile in return.

"Point taken!" Ioane laughs for a moment, then turns the majority of her attention back to watching the wing-gestures of the other two darters and her flight information displays. Following Penny's lead to keep the formation in line is simple enough—reflexive, even, considering how long the three of them have been flying together.

After a brief silence, Nyx's eyes meet hers in their reflection in the front of the darter's canopy bubble. "Do you think there's any chance we *won't* find a melon on the last moon?"

"The way things have gone so far today? I'd say it's slim." Ioane shakes her head slightly. "Just means we'll have to take all of them out after we get the first one, that's all."

"...And means that the things the Novans were doing here are more important than Reba and I ever suspected." From the sound of it, Nyx does their best to stifle a sigh.

"Y'all had no way of knowing about it," Ioane points out. She pauses to adjust her speed a touch now that they're further out from the fourth moon. "I'd wager they'd have turned Mayview into a stealth base by now if you hadn't been keeping up your little jungle, too. The Fleet owes you both a debt for that—beyond the one for not finding you sooner."

A glance up at their reflection tells her that Nyx is staring out at the stars again. They've been doing that in silence off and on for most of the tour of the moons. She's not sure if that's entirely to do with them being Florivan and needing to keep themself oriented with where they are in space, or if there's something more to it.

"Hmm... Possibly? I... wouldn't be sure we've made *that* much of a difference."

Ioane knows that tone of voice, though, even if she's only known Nyx for two days now. She can't claim to understand exactly what everything they've gone through has been like, but having all of it dredged up and fresh on their mind can't be comfortable. A memory of her own of dear friends now lost flits through the part of her mind that isn't focused on flying—ones who would have known what to say, for sure. She takes a breath and dismisses the thought. SCV *Athene*'s fall was long enough ago now that she can manage to do that without much difficulty.

The dismissal comes with both the expected echo of a certain psychologist friend's bell-toned voice encouraging her to make time to reminisce with the girls later and a *delightfully* absurd idea for the present moment. It's too good a thought not to try running with it.

"Say," Ioane asks, turning back to Nyx again, set on *distraction* since the two of them still have a few hours worth of work to do and a darter is hardly the place for dwelling on anyone's past. "Want to try your hand at this for a minute?"

The offer has the desired effect, if the sudden, shocked twitch of Nyx's ears is any indication. "*What*? You can't be serious."

"We've got a nice straight shot to the last moon, and about oh... twenty minutes before we get to a point where I have to actually do much. I can talk you through the basics, easy!"

Nyx's three golden eyes are wider now than she's ever seen *anyone's*. "I'm not sure that'd be wise..."

"I promise I won't let you crash! Besides, I'm right here to take the bird back if you need me to." Ioane smiles to them in the most encouraging way she can. "It looks like you're going to be flying with me quite a bit over the next few days, Nyx—I like knowing my copilots know how to pick up if I need them to. Makes me feel safer."

Nyx hesitates, a light swish of their tail punctuating their words when they finally do speak. "Reba was right about you darter pilots having *very* different definitions of 'safe' from the average human, you know?"

"We take pride in it!" Ioane stifles a giggle. "Takes a bit of an odd sort to want to fly these birds for a living to begin with. So, is that a yes?"

"Well...sure." Once again, just a hint of a smile crosses Nyx's face. "Just for a minute or two, though, Abigail— and I still don't understand why you want to show me."

"Great! Just let me warn the girls." Ioane turns back to her controls and pulls down the microphone bar from her headset. "Just a heads-up, Penny," she calls, "I'm set on giving my copilot a quick flying lesson as long as we're out here. You mind?"

"I heard—of that. S—gain?"

It takes three repetitions of the question and answer before the two of them are able to understand everything through the interference and Ioane has her clearance. Subtly enough that only she could tell outright, both of her wing-sisters move to loosen the formation so they can all slow down to a more leisurely cruising speed.

"There we go!" Ioane flips up her microphone bar again. "The girls are going to let us take point for a bit—they'll match us, so don't worry about trying to fly around them or keep up or anything like that."

"I'll... try not to. You're sure about this?"

"I'm sure! It'll be fun!" Ioane chuckles. She's only ever given one impromptu flying lesson that didn't include a healthy amount of nervousness on the part of the copilot. Granted, that had been Celadon, and they have the sort of personality that would have made for an *excellent* darter pilot had they been human.

"If you say so…" The hint of amusement in Nyx's tone bodes well, at least, even if the rest of their voice seems to be apprehensive.

"I do! Now, copilot's controls are split into the two flip-out panels on either side of you—right is weapons, left is flight. Conveniently, you'll only need the left set and the holoscreen display that should be projecting in front of you now…"

One brief explanation of the flight controls later, and she's got Nyx showing more interest than nerves.

"All right… and you're *sure* you want to let me have control of this 'bird' of yours?"

"Sure! Gives me a chance to relax for a few minutes. Now, I have master override if I need it, and I can switch back to control from up here whenever I need to, but the manual switch for you to take them is that analog button on the top of the panel. Sort of an 'emergency precaution' thing that we hardly ever use, but it's useful for training folks."

"Hardly ever use?"

"Well, we're not one of the squadrons who typically *have* copilots to fly with." Abigail laughs. "Much less ones who end up needing to fly. Now, I've set the speed regulator so you won't be able to go any faster than this. Ready?"

Nyx lets out a nervous bell-like laugh. "No, but go ahead."

"She's all yours!" Ioane switches her darter over to copilot control, bracing for the inevitable jerk to one side and sideways rolling that first-time fliers tend to pull on accident.

She's not disappointed.

"Abigail—"

"—Ease out of it, Nyx, you're doing fine!" She chuckles, remembering all too well her first tries at keeping a darter in line. "Smooth motions work better, especially from back there."

"...Smoother?" Nyx over-corrects to the other side, twisting the darter into a roll the other way.

"Small movements give you big results, especially because we're in microgravity." Ioane turns her to the darter's readouts just in case she does need to take back the controls. "You have to feel the bird as an extension of your body."

"Right..." She hears Nyx take in a breath and slowly let it out. Within moments, the darter is righted to a steady position and flying forward.

"Stellar! Just keep on like that—now slowly turn us back in the direction of the last moon. Your holoscreen guidance display should have that up to show you where it is, but since you *have* a sense of where all of the celestial bodies are anyway, feel free to use that instead."

"You have *far* too much faith in my abilities, Abigail." Nyx sounds like they're relaxing in spite of their protests.

"I'd say I have precisely the right amount of faith in them!" She turns back briefly with a grin for emphasis.

Nyx just twitches an ear at her and keeps all of their attention focused on the controls.

"Just do your best to head us in the right direction. It's..." Ioane has to pause to pull up a conversion chart. "You'd call it six by four-E and twelve, I think, from here."

"Ah... four-A, actually, assuming you're calculating that with Mayview as the primal... and what, the first three moons and your sisters as cardinals?"

"That was the attempt. Forgive me, Nyx," she says, "I've had about four days of actual Nav training—long story, that—the rest of my knowledge comes from trying to help Sarge double-check his 'homework.'"

"It wasn't a bad attempt, Abigail. I'd say you could pick up and learn to be a good Navigator far more quickly than I'll ever learn to fly this thing."

"I'll take that as a high compliment."

"It is one. Now, how do I turn, again?" Nyx lets out another nervous laugh. "We seem to be heading in *entirely* the wrong direction at the moment."

"Gently," Ioane replies, "like you're leaning on the tip of the wing..."

WHEN REBA FINALLY RETURNS TO THE HANGAR, Potts is sitting up on top of the wing of his darter again with his legs dangling over the edge. Below him, Rudy is right in the middle of several neatly arranged concentric circles of parts and pieces on the floor, busily rearranging them. It's a good perch for staying out of the way—which is, at the moment, his job almost as much as playing radio control for the Musketeers is.

"I thought ye were putting the thing back *together*?" Reba asks, setting her backpack down on the nearby makeshift table next to Nyx's model of the Novan jamming station.

"I did." Rudy doesn't look up from the small electronic components in his hands. "As much as I could in these conditions, at least—did you find any of the stuff on that list I gave you?"

"We did." Reba begins unpacking the contents of her bag. "And we brought food—the two of ye are going to take a break for lunch whether ye like it or not."

Rudy glances up to her with a wry smirk now. "Doctor's orders, I take it?"

Reba crosses her arms, taking on the same sort of teasing expression. "Do I need to *make* it an order?"

"Not if you let me finish laying all of this out first."

"Deal." Reba turns her doctor tone on Potts now. "Julian? Tell the rest I've got food for them too once they land, will ye?"

"Will do, but it'll be another hour or two before they get back." Potts pulls down the microphone bar of his headset. "Mayview Control calling Musketeers."

"—*here, Sarge*—" Major Albright replies.

There's even more static surrounding her voice now than the last time she called in. He doesn't like that at all, but it makes sense, considering that she's somewhere around the edge of the short-range radio's *normal* signal range. It takes him three times as long to relay Reba's message as it had any other so far. When he's finally done, he becomes aware of the conversation she and Rudy are having below him.

"So all of that mess were part of the engine what fell off?" Reba gestures vaguely at the collection of darter bits on the floor.

"Oh, this? No, I got that reattached while you were out—I'm just waiting for the bits I sent you to find so I can get it *working*." Rudy absently waves towards the rear of the craft.

"So what are ye doing in the floor, then?"

"*This* is all components of his communications array." Rudy pauses to set one of the small components in his hand into the correct spot in his mosaic. "We've run into what you might call a bit of a complication."

Reba raises her eyebrows and looks between Potts up on the darter's wing and the mechanic sitting in the floor. "Complication as in... with all of that mess? Or something else?"

"This mess is a *solution* in the making," says Rudy, standing and dusting his hands off on a rag tucked into his belt. "So we can get out of the trap we've stumbled into before it gets sprung."

Reba sets her hands on her hips. "What in the stars are ye talking about?"

Potts flips the microphone bar back up on his headset now and looks down to his friend with a laugh. "You've been hanging out with Celadon too much, Rudy—you're talking all cryptic again." He hops down from the darter's wing as punctuation, careful to walk *around* the parts on the floor rather than through them. He learned his lesson the last time he accidentally stepped on something fragile by mistake.

"Very funny, Sarge." Rudy rolls his eyes. "I'm choosing to take that as a compliment."

"I'd say ye *both* be cryptic—are ye going to tell me what's going on or not?"

Wyndi pokes their head up out of Reba's pocket now and yawns, apparently awakened by the conversation. They brighten when they spot Potts and have soon returned to their usual perch on his shoulder, chattering excitedly in kitten squeaks the whole time.

"Hey, there, Wyndi." Potts chuckles and gives the kitten's ears an affectionate ruffle. "Did we wake you?"

Wyndi nuzzles softly against his beard and then waves their tail excitedly before making an acrobatic leap to Rudy's shoulder, now that he's come over within leaping distance. Potts can't help chuckling at that. Wyndi might be *his* fuzzy little ward and copilot, but it's no end of amusement to him that one of their favorite people in the galaxy is his squadron's grouch of a mechanic—and no less because after four years, Rudy's finally given up on trying to protest about the kitten's attentions.

Rudy pats Wyndi's head and then wordlessly passes them back to Potts so he can have his lunch without a curious kitten trying to share it. He looks back to Reba. "To put it simply? The 'complication' is that this little jungle of yours is at the center of a technological spiderweb—and we have no idea where the bloody spider is lurking."

"I understand that *just* enough to be concerned, mister Rudolph." Reba shakes her head. "What sort of a spiderweb have ye found, then?"

Rudy gestures lightly with a piece of celery in the direction of the hangar's doors. "All that interference we've run into isn't just from the melon here. There's a whole network of the bloody things placed on the moons, too—enough, I'm sure, that if they ever fully activated it, we'd lose relay connection and radio as far in as the *next* planet... and possibly be cut off from most things outside Kapteyn's solar system altogether."

"Ye don't think it's activated *now*?" Reba looks up from all of the gathered electronic parts she's now unpacking from her backpack.

"No. If my guess is right, they're not done planting melons yet. If they really plan to do what I think they are, they'd need stations on most of the asteroids along Mayview's orbit too so the whole system would be surrounded..." Rudy takes a bite from his celery as punctuation. "Besides, if it *was* fully activated, we wouldn't have short range at all."

"Ah." Reba looks between him and Potts again, raising a hesitant eyebrow. "And this 'spider' ye mentioned is... What, some Novan battle cruiser lying in wait around here in Mayview's shadow?"

Potts rubs awkwardly at the back of his head. "There's a pretty good chance of something like that, yeah. It'd certainly explain why they came after us yesterday... and probably your Novan-cicle collection, too." He shudders involuntarily at the thought of Reba's Novan prisoners in their eerie stasis-pod slumber. Somehow, even in induced hibernation and still perfectly disguised as elegantly beautiful humans, the ones she'd shown Potts and the Majors yesterday were even more frightening than the last Novan he'd met—and *that* one had dropped her disguise altogether and been aiming to devour his brain the last time he saw her.

Reba sighs softly and seems to be quietly considering all of this for a few moments before she speaks again. "I suppose I see what ye mean. So, what do we do now, if we're going to get in touch with the ship that's picking us up? Ye don't exactly go breaking bits of a spiderweb without expecting the spider to make an appearance."

Potts makes an exaggerated gesture to Rudy with a knowing smirk. "At the moment? We all give thanks that the Majors brought *him* along, because if there's anyone who can manipulate a radio system enough to get us through to *Aegolius*..."

Rudy shrugs. "I'll try my hand at it, at any rate. The hard part is going to be getting the carrier signal tuned right." He pointedly inspects the ration bar in his hand. "Last time I pulled a stunt like this, I was burying that with background interference... and I don't exactly have access to those frequencies at the moment."

"Do I *want* to know what happened the last time?" Reba looks between the two of them with the same disapproving glint in her eyes she used to get every time Potts came in from darter pilot training with a new injury for her to treat.

"Long story short?" Potts pauses to give one of his strawberries to the eager little Florivan kitten on his shoulder. "The two of us were stranded in deep space with *Aegolius* when she got separated from the rest of the Fleet on the way to a battle and had to stay under radio silence... and the only reason the Admiral didn't throw the book at *him* for disobeying orders and rigging my darter so my radio could sort of tag in to the nearest ship's Nav intercoms—and *me* for flying out to use his rigging to call for help—was that her jumper would have died if we hadn't."

Reba's eyes widen for a moment, and then she shakes her head. "Ye'll have to tell me the whole of *that* later."

She goes back to unpacking things from her backpack. "I think Wyndi found everything what were on ye list, Mister Rudolph. If ye need anything else, I may as well take ye back to the storage rooms to look for yeself."

"Thanks. Considering that I'll probably have to move my bloody 'imaginary relay' system to one of the other daters, I'll take all the spare parts I can get."

"Imaginary relay?" Reba asks, making little air quotation gestures and a suitably skeptical expression to go with them.

"The bit of farm-rigging I did last year that Sarge was referring to. It's going to take another day at least for me to get *his* bird safe to fly again, and the only way the system has a chance of working is if we can get it and him far enough out of range of the bloody melons to turn the carrier wave on." Rudy lets out a bit of a huff.

Potts chuckles and gives Reba a soft conspiratorial nudge. "He's a bit sore about Admiral Marvin calling it 'imaginary,' still, if you can't tell. The joke is that it doesn't and probably *shouldn't* work... except that for a handful of us, it *does*."

Once again, Reba gives him that look she usually reserves for when she knows he's done something to get both of them into trouble and is just waiting to find out what it was. "I'm not sure I understand, Julian."

"The folks at Intelligence and Research *tried* to replicate my rig and results, and even though they finally admitted that the bloody *theory* is sound—a long shot, granted, but *sound*—they couldn't get it to work at all anymore than we could for anyone but this fool, Li, and the Ranger who came to our rescue back then," Rudy grumbles. He waves his hand in a vaguely dismissive fashion. "A friend of mine back at the shipyards *does* have some civilian researcher or other who they got it to work for, but that's beside the point. From what I'm told, she's even more of an odd duck than Sarge here is."

Potts chooses not to protest that last remark in consideration of how many times he's heard it. He amuses himself instead by tossing another small strawberry up in the air for Wyndi to catch and nibble on.

"So why…?"

"To put it in terms you can understand, Kiley—no offense—"

"—None taken.—"

"—The rig pokes a little hole in the veil the same way the Relays or the Nav/Quan intercom channels do, with the aim of *finding* one of those intercom channels and tapping in like a second jumper's earpiece would once contact is made." Rudy grunts with his characteristic annoyance at a thing which has not been cooperative with him. "And because Quantum Space just has to make everything bloody difficult and weird, it's the *jumper* hearing and connecting the lines that makes it actually work, when it decides to work." He looks over to Potts with a pointed sort of a shrug. "So far, as near as any of us can tell, it seems the only human voices that any Florivan can hear over the rig are folks who've survived near-deadly miasma exposure."

Reba looks to Potts again, crossing her arms and taking on an equally pointed version of her doctor voice. "I don't believe ye mentioned *that* yet, Julian?"

Potts gives her his most charmingly sheepish grin in return. "To be *fair*, Reba, I don't remember it, and it wasn't intentional. Celadon thinks it was something to do with how Wyndi's parent died… regardless of how or when it happened, I have enough of a sense of which side of the veil I'm on that they're sure it *did* happen, even though I don't really show any other typical signs."

"Ah." Reba gives him a look which says she *will* be demanding a more thorough explanation than this later. "I see." She turns back to the backpack, shaking her head slowly.

Potts resigns himself to the eventual interrogation. He's known since they were kids that trying to hold information back from Reba is a losing battle—*especially* if it's to do with some injury or other that she wasn't there to witness.

Wyndi takes this opportunity to hop down from their current perch and scamper over to help Reba with the contents of the backpack. When she pulls out a certain small black case and sets it on the crate with the other things, the kitten begins squeaking excitedly.

"Shiny!" They look over to Rudy with an expectant waving of their tail. "See? *Shiny*!"

"What, Wyndi? You found something for me?" Rudy chuckles and sets the remains of his lunch aside to join Reba and Wyndi at the crate.

"Ah, that thing." Reba laughs brightly. "I don't know what use it'd be, since nothing of the sort were on ye list, but Wyndi pulled it out of the cabinet at the last minute all the same and insisted we bring it to ye."

Rudy picks up the case and dusts off the label. His eyes take on a startled wideness as he reads it. "You... didn't happen to open this up and see if it's empty or not, did you?"

"No, why?" Reba flashes him a sarcastic roll of her eyes. "And why'd ye think anyone would go and put an empty case back in a cabinet?"

Rudy matches the eye-roll as he slips the latches on the corners of the case up so he can open it. "You've *met* my pilots, Kiely. You tell me."

Reba looks back to Potts now, then nods sagely. "I see what ye mean."

"Hey, now! I only did that once," Potts protests, chuckling. "So, what is it that Wyndi's all squeaky about, then?"

"Shiny!" Wyndi declares, still waving their tail excitedly and keeping all three eyes on the mechanic's face and the case in his hands. The way his eyes go wider when he looks at the contents only makes their tail wave more vigorously.

"Oh, it's bloody *shiny*, you brilliant little magpie—how in the stars did you know I needed these?" Rudy shakes his head, then closes the case back and sets it gently on the crate. His incredulous smile breaks out into a wide grin. "I believe I owe you a donut when *Aegolius* gets here for this one, Wyndi! You just saved me *days* of farm-rigging." He holds a hand out to the kitten.

Wyndi excitedly scampers up into Rudy's arms to accept the offered cuddles.

Potts and Reba exchange equally confused looks.

"Okay, if ye won't ask again, Julian, I will." Reba looks to Rudy and crosses her arms again. "What's in the box? Or was 'intercom spare parts' something important?"

Rudy pauses in his kitten-praising long enough to laugh and make a vague gesture at the case. "Oh, *important* doesn't begin to describe it. Without getting too technical? That's a fresh set of miniaturized relay crystals and a few other bits and bobs that go into Nav headsets and jumper earpieces."

"Shiny," Wyndi adds, with a series of squeaks tacked on for good measure. "Wyndi *find*!"

"Yes, indeed!" Rudy laughs, turning his attention back to the kitten. He spins around in a circle with them a few times, much to Wyndi's delight. "You found *exactly* what I needed so we can rig things up to be able to call your Entile Celadon so they can come get us *off* this bloody rock. Good job, magpie!"

Potts looks to Reba again, shaking his head. "I am going to take this as a good thing," he stage-whispers, "but it's unsettling seeing him this happy about something, isn't it?"

"Aye," Reba replies in a similar teasing tone, "but it be a good sort of unsettling. I'm sure he'll be back to his usual bluster once he starts working on ye darter again."

Rudy rolls his eyes in mock offense. "I'd have some choice words for both of you, but I promised Dons I wouldn't use them where Wyndi could hear."

"I'm sure you would," Potts replies.

"You are right, though, Sarge..." Rudy chuckles softly, still lightly stroking Wyndi's head. "We do need to ask Dons if kittens are *supposed* to be this good at causing helpful coincidences. This is what... the second time today they've pulled out the exact thing someone needed?"

"After your laser saw? Yeah."

"Third," Reba chimes in, giving Potts' arm a light nudge. "Ye forgot to count them *being* the thing ye needed in the first place."

"Technically, they're still in trouble for that one..." Potts tries his best to sound firm as he gives his little counterpart a knowing look.

Wyndi, though, is too busy tucking themself into the largest inner pocket of Rudy's vest for a nap to add any more comment than a self-congratulatory squeak.

16

THE FOUR PILOTS, NYX, AND DR. KIELY SIT around a small table in the flower-filled 'lair' the two castaways have made for themselves in the lowest level of the complex. With Rudy working on the sort of tedious small-scale coms installations that he's made it clear he *doesn't* want anyone but Wyndi attempting to help him with, there's not much left for the six of them to do except play a friendly game of cards or four and wait.

"Hmm..." Ioane looks over the top of her hand and studies the faces of the two grinning pilots on either side of her. "So you two *really* think I'm going to believe that you've got two pairs of roses and a lady's slipper between you?"

"That's my bid, Abi," Penny says, setting her half of the cards in question face down on the table. "Now can you beat it or are you going to call us on this bluff you're imagining?"

Anna does the same, absently readjusting her headscarf afterwards. Whether she's doing that as a *conscious* tell or not is anyone's guess. Half the fun of playing cards with the woman is picking games where probability doesn't factor in enough to make it easy for her, though.

Ioane grins. "Oh... I'd say I can beat it. We've got a full crop of Kudzu between us, and I'd be *delighted* to see you take that off our hands."

Nyx's third eye meets her glance across the table, while their lower two seem intent on studying their cards. They twitch an ear with what she's come to recognize as amusement and slide three cards face-down in a neat little stack towards her. She sets her own pair of vine-decorated cards face down on top of Nyx's three. Four rounds into this game, and she's already determined that they're a better partner for Snapdragon's Garden than Sarge will ever be. That might come with the territory for a botanist, though.

"Well, Doc?" asks Penny, turning her attention to the woman sitting beside her now, "You getting in on this?"

Dr. Kiely exchanges a wordless glance with Sarge, then laughs and holds her hand out to him. He passes the large stack of cards he's holding to her with a slow, knowing shake of his head. She shuffles her own mass cards into his and sets the whole pile down in amongst the grapes the six of them have been making bets with. "Oh, that about does us in, I'd say—I've had me fill of picking up a pile of dandelions every time one of us tries to call ye bluffing as it is."

"Fair enough!" says Penny. She taps the table in front of her expectantly. "Well, Abigail? Show us the kudzu, then—I know a bluff when I hear it."

Ioane looks to Nyx, who nods with a knowing smile. One by one, she turns over the cards from their final bid of the round. Five matching vine-and-leaf decorated cards stare up from the table. "Behold! Our crop is *bountiful*!"

Anna laughs, tossing the rest of the cards from her hand into the pile in the center of the table. "Nice one coordinating that play, you two. You got us."

"What can I say?" Nyx quips with a wry smile and a dramatic wave of their tail, "If I know *anything*... it's how to make vines grow where people don't expect them."

"That ye do," Dr. Kiely agrees, standing and stretching some stiffness or other out of her limbs. "And considering that ye beat me at two-player every time, I'm not surprised the two of ye are dominating the table."

"We can switch up partners for the next round if you like, Doc," Penny says, collecting all of the cards from their various piles. "We usually do sooner or later to balance out Sarge's luck."

"I'm not *that* bad at this, am I?" He protests with only mock annoyance; the grin he's wearing is threatening to break out into a chortle.

"No..." Anna stifles a giggle. "But you have to admit you don't play nearly as well when Wyndi's not around to distract people from how bad your poker face is."

"I..." Sarge does laugh now, shaking his head. "Guilty as charged, Major."

"Well, Doc?" Penny asks, shuffling the cards as punctuation. "Want to rotate partners for the next round?"

"Nay," Dr. Kiely chuckles, "I think I'll keep him for a while yet. It just ain't right to leave the poor man feeling unwanted."

Ioane catches a particularly telling sort of mirthful expression crossing the faces of her wing-sisters in unison. She just shakes her head. Dr. Kiely is lucky that the two of them are trying to keep their teasing to a minimum tonight. Normally, neither of them would be able to resist giving Sarge a hard time for a remark like that.

"Thanks for the vote of confidence, Reba." The man in question is turning pink around his ears and *pointedly* looking away from all of them. He tries to be casual about trying to stack what few 'betting grapes' remain in front of him into a little pyramid, but to anyone who's been around him for long it's clear he's just making an excuse to avoid eye contact with anyone who might start giggling at his expense.

Ioane isn't the sort to get in on the good-natured teasing most of the time, in no small part because she can usually only pick up on the opportunities for it because of that particular look Penny and Anna get, or because of Sarge's habit of getting preemptively embarrassed if one of them is around to witness his usually-doomed attempts at flirting with people. She saves her teasing for all of the *other* embarrassing things he and the girls do that aren't to do with their respective love lives.

As usual, Ioane takes up her role as the changer of awkward conversational topics with pride. "Well, Sarge, since you're the one talking this round," she says, glancing over to Nyx with a conspiratorial wink, "we could spot the two of you the opening bid and say... two cards? Just to make it interesting."

"I could get behind that," Sarge laughs. "I can't say it'll make much of a difference, but I'll take any advantage I can get at this rate."

Dr. Kiely shakes her head ruefully. "Ye should have held out 'til she offered ye four cards, Julian—we might stand a chance, then."

"Ah, now, Reba!" Nyx leans over and gives the doctor a playful nudge. "Where's the fun in making it too easy for you?"

"Cheeky." Dr. Kiely nudges them back, then settles into her chair with an easygoing grin. "But fair enough."

"I'd say we're ready to start, then!" Penny dramatically shuffles the cards one more time and then leans over and plops the deck in front of Nyx with a flourish. "Appropriately enough, it's your turn to be our head gardener."

Nyx chuckles and picks up the deck with their lower hand. "Abigail," they ask, turning their third eye to her while their lower two remain focused on the cards their upper hand is flicking around the table face-down with a practiced ease, "am I right in assuming that one of your wing-sisters here is going to continue to make that joke *every* time it's my turn to deal?"

Ioane nods sagely. "It's too good of a joke for them to resist." She'd made the joke first herself, after all.

"Well, I'll just have to think up something dreadfully witty to pester them with in return, then." Nyx sets the remaining cards in the center of the table and taps it with one finger. "But for the moment, there's a Snapdragon sleeping in here, and I would *hate* to wake them up early…"

Ioane nods, raising a finger to her lips in a hushing gesture. Penny and Dr. Kiely mimic the gesture, since they too are silent partners this round.

Nyx winks at her, then turns to Sarge. "Now, I believe we gave you the opening bid… and two cards. Where do you want those to come from?"

Sarge glances down at the cards he's holding, then looks to Dr. Kiely. She shakes her head subtly; he laughs and pulls two cards from his hand. "I'd say these can go. I'll be picking more dandelions than I can handle before long, I'm sure."

"Fair enough!" says Nyx, taking the cards and slipping them into the middle of the draw pile they'd left in the center of the table. "Which reminds me that I need to harvest some of mine before they go to seed…"

"In the *game*?" Sarge asks, raising an eyebrow.

"Oh, no! I have them down on level two with the rest of the salad greens." Nyx chuckles. "In the game, it is not yet time for dandelions to sprout—unless you're making that your opening bid?"

"No, no, just give me a moment to think…" Sarge furrows his brow and looks between the remaining eight cards in his hand and Dr. Kiely for a while, then finally seems to come to a decision. He nudges one of the grapes from his fallen pyramid into the center of the table near the draw pile. "We'll open at two Cattails over a—ah, I always forget what it's called—a trio of whatever the pink flowers with the leaves that look like three little hearts attached at the points are."

"You do this every time we play, Sarge," Anna laughs. "How do you not know what the names of the cards are by this point?"

"Because it's one of the two Shamrocks and I always get them mixed up with the other one that's three round-ish leaves with the fluffy ball flowers."

"Wood Sorrel," Nyx supplies, seemingly holding back a laugh. "That's the one you're trying to bid. The other one is Clover."

"Ah! Thanks, Nyx—three of those, then." Sarge triumphantly sets two of his cards face-down on the table, then takes the three Dr. Kiely is holding out and adds them to the little pile.

Anna shakes her head. Across the table, Penny is stifling a laugh. "Whatever they are, you said there were *two* Cattails with them?" She adjusts one of the folds in her headscarf while she's staring at Sarge, just as she usually does when she's sizing up whether someone's bluffing or not.

"Yep! You want to challenge that, Major?" Sarge grins back at her.

"Hmm…"

While the two of them are having their little staring contest, Nyx's lower pair of eyes glance at their cards, then make contact with Ioane's questioningly. She looks down at her own. One of the deck's nine cattail cards is in her hand. She looks back up to them with a light shrug. She knows Sarge well enough to know that he had to have been honest about the cards *he* put down, but she doesn't know Dr. Kiely well enough to have any real guess there.

"Nah," Anna says at last, giggling and tossing a grape into the center of the table. "I'll let you have it this time. It's always sad when you get caught on the first round…"

Nyx tosses a grape in as well. "Oh, I don't know, Major—if I know Reba, she's *counting* on all of us having pity on him."

"Does that mean you're calling him out, Nyx?" Anna raises an eyebrow.

Nyx shakes their head. "Not this time, even though I wouldn't be surprised if Reba slipped a cabbage or two in with that—*we* are trying to give them a fighting chance on the first round, after all…"

Ioane holds back a giggle for the sake of being silent and avoiding any penalty draws. Half the reason she and Nyx have been winning, in her opinion, is that between the two of them they know all of the others' ways of playing too well—and, to a certain extent, that they'd picked up on each other's body language quickly during the first two rounds. Nyx is an easy partner to play with, too, particularly since they'd learned the same regional variation of the game when they first moved to Mayview that Ioane herself had grown up playing. They might be running the standard rule set out of consideration for the others, but the strategic quirks one picks up from the Mayview variant's host of extra penalty rules make for a team that's hard to beat in present company.

"All right, then." Anna rolls two grapes into the center with a calculated precision. "We'll bid up to a pair of those Wood Sorrel… and a Blueberry Bush."

Penny wordlessly passes Anna one card to go with the two she's pulling out of her hand, then nonchalantly sets about re-tying one of her ponytails. Penny theoretically has an advantage at games that require a good poker face, thanks to the tint of her protective wraparound glasses somewhat obscuring the movements of her eyes. Even with that, though, the woman has enough tells that she's almost as easy to read as Sarge is, if one knows her. To Ioane's eyes, the ponytail adjustment is more a sign that she's trying to strategically entice someone to call her team's bluff than anything.

Sarge laughs. "You really are going easy on me, aren't you, Major?"

"Who, me?" Anna raises her eyebrows, otherwise leaving her face cheerful but ambiguous. "Since when do I do that?"

"Point taken." Sarge shakes his head. "Well, it's your option to call first, Nyx, but if you don't, I will."

Nyx smiles softly, even as their eyes meet Ioane's own and hopefully catch the near imperceptible shaking of her head. They clearly pick up her meaning, too. They roll two grapes into the center of the table to join the rest and then lean back in their chair, folding their cards together into a neat stack in their lower hand and gesturing to Sarge with the upper. "I'll let you have the honor, Julian, if you want it. You *do* know these ladies better than I do, after all."

Sarge grins. "You may regret that, but okay! Show us those blueberries of yours, Major."

His grin disappears immediately as Anna turns over the three cards to reveal first two matching Wood Sorrel cards and then the requested Blueberry Bush.

"Here you go, Doc!" Anna says, cheerfully scooping up all three of those cards and the still-face-down ones Sarge had bid to begin with and passing them across the table.

Dr. Kiely rolls her eyes lightheartedly and accepts the two piles, setting the revealed ones beside her in her penalty pile and all five of the unknown ones back in her hand.

"And that's two cards for *you* to draw, Sarge, for daring to doubt our honesty!"

"Fine, fine." He reluctantly reaches for the draw pile. "I could have sworn you were bluffing there..."

Five rounds of bids later, and once again Ioane and Nyx are down to four cards between them, she holding one and they three, while Anna and Penny have four apiece. Sarge's team, on the other hand, has the majority of the rest of the deck either in play or in the rather large pile of face-up cards beside Dr. Kiely.

"Well," says Anna, grinning and tapping the small pile of cards from her latest bid, "if neither of you are going to try calling me on this one... I believe that makes it your bid, Nyx. What are you holding?"

"Quite eager to have this round over with, aren't you, Major?" Nyx's tail subtly swishes behind them with an easy grace. Their third eye meets Ioane's glance with a light flicking motion to the single card she's holding.

Ioane flashes them the briefest of smirks and leans across the table to set it face-down in front of them. Holding on to the card that only incurs penalties when it's revealed until the end of the game is classic Mayview-rules strategy, and one she hasn't had the chance to test with Nyx before now. Considering that she *drew* the thing in her opening hand and hasn't moved its position when she's had other cards to hold, though, she can only hope that Nyx has been paying as close attention as she thinks they have. That's half the fun of this game, in her mind: learning to read the play style and body language of your teammate enough to know what they have and how to play it without cluing any of the opponents in to your plans.

Nyx chuckles softly, setting their own three cards down on top. "Three dandelions... and the Snapdragon."

"Oh, really, Nyx," says Anna, laughing, "*now* you decide to bluff us?"

"Is that what you think I'm doing, Major?" Nyx tilts their head to one side and makes a vague gesture at the cards in front of them. "You're more than welcome to challenge our victory."

Anna stares at them skeptically for a few moments and then looks over to Sarge.

Sarge and Reba exchange a glance; she shakes her head, holding back laughter. "Well, if I've picked that snapdragon up at some point, there are too many cards in my hand to tell where it is... but we're behind enough on points as it is." He rolls his last betting grape into the pile. "If you want them called, you'll have to do it yourself."

"You're *learning*, Sarge." Anna laughs and tosses in a grape herself. "All right, Nyx, I can't resist calling your bluff. I halfway believe the dandelions, but that's it. What do you really have there?"

Nyx wears a serene smile, naming each of the cards as they turn it over. "Why... Dandelion... Dandelion... *Dandelion*—"

"I am so glad I didn't call that one," Sarge mutters.

"—And here's the Snapdragon! All refreshed from its nap and ready to chase away trespassers." Nyx's smile has shifted into a wide grin.

"*How*?" Anna asks, even as Penny is giggling and picking up all of the bid cards that the two of them have now earned. "I could have sworn that would still be in the draw pile, considering how many cards we've all been passing back and forth without it showing up..."

"I've had it since we started," Ioane says triumphantly, now that she's no longer required to stay silent by the rules of the game.

"*You*—" Anna shakes her head, laughing. "—Of *course* you did, Abigail. I'm starting to remember why we usually pair you up with Sarge when we play..."

Sarge looks to her now, raising an eyebrow. "I know *one* of us has just been insulted, Major, but I don't know who it was."

"I'd say it was both." Ioane rolls her eyes, then reaches across the table to offer a congratulatory handshake to her partner. "Good job coordinating that, Nyx!"

"Likewise, Abigail," they reply, accepting the gesture. "And as fun as this has been, I think it might be wise for us to pick a different game for a while... especially since I need to step out and make sure those water circulation pumps I adjusted earlier are still running correctly."

"Ye know ye ain't obligated to keep the jungle running, now that we'll be leaving?" Dr. Kiely asks, looking over to the Florivan with a hint of concern in her eyes.

"I know." Nyx stands and sets a hand on the doctor's shoulder briefly before they head towards the door. "But on the off chance that the Fleet *will* be taking this place over after we leave, I'd like not to leave the equipment in too much of a state for whatever poor horticulture team they bring in to tame my jungle to handle."

"All right, then—do me a favor while ye be down that way, Nyx? Let Mister Rudolph know I'm expecting him and Wyndi to join us for tea this evening, urgent work to be done or no." Dr. Kiely's concerned tone shifts into something more firm and professional as she says this.

"Do you need any help?" Ioane offers, halfway to standing as well. Truth be told, she wouldn't mind taking a break from thrashing her fellow pilots at cards herself.

"Ah, no, not really—but thank you." Nyx turns back long enough to smile at her, and then disappears through the curtain of vines hanging over the door.

While Penny and Anna are playfully arguing with Sarge over which game they should switch to now, Dr. Kiely shakes her head with a small, nearly inaudible sigh and gets up to refill her near-empty glass of water.

Ioane follows, her own empty cup in hand. "Do you think they're okay?" she asks softly.

"Nyx? I'd say they be as okay as they've been..." Dr. Kiely shakes her head again. "It just be a long day. They probably need to take some time to re-center a bit, even if it do seem they've been enjoying playing with the lot of us like this."

Ioane nods lightly, accepting the water pitcher from the doctor to fill her own glass. "Good. I worried that we'd pushed them too hard with the flight today..."

"Nyx be good about saying when they've hit their limits." Dr. Kiely takes a sip from her refilled cup. "Better than I be, even."

"Hmm." Ioane studies her expression for a moment. "And how *are* you holding up, then?"

Dr. Kiely forces a laugh, glancing back over to the animated argument around the card table. "It's been *silence* here for four years... I ain't used to so much company, anymore. But it's good to have ye, even if playing cards with ye be exhausting."

"I can see how it could be." Ioane lightly reaches up with her free hand to brush a stray lock of hair behind her ear. "You should see the chaos whenever we manage to get Celadon in for a game—you'd *swear* they can read people's minds. Drives everyone to distraction trying to figure out how they do it, too."

Dr. Kiely shakes her head again, smiling softly now. "Like ye and Nyx have been pretending to all afternoon?"

"Oh, worse, I would say—Nyx and I made a surprisingly good team, sure," Ioane replies, half chuckling, "but Celadon? They always seem to be six moves ahead of the rest of us no matter what gets bid."

"Their Navigator must be a decent player himself, to be able to keep up with that."

Ioane grins. "Believe it or not, he's not much of a Snapdragon fan, as far as I've ever heard; more of a poker guy, and a hard one to beat at that. Whenever Celadon's played with us, it's been as *Rudy's* partner—and I tell you,

Dr. Kiely, when the two of them play together you'd think they were seeing all the cards face up."

"Well, then," Dr. Kiely says, stifling a giggle, "once we all be safely on a ship with ye friends, we'll just have to get ye and Nyx in a match against the two of them and see who comes out on top."

"Oh, now, that could be *fun...*" Ioane pauses to take another sip from her water. "I won't hold out much hope for us winning, though."

"I'll cheer ye on." Dr. Kiely gestures towards the table with her glass. "And it seems they've finally decided on a game."

"So it seems they have." Ioane shakes her head when she sees what the other pilots have picked. "I may just sit this one out and watch. Sarge and Anna get a bit overly enthusiastic and competitive when they start building card castles."

"Oh, do they?" Dr. Kiely raises an eyebrow. "I know he and Edwin used to get heated about it..."

"Well... let's just say you might need to get your first aid kit out to deal with any card-cuts—usually at least one of them manages to hurt themself by the end." Ioane stifles a giggle.

"Ah, that sounds familiar." Dr. Kiely shakes her head. "Did Julian ever tell ye that's how he broke an ankle once?"

"An ankle? But... *how*?"

"Slipped on one of the cards after his castle fell down, trying to go after Edwin's in revenge." Dr. Kiely chuckles. "There were a two-month ban on card castle building while he were healing, too."

"Yours, or their uncle's?"

"Both."

Ioane looks over to the flurry of activity on either side of the table. As usual, Penny has all of three of cards shakily balanced in front of her. Meanwhile Anna and Sarge are already busy competing to snatch the 'best' cards from each other to start their second tiers. She shakes her head. "We may need to intervene before it gets to that stage."

"True... but I be up for some spectating until then if ye be!"

"Sounds like a plan to me. Card castles are more fun with Wyndi around. They like to slip cards out of the towers and bring them to me while everyone else is distracted."

"Oh, now, *that* I'm looking forward to seeing for meself."

"Abigail!" Penny calls from the table, excitedly, "Look! I got a fourth card to stay this time!"

"Good job, Penny! I see it!" Ioane refreshes her water again and then nods to the doctor. "Come on, then, might as well get your obligatory joke about the sort of things darter pilots do for fun in now."

"Who, me?" Dr. Kiely asks, putting on an innocent face. "Tease the lot of ye for playing children's card games in ye off time?"

"You wouldn't be the first."

"Well, then..." Dr. Kiely takes on a conspiratorial smile and leans over, dropping her voice to a whisper. "We've got the rest of them stashed away right now, but there be cards enough in that cupboard over there to build a tower what goes up to the *ceiling* in here—and we walked around it for at least a week before it finally decided to fall down."

Ioane can't help laughing. "Now *that*, Dr. Kiely, I would have loved to see."

★

WHENEVER NYX YRITAL FINDS THEMSELF feeling off-center, they gravitate towards the calming stillness of tending the plants in their care. Even as a kitten, whenever they became separated from their littermate in their explorations of their parent's starship, they would wander into the nearest hydroponics bay and find a nice cozy plant to sleep in until someone came looking for them.

In the long years since their return to Mayview, Nyx has focused the majority of their personal pain and anxiety into the cultivation of their gardens. There is something about working with their plants that is centering, be it pruning the vines or setting new generations of seedlings into their new homes. The little jungle filling the outpost is testament, in a way, to how hard it was at first for them to accept everything that had happened to them and Reba.

On this particular evening, Nyx finds themself both happier than they've been in years and restlessly unfocused. As much as they truly did enjoy playing cards with their new friends, it's nice to have an excuse to step out into the quiet of their vines for a while. Their routine of chores and maintenance tasks is relaxing in its simplicity compared to everything they've been through in the last few days. It's not long before they're able to calm their thoughts enough to find their center.

Once all of their jungle chores are done, Nyx heads down to the outpost's hangar to check on their cousins as per Reba's request. They come through the door just in time to see a silver streak of kitten scamper down from the darter where their human cousin has his upper body wedged into an access port over one wing and into the bag of tools in the middle of the array of parts and pieces on the ground below. As they approach, Nyx hears soft squeaks of concentration from within the bag. Soon, little Wyndi pops back out again dragging a green-handled tool of some sort.

"Hmm... better make that the point-zero-two microcircuit probe, Wyndi, now that I think about it," Elias calls down, his voice echoing from within the darter. "We don't have enough bloody spares to risk overloading things."

The kitten squeaks a cheerful acknowledgment and sets the larger green-handled probe they'd been fetching back into its spot in the bag in exchange for the correct size one. They hold the probe between their lower set of hands as they scamper back and climb up onto the wing of the darter where the mechanic's legs are sticking out. They tap on one of his feet to catch his attention before slipping up into the limited bit of free space inside the access port where he's working.

"Shiny?" Little Wyndi's voice echoes now from inside the access port.

"Yes, that's the one. Thanks, magpie. Think you can wrangle one of those spools of fine-gauge optical cable up here next?"

Within moments, the kitten is scampering back down into a box where all of the spools of different wires and cables are piled.

Nyx walks up to the box and makes a small trill of greeting.

Wyndi squeaks cheerfully in response and hops up into their hand for a few moments of clearly-appreciated cuddling. Oddly, the kitten seems to be wearing some sort of technician's anti-static wristband as a collar and a second one as a belt beneath their second pair of arms.

"Hello, Wyndi." Nyx gives their little cousin's ears a gentle scratch. "Still hard at work?"

"Wyndi *help*!" The kitten replies with a happy swish of their tail. Wyndi abruptly seems to remember that they're supposed to be helping *now*, and leaps gracefully back from Nyx's shoulder into the box of spools. It only takes a few moments for them to find their prize and begin dragging it up out of the box.

"Here," says Nyx, offering their lower hand, "let me."

Wyndi gives them a grateful trilling squeak and lets them take the spool before scampering back up onto Nyx's shoulder. They gesture excitedly towards the darter where Rudy is waiting.

Nyx climbs up onto the darter's wing, holding the spool with the end of their long prehensile tail so they can have full use of both hands. "I'm not sure what this is, Cousin Elias," they say once they're safely sitting on the wing beside the man's legs, "but Wyndi seems to think you want it?"

"Ah, hey, Nyx—didn't hear you come in." Elias slides out onto the wing from the access port to inspect the offering. "Yeah, that's what I asked for!" He pulls a small pair of cable nippers out of one of his vest pockets and begins unrolling sections of the hair-like optic cable and snipping it into lengths. "I take it someone's sent you to check on us?"

"Reba did, yes." Nyx absently occupies their hands with kitten-cuddling while they talk. "She said to tell you that you're expected to come join us all for tea. If you don't manifest, I wouldn't be surprised if she comes after you." Their tail swishes with amusement. "That's about two hours from now, though."

"Sounds like her." Elias half chuckles. "Well, no need to get the good doctor all riled up just yet. I should be at a decent place to stop by then anyway."

"That's good. I've been on the receiving end of her 'if you don't rest I shall *make* you rest' lecture more than once myself—probably best to avoid having her bring it out today."

Elias gives them a look over the length of optical cable he's measuring. "Yeah, I can see you being the type to need the lecture."

"Guilty as charged." Nyx smiles, twitching one of their ears softly. "I *might* be the type who tends to forget how long I've been working when I get absorbed in things…"

"If that means you have to be reminded to stop and eat," Elias teases, tucking his cable nippers back into one of his vest pockets, "then I am not surprised at *all* that Li is related to you somehow. He and Dons both get like that, actually. Now, me? I usually know when to stop and take a break…" He laughs, reaching out to ruffle Wyndi's ears. "And you might have noticed that my little assistant here is pretty vocal when they're hungry?"

"I had noticed." Nyx stifles a laugh of their own. "Kittens do tend to be, though."

"Speaking of which…" Elias holds the spool out to Wyndi. "You can put this back in the box now, magpie. I've got all the bits I need. We'll take a few minutes break before we get back to it, but if you can find the bag of cable link ends for me in the meantime, that'll be a help."

Wyndi squeaks happily and takes hold of the spool, disappearing once again as a silver streak over the side of the darter's wing.

"You've trained them well, it seems," Nyx notes. "Reba was saying they could actually identify all of the parts you sent her to find?"

"They can, for the most part—not so good at reading the bloody labels, yet, but if I show them what things look like, Wyndi can usually pick them out." Elias chuckles and leans back against the darter's side, rolling his lengths of cut optic cable up into a neat bundle. "Sarge's had to leave them with me often enough that they've sort of imprinted on the work I do. I taught them the names of the tools so

I could ask them to *return* the things they'd 'borrowed', though."

Nyx nods with an amused flick of their tail. "That's how I got my start in botany, you know? According to Nida, I spent half of my kittenhood escaping from them and pestering poor Lt. Howards in *Deinocheirus'* hydroponics bays..." They can't help smiling at the vague memories. Their kittenhood was a long time ago, now, but they do still remember bits and pieces of their days riding around on the old botanist's shoulder. "From what I'm told, most of my portion of the stashes of shiny things Thalassa and I had when we were Wyndi's age was just seeds and flower petals."

"I can see that." Elias tucks the neatly-bundled cables into another pocket inside his vest and stretches out his limbs. After a moment, he looks back to Nyx with an odd sort of curiosity in his eyes. "How are you holding up, then?"

"Hm? Me?"

"Yes, you. With all the bloody flying and whatnot—I didn't really hear much of how things went up there aside from what you and the girls found with the melons and the frequencies I needed to get this rig to slip through." A note of genuine concern colors his tone, although Nyx's not entirely sure why.

"Oh. It went as well as one could expect, considering what we're dealing with." Nyx absently begins straightening out the fluff on the end of their tail. "I still almost can't believe that there's one of these... melons... on every one of Mayview's moons, but I *saw* them. I almost wouldn't be surprised if those had been built before Reba and I got trapped here, even." They sigh softly. They don't want to bring up the memories of everything that happened surrounding their arrival at this place again.

"I wouldn't either. Wouldn't be surprised if some of them came after, too, though—can't quite fathom why they've not turned this bloody resonance network on yet, unless there's some bigger scheme at work than just causing coms interference." Elias pauses, taking a few moments to stretch out some different apparent stiffnesses from his limbs. "But speculation on that isn't really our place. Flying with Ioane's not bothering you too much?"

"No," Nyx replies, grateful for the slight change in subject. "It's... almost nice, actually, when no one's shooting at us. Very different from being in a shuttle or on a proper starship, of course, and there's so little barrier to the outside it's almost easy to forget one's in a spacecraft at all—" They stifle an unbidden giggle. "—If it weren't for the danger, I could actually learn to enjoy it, I think."

"I'll take your word for that." An almost imperceptible shudder crosses the man's body. "I know too much about how the bloody birds work to like being in them, even if I weren't..." he trails off with a vague gesture.

"Particularly unsuited for flight of any kind?" Nyx completes, raising one of their eyebrows partway.

"That's one way of putting it."

"And yet, you work on a Fleet starship doing... this?" Nyx makes a vague gesture towards the access port and their human cousin's array of tools and parts.

"Starships aren't a problem as long as I don't try to sleep during Quantum Space transit." Elias shrugs. "And when I signed up for the bloody job, I was in a *planetside* position at the shipyards. Never thought I'd wind up at the Orbital, much less assigned to the Fleet's smallest and most trouble-prone squadron." There's a bit of a fond, amused sparkle in his eye as he says this. He drops his tone down to a conspiratorial whisper. "Don't tell the Musketeers, but I wouldn't change that last bit for all the stars."

Nyx gives him a reassuring pat on the shoulder. "Don't worry, Cousin Elias. I won't ruin your reputation with them."

"Thanks." He lets out a small chuckle. "They're hard enough to manage as it is."

Wyndi returns now, scampering up into Elias' lap with a cloth pouch in tow that's almost as big as themself. "See? Shiny!" they declare.

He takes the pouch and opens it to inspect the contents. "Ah, that's the ones! Good kitten."

Little Wyndi squeaks triumphantly and accepts the head-pats and cuddles of appreciation with no small amount of pleased tail-swishing and purring.

"Has anyone ever told you that you're good with kittens?" Nyx asks, not trying to hide their amusement at the scene.

"Once or twice." There's a pleasing warm softness to his smile now. Nyx has the impression he'd try to conceal that if anyone else was there to see it. "Really, I think it's just that Sarge has had to leave this little pest with me too often."

Wyndi looks up to Nyx with wide, contented eyes and wraps their tail around Elias' wrist, since he's still absently petting them. "Mine."

"So you've said, Wyndi." Nyx can't help chuckling as they reach out and give the kitten's ears a ruffle themself. After a moment, Wyndi seems to take this as an invitation to climb over into their lap instead.

"Well, Nyx, thanks for the excuse to get some fresh air," Elias says now, stretching again and brushing the wisps of shed kitten fur off of his trousers. "You're welcome to sit here and distract Wyndi while I get these cables installed, if you like."

"I think I'm obligated to," Nyx replies with a smile, snuggling the kitten a little closer. "Although I'd hardly call *this* fresh air. I'll take you on a walk through one of my gardens later; that's where the best air is around here."

"I'll take you up on that." He shimmies his upper body back into the access port. "And if you don't mind staying for a bit," Elias adds, his voice echoing inside the darter now, "I could use an *adult* ear to tune the relay crystals once I get them installed."

"I'll see what I can do." Nyx hesitates. "I'm sorry I can't be more help to you with all of this..."

"There's not exactly room enough in here for two," Elias quips. "Well, unless Wyndi's one of the two, but even then they have to remember to keep their tail out of the wirings."

"You know what I mean. If we'd been able to salvage the shuttle, or if I could... well." They run out of words before they can finish the thought, and turn their eyes back to the contentedly purring kitten who seems to be falling asleep in their lap.

"My mum had a saying, Nyx..." There's a pause and a low grunt as Elias shifts his position, likely to better reach some component or other within the narrow access space. "What is *is*, and y' work from the 'is' forward... and if y' keep your eyes on what y' *can* do, the forward will sort itself out."

Nyx finds themself smiling in spite of the uncertain mix of emotions that's making their tail twitch. "Your mother would get along wonderfully with my Nida, I'm sure."

"Oh, I wouldn't doubt she would have." Elias chuckles. "Of course, it's all just a nice way of saying not to bloody dwell on it when you're already doing the best you can with what you've got—and from what I've seen, you've been doing that all along."

"Thank you."

"No problem."

Quite some time passes in silence, save for the sounds of whatever alterations Elias is making to the darter and Wyndi's loud, contented purring. Nyx is left alone with their thoughts, although calmer somehow than they'd been before. They can see now why the kitten and Elder Celadon both seem to favor this human, despite his pretense of bluster and the sharp, fiery temper Abigail had described during their mid-flight conversation earlier.

Soon, Elias slides back out of the access port and hops down off the wing. "That should do it for now. Think you're up for crystal tuning still?"

Wyndi immediately wakes up at the sound of his voice and bounces out of their lap, making a graceful leap off of the darter's wing and onto the mechanic's shoulder.

"I'll give it a go," Nyx says, free now to stand and stretch out their limbs. It's been a long time since they were an apprentice practicing Nav/Quan drills, and they certainly don't feel up to making any jumps through the Strange, but they still remember their basic skills. They're Florivan, after all. "How do you want to do this? I don't really have a Drive Bay here to run the simulation in."

"Hmm... Is there something like a closet or a sealable room in this place that we could convert to a sim box for you?"

"Ah! Yes, there's a storage chamber off the hangar that way which could work." Nyx gestures in an appropriate direction with their tail.

"Good. Let's get you set up and see if we can't make my little nonsense rig play nice for us..."

At Dr. Kiely's request, Ioane goes with her Wing-Sergeant to retrieve Nyx, Rudy, and Wyndi from the hangar when it's time for dinner. She finds it amusing, in a way, that the doctor is insisting they all make an effort to eat and sleep regularly despite the relatively pressing nature of the situation they've found themselves in—but she *certainly* wouldn't be interested in arguing the point herself. Ioane has never been one to argue with medical personnel in the first place, unless there's a very good personal reason for her to disagree. Usually, she can't find one. She's more the sort to negotiate than to argue to begin with.

Sarge shakes his head, doing his best not to trip on the grape vines the two of them cut the first time they came through this corridor. "I don't know why she's set on us all eating together," he says, in what Ioane thinks is the fourth iteration of the statement since they set out. "I *tried* to tell her that Rudy tends to keep his own schedule…"

"Now, Sarge," Ioane chides, forcing herself not to laugh. "You've known her longer than any of us. Do you really think a little thing like *that* could change the good doctor's mind?"

"It's… not particularly easy to change Reba's mind once she's set on something in the first place, no," the younger pilot admits, awkwardly running a hand through his hair. "I just don't get the *why* of it, that's all."

"Well, think of it this way: She and Nyx have been alone here for *how* long?" Ioane gives him a gentle nudge and a knowing look. "Having the lot of us around to share meals with them means something important to her, even if she's not asking us to in those words."

Sarge is silent for a moment, then shakes his head. "You're probably right, Major. She was like that when we were kids for a long time, too, now that I think of it… used to coerce Edwin into taking us on picnics after school most days and everything."

"I wouldn't be surprised if she did, from what you've told me." Ioane smiles softly. Her Wing-Sergeant is a sweet sort of a fellow, when he's not off getting himself into trouble. "Now! I don't know about you, but *I* don't want to get on Dr. Kiely's bad side for letting the rest of our little 'family' get away with skipping meals."

Sarge chuckles as the two of them walk into the hangar. "Me neither, Major. Shall we collect the strays?"

"Naturally!" Ioane strides up to the wing of her darter and calls to the legs of the mechanic who's wedged inside one of its access ports, "So! Do you think your patient will live to fly another day?"

"That depends *entirely* on whether the bloody madwoman who flies this bird will try to stay *out* of the line of fire for once," Rudy bellows back, his voice echoing from within the darter's body.

Ioane laughs brightly, setting her hands on her hips. "Oh, now, Rudy, where's the fun in that?"

"Bloody darter pilots," Rudy mutters, shimmying out onto the wing now. "Your bird's fine, Ioane, and I'm in the middle of tuning the intercom rig." He stands and reaches into the cockpit, then leans down off the wing and holds out her radio headset. He's already wearing the spare one he keeps with the rest of his repair kit, although he has the microphone bar flipped up. "Here, make yourself useful so I can finish this up—you too, Sarge, go on and get yours, I want to double-check the tuning on your bird too tonight, even if you won't be flying tomorrow. Nyx can hear me well enough, but *you're* the ones that'll have to pull this off. Fine-tuning's always easier if I don't have to talk at the same time."

Ioane shares a look with Sarge that's more amused than not. They both know what their squadron's mechanic can be like when he's in the middle of something. She laughs again and takes the headset, climbing up onto the wing to join Rudy. "Fine, but after this, we're expected elsewhere."

"Reba sent us looking for you, you know," Sarge adds, calling back over his shoulder as he's walking towards his own darter.

"I figured," Rudy calls back, "and we'll be done with this soon enough." He rolls his eyes and pulls the microphone bar of his headset back down. "All right, Nyx, sorry about that. Sarge and Ioane are going to help us finish this up so you can come out of your box and convince Kiely not to be irritated about us being a touch late for tea."

Ioane gets her headset in place and turned on in time to hear Nyx laughing. *"That sounds like a plan, Cousin Elias. We're ready to continue whenever you are."*

"Where is Nyx, anyway?" Ioane asks, tilting her head curiously to one side.

Rudy makes a vague gesture in the appropriate direction. "We sealed off and set up an empty storage room for them to run the simulation from—and if you're looking for Wyndi, that's where they are too."

"I had wondered..." Ioane pulls down the microphone bar of her headset. "Okay, then. Can you hear me at all, Nyx?"

There's mildly static-laden silence on the other end for a few moments. This doesn't surprise Ioane at all; half the reason there are so few people qualified to be Navigators in the world is because the entire operation depends on whether or not the Florivan jumper on the other end of a Nav/Quan intercom system can hear their human counterpart's voice or not. As far as she knows, it's a matter of personal familiarity and instinctive compatibility at work, as well as the jumper's own skills and experience.

The silence only lasts for a moment, though, much to Ioane's surprise.

"*Hello, Abigail!*" Nyx's voice rings clearly in her earphone, complete with their usual wind-chime-like Florivan undertones.

"Nyx! You can hear me?"

"*Yes, there's still a bit of static in the channel but I can hear you now.*" She hears them laugh again, and then what sounds like excited squeaking sounds in the background. "*Wyndi can hear you too, since I have you on a speaker instead of an earpiece—they're very happy about that.*"

"I don't know *how* you're getting anything done with them on your shoulder," Ioane teases, making herself comfortable in a cross-legged position with her back to the body of the darter beside the access port Rudy's still rearranging himself into. "But I'm glad you can both hear me, since I've been conscripted to help with this."

"*They're better behaved than you give them credit for, Abigail! Besides, we're only running a simulation… but they do seem happy to get to be in the fringes of the veil.*"

"*Wyndi helping!*" the kitten's voice squeaks in the background, just on the edge of what Ioane can hear.

"Yes, Wyndi, I'm sure you are," she says, unable to hold back a giggle. "You ready for us, Rudy?"

"I am *now*," the mechanic replies, with a tone that makes her certain he's rolling his eyes. "You said the static was worst on the low end of the channel, Nyx?"

"*Yes… I moved your speaker closer to my good ear and it's sill there. I think there's a ringing on the higher end, too?*"

Ioane is not surprised in the slightest that Rudy's voice carries over the modified intercom system well enough for Nyx to have been helping him tune it across their simulation jump. With all the time he's spent around

Wyndi and Celadon, he probably understands Florivans just as well as the average Navigator. Granted, she knows he helps *Surnia*'s Nav/Quan team with their equipment too from time to time, if they need an additional pair of hands. She counts all of that among the many reasons that her squadron was right to steal the man from the shipyards—it always pays to have a mechanic with uncommon additional skills, sooner or later.

"We'll work through the lower end first, then." Rudy pauses to nudge her leg with his foot. "Just keep up a conversation on this end, Ioane. Nyx and I will handle the rest."

"Gotcha." Ioane chuckles. "Okay, Nyx... so after you left, Sarge and Anna got into one of their little card-castle-building competitions—"

"*—A bit more, Cousin Elias, that's almost cleared it up—go on, Abigail. Who won?*"

"Jury's out on that." Ioane shrugs. "After all of the cards from their tiebreaker round fell on him, Reba called a time-out and—"

"*—Ah! That's it. Stop there, she's nice and bright now.*"

"*Shiny!*" Wyndi's distant voice chimes in.

"Good," says Rudy, echoing from within the darter. "You still hearing that bloody whistle?"

"*Just a touch on the higher end.*"

"That'll be the number eight crystal... keep going, Ioane, this should be the last one."

Ioane chuckles. "Just what I wanted to be today: another piece of equipment for Wyndi to decide to carry off and hide somewhere with the rest of their shiny things."

Nyx's laugh is a very pleasing sort of wind-chime-toned sound, she decides. They still seem a bit out of practice using it, but it's nice to know that she can crack them up. *"Oh dear,"* they say between giggles, *"that would be a sight to see…"*

"How's that whistle, Nyx?" Rudy is clearly holding a laugh of his own in.

"Ah! Just a touch more and you've got it."

"Does that mean you need me to keep babbling and cracking bad jokes?"

"I wouldn't mind if—ah! That's done it, Cousin Elias. I don't think you need to adjust anything else."

"Good," says Rudy. "Just let me close this bird up and get Sarge's darter set up to call into your channel and we can check the tuning on *that* and be done for now."

"Sounds good to me—and you really didn't have anyone to tune your rig with when you first used it?"

"No, this is a *luxury* in my world." Rudy slides out of the access port. "Thanks for the assist, Ioane. Mind keeping Nyx on the line for a few minutes while I get things sorted with Sarge?"

"Not at all." Ioane grins. "This is kind of fun."

"Does that mean we're in danger?" Nyx quips over the radio.

Rudy rolls his eyes at the air and turns his attention to sealing the access port.

Ioane laughs. "Not at the moment! Not *everything* I consider fun is a threat to life and limb, you know."

"Of course not… but most of it seems to be." Nyx giggles softly. She can hear Wyndi giggling with them. *"So, what happened with the card castles?"*

"Well, like I said, they ended up at a tiebreaker, and then all the cards fell on top of Sarge..."

Twenty minutes later, Ioane finds herself knocking on the door of a small storage room adjacent to the hangar. She can still hear Sarge discussing with Rudy how long it'll take to get the reattached engines of his darter to actually function somewhere behind her. As usual, Rudy seems to be taking great delight in giving the youngest of his pilots a hard time about how much damage there is to repair. It's just as amusing as ever, in Ioane's mind, but she has other things to do besides listen to the boys banter today.

"Nyx? Are you clear to open the door?"

"Ah! Just a moment, Abigail. I have to sort out one last thing..." Nyx's voice is muffled by the door. She distantly hears Wyndi squeaking something, too, but she can't make out what it is.

"Take your time." Ioane laughs lightly and takes the opportunity to stretch some evening stiffness out of her back. "I'll be here."

A few moments later, the door creaks open. Nyx emerges, Wyndi perched on one shoulder and a thick towel draped over the other.

"My apologies for the delay, Abigail," Nyx says, their upper hand reaching to lightly stroke the kitten's head. "We had a bit of trouble getting the towel un-stuffed from under the door."

"I was *wondering* what that was about!"

"Well, yes... the door sealed well enough everywhere else, but the base of it had a gap that we needed to do something about. Luckily, this was sufficient to fix it so I could manage the simulation safely." Nyx smiles at her, gesturing at the towel. "Wyndi and I weren't about to let any trace miasmas out to bother the rest of you, after all."

"Of course not." Ioane nods.

She understands just enough about Nav/Quan things from hanging out with the handful of Florivan friends she's had over the years to know the significance of what they're talking about: when the Quantum Space Drive is engaged for a jump on a starship, the Drive Bay is filled with the miasmas of Quantum Space itself and sealed off from the rest of the ship's "Normal Space bubble" to protect the humans within from the potentially deadly effects of exposure. Florivans like Nyx aren't affected the same way by miasmas, though. From what she's been told, kittens like Wyndi even *need* to be exposed regularly. Jump simulations for testing equipment and training Navigators, too, involve a sealed simulation chamber of some kind and smaller amounts of miasmas.

That, though, is very much the extent of Ioane's knowledge of such things. She's never really had cause before to wonder just how the simulations work, any more than she's had reasons to ask about the workings of the Drive itself. Her interests have always been centered around piloting, and since darters have yet to be adapted for flying in Quantum Space, her curiosity about the subject is limited.

Wyndi takes this moment to leap over to Ioane's shoulder and give her one of their characteristic "you have been gone from my sight for too long" nuzzles. She chuckles and gives them a few soft scratches around their ears in return. Ioane has known the kitten long enough that she's used to needing to reassure them that she is, in fact, still okay on a regular basis.

"Do you think Julian will believe me if I tell him how well-behaved they were?" Nyx asks, twitching their ears in amusement.

"No, but I'm sure they were." Ioane offers them her arm. "Shall we? I believe Dr. Kiely is expecting us by now."

Nyx sets both of their hands around her arm with a soft smile. "Yes, I'm sure she is." They pause, their third eye glancing over at Rudy and Sarge. "Should we wait for the two of them to finish?"

"I think they'll be along soon enough." Ioane looks up to the kitten on her shoulder. "Wyndi? Be a sweetheart and go tell your menfolk to wrap it up and come to dinner, will you?"

Wyndi makes one of their adorable miniature versions of a pilot's salute and leaps from her shoulder. They scamper off in the direction of Sarge's darter with a cheerful series of squeaks.

Ioane looks back to Nyx with a grin. "See? That's sorted. Those two are Wyndi's responsibility to begin with, really."

"The poor kitten has their hands full, I'm sure." Nyx seems to be holding back a laugh. "I'm glad they're being raised by such a good family. It's obvious they're happy with your squadron."

"We're lucky to have such a helpful little mascot," Ioane replies as the two of them step out into the corridor. "And cute, too! I'll have to get Anna to show you the 'pictures of Wyndi being the most adorable troublemaker in the galaxy' file she keeps on her pocket-com later." She stifles a giggle. "She's got a whole set of images from the time we helped them bury Rudy in the sand and they built a shell-nest on top of him, even. Wyndi made the *cutest* fuss when he finally woke up—Celadon had to negotiate with them in the end so they'd let the poor man get up before the tide came in."

"I look forward to seeing those." Nyx's tail swishes to match the amusement in their wind-chime toned voice. "Reminds me of some of the stories Nida tells about me and Thalassa as kittens."

"Now that sounds promising..." Ioane pauses, then shakes her head. "It's hard to picture *you* as a little silver-furred scamp, though."

Nyx gives her a playful nudge with the tip of their tail, since both of their hands are still resting on her arm. "Would it be easier to picture if I made you chase after me to retrieve something shiny I'd borrowed? Or would you prefer to find one of your boots filled with flower petals?"

Ioane laughs. "Point taken—I don't mind flower petals, to be fair, but I'm up for a good game of tag after dinner if you are! Just bear in mind that the others will probably want to play too... and Penny tends to pull out her judo moves to catch people when she's the one chasing."

Nyx shakes their head, giving her a slight eye-roll. "Why am I not surprised at least one of you does? Or that you play tag often enough to know to warn me?"

"What can I say, Nyx?" she quips, "we dance with death for a living and play children's games in our downtime—such is the baffling but exciting life of the darter pilot!"

"'Baffling' is a good word for you, Abigail," Nyx replies, chuckling. "But you're good company, all the same."

Ioane grins and pats their upper hand. Considering that she's only known them for a day or two, this feels like a very high compliment. "Likewise, Nyx."

THE NEXT DAY, POTTS FINDS HIMSELF IN THE co-pilot's seat of Major Ioane's darter. It's hardly the first time he's flown with her like this, but as usual he'd much prefer to be up in the front seat of his own bird. He glances out of the canopy polyglass at the other darters flying alongside them. Major Albright has Nyx in tow today to compensate for the interference clouding all of their proximity scanners. In Potts' opinion, Nyx seems to be settling into their unexpected role as part of the 2nd Squadron quite well—although it's clear they'll be happier once all of this is over and they don't have to worry about watching the void for strikers anymore. He doesn't blame them for that one bit.

Thinking of Nyx, Potts is reminded of his own little Florivan counterpart. On a half-serious whim, he leans down and reaches into the small space underneath the copilot's seat. Thankfully, no small curious hands reach back to tap his hand this time. Of course, he *had* seen Wyndi waving from Reba's shoulder when they left Mayview, but he wouldn't put it past the kitten to have somehow been able to stow away for this flight anyway. Withdrawing his hand and absently stroking his beard, he chuckles to himself. He's fortunate, he knows, that Wyndi has taken to Reba so quickly; otherwise, they'd have put up far more of a fuss about being left behind with her and Rudy.

They've just gotten into a loose orbit of the outermost moon when he sees Major Albright's darter subtly waggle its wings.

"All right, Sarge," says Major Ioane, turning around halfway to look at him for a moment. "There's Penny's signal! I'll keep an eye out in case she and Nyx spot anything. Go ahead and fire up the rig and let's see if anyone's there to hear us."

"Yes, ma'am!" Potts taps in to the copilot interface to turn on all of Rudy's adjusted intercom relay systems. "Carrier wave is on... and channel is open." He pulls down the microphone bar of his headset. "This is darter 2-M-3 from SCV *Surnia*. If anyone within range can hear me, answer back."

Five minutes pass in silence before he repeats the hail, then another five, then another. Still, there's no sign of any response. Potts continues the pattern; patience is their only option to make this work, and he knows it.

"So, Sarge," Major Ioane asks after what must be the fifteenth repetition, "out of curiosity, last time you got this imaginary com-link rig to work... how long *did* it take for someone to hear you?"

Potts has to pause to think about it. He shrugs. "Well... long enough that I didn't have enough charge left to get back to *Aegolius* on my own because I'd coasted so far out after I hit half on my gauges. Wound up waiting around for the Rangers to pick me and Wyndi up on their way in after we made contact. So... six or seven hours at least?"

Major Ioane groans dramatically. "I shouldn't have asked."

Potts chuckles. "Well, what we're really waiting on right now is for me calling to coincide with Celadon actually making a jump. Last time, we were out in deep space and there weren't many ships within range. We know that this time *Aegolius* is in the area and heading our way. If Rudy and Major Toussaint calculated the timing right, that shouldn't take much longer."

"And if they didn't, we'll be up here as soon as we charge up to start calling again." He sees the Major shake her head in the reflection of the canopy bubble. "Keep at it, Sarge, they're bound to hear you sooner or later."

"Yes, Ma'am—they will, you know. Celadon's heard me well enough when Lt. Hsu's had me run jumps for training, at least." Potts pauses to double-check his readouts of the rig to confirm that it's all still functioning properly before tapping the button to activate his microphone again. "This is darter 2-M-3 from SCV *Surnia*. If anyone within range can hear me, answer back..."

★

Another half hour passes without so much as a crackle of static in response to any of his attempts.

"Say, Sarge?" Major Ioane turns around halfway again with a curious sparkle in her eyes. "Here's a thought. You're using a standard darter distress call, short the 'tarantaras'—but you aren't calling just anyone in the area. Celadon's used to running those training jumps with you, aren't they? Try using your Nav voice and see if that makes a difference."

Potts flips his headset's microphone bar back up. "'Nav voice' is just me talking, Major," he says, making air quotation gestures with one hand for emphasis. "Nothing all that special about it."

"Really? There must be something to it, considering how picky every Florivan I've ever met is about who they work with. Not to mention how many humans they *can't* hear."

"It's more about how easily they can imprint on you, from what Celadon and Indigo have told me."

"Ah. And yet, there's only *four* people in the galaxy as far as we know who can even use a rig like this—and the first jumper you ever contacted with it hadn't even heard of you before, much less met you." Major Ioane takes on a lightly lilting tone which, in his experience, often precedes her being the one to get the two of them into trouble. "Makes me *wonder*, Sarge..."

"Me too, but it's hardly the time for wondering about things I can't remember." He thinks on her suggestion for a minute or two all the same, absently running a hand over his beard. "Still... maybe you've got something there. Nav does use different protocols for making contact, at least."

"I thought it did." Major Ioane turns back to her instruments with a vague gesture out at the stars. "I can never remember what they are aside from using the jumper's name, but it stands to reason that if you're trying to call through the veil on a farm-rigged Nav intercom, you should call the way they've *trained* you to call."

Potts lets out a small self-deprecating laugh as the realization dawns on him. "*Stars*, Major, I wish you'd said that an hour ago!"

"Well!" He can hear the grin in Major Ioane's voice clearly even if he can't see it. "At least they should be well into the jump cycle by now, if the time on *Aegolius* is as late as we think it is. Give it a go, Sarge. Let's see if you can't catch our favorite Elder's ear this time."

"Yes, Ma'am!"

Potts cracks his knuckles, then pulls his microphone bar back down and does his best to focus on imitating the tone of voice Lt. Hsu always uses when he's running jumps. He may only be a Navigator-in-training, but he's been training under the best Nav/Quan pair the Fleet has—the ones who lead the rest of the Fleet's jumpers, even—and *that's* who he's trying to reach. There's no need to be vague in his hails at all.

"This is Julian Potts of the 2nd's Musketeers," he calls, dropping the darter pilot's regulation code signs for the Navigator's all-important familiarity. "Celadon Toreval, if you have *Aegolius* somewhere that you can hear me, we need your help."

There's silence for a minute, then two, then five. He thinks for a moment that he hears a soft undercurrent of static start humming over his headset.

"Well?"

"I'm not sure, Major, but something's changed—Celadon? Can you hear me?"

There's another long moment of silence, save for the soft hum. Then, just as Potts is about to repeat the hail, a distinctively *familiar* bell-toned laugh fills his ears.

"*I knew you weren't dead, Julian! How's my favorite hitchhiker today?*"

"Celadon!" Potts lets out a relieved laugh of his own. "You have no idea how happy I am that this is actually working."

"It's about time!" Major Ioane cheers brightly and briefly takes the darter into a roll to signal to the rest of the Musketeers that contact has been made.

"*What sort of new and exciting trouble have you gotten yourself into this time, then, Julian?*" asks the Florivan voice in his ear, equal parts amusement and concern. "*I know you wouldn't be using Elias' little trick of the imagination to get in touch with us unless something was wrong.*"

Potts runs a hand through the back of his hair awkwardly. "'Wrong' doesn't even *begin* to describe it..."

"*Oh, dear—Li? Would you mind getting Jenny on the line with us? I have a feeling she'll want to hear this, whatever it is.*"

"*Will do,*" says the equally familiar lightly accented human voice of Celadon's Navigator. "*Hold on a few minutes, Sergeant. I'll have to get someone to wake the Admiral for you.*"

"Thank you, sir." Potts wasn't necessarily expecting that he'd have to talk to Admiral Marvin directly today. It's a thought that's only made more intimidating by the fact that she's going to have her sleep disturbed in the process.

"In the meantime," says Celadon, *"I'll keep you company. You all made it to Mayview safely, then?"*

"Yes, we did—all of us, kittens and spacesickness-prone mechanics included." Potts chuckles softly. "We've got some extra hitchhikers with us, though…"

Some time later, Potts is climbing down from the wing of Major Ioane's darter, having returned to Mayview without incident. He's quite grateful for that, too, considering how much has happened over the last few days.

"Sarge!" A particularly gleeful series of kitten-squeaks accompanies Wyndi's excited leap up into his arms. As usual, after the initial hugging of his neck, his little counterpart begins swiftly checking him over for any sort of injury.

"I'm fine, Wyndi." Potts chuckles, lightly stroking the kitten's ears in an attempt to settle them down. "I don't *always* get hurt when I'm out of your sight for more than an hour, you know."

Wyndi begins purring softly, but then makes a point of catching his right hand with their own lower pair and gently inspecting the small translucent bandage wrapped around one of his fingers with their upper hands. Their three small golden eyes look up to his with a pointed expression and a small squeak of disapproval as if to say that *this* is proof enough that he needs constant tending.

"Oh, now, not this again—I told you last night that this is just a little cut from building card-castles with the Majors." Potts shakes his head and looks over to Reba, who's finally caught up to the kitten and come to greet him. "I swear, they fuss over me for every little scrape even more than you did when we were kids."

Reba arches an eyebrow at him, although with a wry smile. "I can't say I blame the wee beastie, Julian."

Wyndi lets go of his hand and does their best imitation of the disapproving doctor stare Reba always uses on him, crossing both pairs of arms across their chest. Their tail swishes slowly to match. "Mine," they remind him, in a tone that he can't mistake.

Potts chuckles again and pats them on the head. "I know, I know. I'll try to be more careful next time. Promise. But see, nothing new for you and Reba to be concerned about."

The kitten seems to consider this, then squeaks happily and climbs up to Potts' shoulder once more, hugging his neck again and giving his bearded cheek a small nuzzle.

Major Ioane, slipping down from her darter's wing to stand beside him, finally succumbs to the giggles she's clearly been trying to hold in. "If that's not the *cutest* thing I've ever seen, Sarge, I don't know what is."

"They've only known Reba for three days," Potts tells her with the most dramatic tone he can muster, shaking his head with mock sadness, "and the two of them are already starting to gang up on me. I'm doomed, aren't I?"

"Seems you are!" Abi gives his arm a nudge. "But I'd say being well looked-after is the least of your worries right now."

"...Point taken."

Reba crosses her arms in exactly the way Wyndi had been imitating, then silently rolls her eyes. "I'd say it ain't. Do ye have any news for us?"

Rudy also approaches now from the direction of Potts' own darter, dusting his hands on the ever-present rag at his belt. "I'll second that question—did the bloody rig work this time or not?"

Potts looks to Major Ioane, then over at the two darters whose pilots have just climbed out of them; Major Albright is helping Nyx down from her darter's wing. He looks back to Rudy, unable to conceal his grin any longer. "Celadon says that you need to tune the rest of the whistle out of the high end before I try to call them again."

A matching grin spreads across his friend's face. "Good. Glad to hear you got through to them! It took you long enough—And I *did* tune that whistle out once already." He casts an amused glance to Major Ioane. "You and your fancy flying probably shook one of the bloody crystals loose."

The Major laughs, just as the others come to join them in their little circle beside her darter. "Now, is that *really* my fault, Rudy? I'd have thought you'd known me long enough to take my fancy flying into account by now!"

Rudy rolls his eyes. "We're lucky it worked at all, I'm sure. But you *did* get through to Dons in the end?"

"We did," says Potts. "Celadon also said to tell you 'hi' for them... and something cryptic about naming a pair of secrets you've held for them? I didn't understand that bit well enough to remember their exact words, and that was about the point when the Admiral got on the line with us, so I didn't get a chance to ask about it."

Rudy looks at him for a moment, then chuckles. "Don't worry about it, Sarge, I got the message anyway—just a bit of family business to look forward to once we get off this bloody rock, that's all."

Potts has a suspicion or two now of what that might be, judging by his friend's reaction, but it's hardly the time to pester him about it. As if to highlight that, Major Albright sets her pale hand lightly on the one of his shoulders that's free of perching kittens.

"Getting off this rock being the priority," she says to Rudy, although not without a touch of amusement in her voice, "did you get that bird where it can?"

"Surprising as it may sound, Albright," the mechanic replies, the grin on his face returning to his more usual wry smirk, "your d'Artagnan here managed to have enough of a bloody engine left that I *could* fix it. I've got some small tweaks and dusting left, but it'll fly by morning."

"Good! That makes things simpler!" Major Albright gives Potts' shoulder a light pat before crossing her arms. "We should have our end of the plan ironed out by then."

"Do I need to go pick some more melons for you to plan with?" Nyx asks, sounding halfway between serious and teasing.

"No," says Major Albright with a smirk, "as long as you think the model you made for us is still accurate, at least— although I wouldn't say no to some planning snacks!"

"Planning snacks can be arranged," Nyx replies.

"Snack?" Wyndi repeats, looking up to Potts with an expectant swish of their tail and wide, hopeful eyes.

Potts chuckles and gives their ears a soft ruffle. "Sure, that sounds like a good idea to me, too." He looks over to Nyx. "We'll come with you to carry things. Seems my fuzzy friend here is in one of their 'bottomless pit' moods."

"I *did* feed the wee beastie," Reba tells him. "Don't believe them if they're trying to tell ye otherwise."

"Noted." Potts tries not to laugh at the face the kitten makes in response to this, and fails.

"I don't know about the rest of you," Major Toussaint says, stretching out her arms, "but I'd be more than happy to take a bit of a break to freshen up before we talk strategy myself."

"Same here," Major Ioane adds. "Especially considering that we're all going to spend most of the day in the birds tomorrow even if the plan goes off without a hitch."

"*All* of us?" Rudy raises an eyebrow.

"Yep!" Major Ioane replies, grinning at him. "Can't exactly leave you behind while we go blow up melons and possibly take sizable chunks out of the planetoid!"

Rudy looks between the Majors with a grimace. "I'd almost say I stand a better chance of surviving if I stay here with the bloody shock waves..."

Major Albright laughs and gives the man a playful nudge. "Oh, now, Rudy, don't go grumbling about it already. You can fly with Anna this time!"

"Yeah," says Major Toussaint, grinning, "I'll put one of my symphony recordings on and everything. Been meaning to have you take a look at my inertial stabilizer tuning anyway—it only ever acts up when I'm out on maneuvers..."

"You see what I have to put up with, Kiely?" Rudy looks over to Reba with a mournfully gruff shake of his head. "These madwomen are going to be the death of me one of these days."

"Who, us?" Major Ioane laughs brightly. "We wouldn't dare—Celadon would never forgive us."

Reba seems to be holding back a laugh herself. "I see what ye mean, Mister Rudolph. I think I can do something for it, though."

"It'd be a miracle if you could," Rudy grumbles. "I haven't even heard the whole of their bloody plan and I already don't like it."

Potts is about to say something himself, but he's interrupted by a rather insistent tapping on his cheek. When he looks over, Wyndi is giving him one of their adorably impatient little expressions.

"Snack *please*?" The kitten folds all four of their hands together and swishes their tail.

"Oh, now how can I say no to that face when you're being so polite?" Potts gives them a little scratch under their chin. "Nyx, would you mind...?"

Nyx giggles softly and offers him their lower arm. "Come on, Julian, I have some dragon fruits that should be ripe up on level eight—it'd be a shame to let those go unharvested."

Potts takes their arm with a nod. Wyndi takes the opportunity to leap over to Nyx's shoulder and give them some appreciative snuggles instead.

In a way, Potts muses as he walks with the Florivan botanist up the winding trail to the complex's uppermost level, he's almost going to miss this odd little jungle and the change to his usual routine. All the same, though, he's looking forward to not constantly being tripped by vines.

Part 3: The Battle of Mayview

"OKAY, NYX, THERE'S OUR SIGNAL!" ABIGAIL calls over her shoulder at some near-imperceptible movement of one of the other three darters circling the spot on the outermost moon's surface where the Novan jamming station is sitting. "We're taking point from here—am I lined up correctly?"

"You are," Nyx replies, "and it feels like the others are too."

They keep their gaze and other senses intently focused on the "melon" below them, the other darters, and the boulders anchoring the odd Novan installation to the planetoid's surface. The shimmer of camouflage does little to hide the thing from their eyes, but even the adjustments that Elias has made to the sensor systems of the four darters make little difference in making it perceptible to their human friends. When the time comes, Nyx knows that Abigail is depending on them to help her know where to aim if the melon's camouflage doesn't drop.

Nyx is nervous about this whole endeavor, but that's little excuse for them to lose focus. They don't know how it happened, exactly, but the entire plan for getting rid of the resonance network disrupting communications around Mayview and hopefully being rescued by Admiral Marvin's flagship when it arrives rests on their shoulders. They still doesn't know how to feel about *that*, either. As a result, the tufted tip of their long prehensile tail has been twitching erratically ever since they strapped themself into the co-pilot's seat of Abigail's darter.

"Good! Ready?" She sounds genuinely *excited* about what's about to happen, even though she knows better than Nyx ever will just how much danger all of them are about to be in. Abigail does this sort of thing all the time, though. They're starting to believe Reba's stories about darter pilots being chosen *because* they enjoy putting themselves into dangerous situations.

Nyx takes a deep breath to re-center themself. "No, but go ahead. Let's get this over with."

"Sounds good to me!" Abigail laughs and pulls down the microphone bar on her headset. "Forward to immortality!" she calls to the other pilots.

A chorus of static-overlaid echoes of the darter pilot's battle cry fill the radio speakers. They distinctly hear little Mirawynd's voice chiming in among the echoes.

Darter pilots, Nyx has decided, are an *odd* sort of special—and certainly an unorthodox choice of guardians for a Florivan kitten. If they weren't trying to keep themself from being frightened by the prospect of all of this, they would even find it amusing.

They don't have long to think about this, though. Within moments of the battle cry going up, the three other darters mount their synchronized attack on the boulders at the base of the melon's support anchors. As one, they spiral in, firing a single pulse-laser blast at their target boulder. The shots send up plumes of dust as they make contact with the surface of the rock.

Just as Abigail had suspected from the beginning, once the darters are close enough to the melon, ports on its upper half open and extend some form of cannon out on each side.

"It's going to fire on them!" Nyx says, only dimly aware that they're shouting. "From above!"

"Evasive pattern!" Abigail calls over the radio, still keeping her own flightpath to an upside-down circle above the melon and well out of its range. The transparent bubble of her canopy remains angled towards the little battlefield so Nyx can have a clear view of everything.

The other pilots must hear her clear enough through the interference to act, for just as the melon begins firing blasts of white-hot plasma, each of them dodges with an almost eerily well-timed roll. As one, they redirect their darters out of range and back into a circling pattern around the melon.

"Well—n't beat all!" says Major Albright's voice through the static on the radio. *"Since when—the Nov—ing plasma cannons?"*

"*No clue—*" they hear Major Toussaint call back, "*but it's—ed—ing annoying!*"

"I was looking forward to some good old-fashioned pulse laser dancing too," Abigail quips, "but this is what we have to deal with." She turns halfway back to look at Nyx. "You saw where the canon ports were, right?"

"Yes... about a quarter of the way down from the top of the melon, in line with each of the support bars."

"Okay, then!" Abigail grins and turns back to her controls. "That's what... a hundred and twenty meters up from the surface?"

"Roughly," Nyx replies.

"Check. All right, Anna, Sarge, you two hang tight and cover us! Penny? Draw some fire for me, will you? Nyx and I will take care of those cannons!"

"*Roger—on—mark!*" Major Albright's voice calls back as she moves into a tightening circle around the camouflaged installation. The other two pilots make similar affirmations and pull back further from its firing range.

"We'll *what* now?" Nyx asks, eyes widening as the implications sink in.

"Get me in a good line with the first cannon from above and start a dive straight towards it," Abigail tells them as the co-pilot's display activates in front of their hands. "I'll take care of the rest. With a little bit of luck, I'll be able to get us in and out while they're busy firing at Penny to make the shot."

"You're putting *far* too much confidence in my ability to fly this thing, Abigail."

"What choice do we have?" She laughs. "I know you can do it! Ready?"

"No," Nyx says, reluctantly tapping the button to take control of the darter, "but go ahead—just don't get too mad at me if I get us killed."

"That's the spirit!" Abigail taps into her radio again. "Go ahead, Penny!"

"*For—immortality!*" Within moments, Major Albright is spiraling around the boulders in a dizzyingly erratic pattern of dives and changes of direction and altitude. The three plasma cannons at the top of the melon extend and begin firing, although none of them can manage to hit her darter.

"Oh, yes," says Abigail, seemingly content to watch the show since she's not the one flying at the moment, "ten-second reload and charge-up time! Now that's a stroke of luck for us!"

Nyx doesn't reply. They're too busy doing their best to focus on getting Abigail's darter into position without pulling it into any accidental barrel rolls. It takes a minute or two, and then they have the nose of the darter angled down in a sharp dive directly towards one of the extended plasma cannons.

"It's all yours, Abigail!"

"Stellar!"

Nyx is relieved for a moment as they feel her take control of the darter—and then *terrified* as they realize that she's pushing it to full throttle without coming out of the dive. She fires her pulse lasers as they come into range, destroying the first of the plasma cannons just as it's charging up to fire on Major Albright. She pulls up into a high loop just before she can crash into the smoldering Novan device.

"Woo! One down, three to go!" Abigail cheers, guiding her darter back around into the same high circling pattern she'd started in.

"You could have *warned* me that you were going to do that!" Nyx peels their lower hand's fingers up off of the armrest of the copilot's seat. "I was sure we were going to crash into it."

"Sorry, Nyx—but you did great!" Abigail is beaming as she turns around in her seat briefly to lock eyes with them. "Best copilot I've had in ages!"

"...Thank you." Nyx's ears twitch, but they find they're *pleased* somehow to hear her say this.

"Now," asks Abigail, turning back around, "get us lined up for the next one, will you?"

"Fine..." Nyx shakes their head as they take the darter's controls back. "...But try to pull up a little sooner this time? You nearly scraped the paint off this bird of yours with that stunt."

"Warning duly noted!" Abigail laughs brightly. "It's a bit hard to avoid crashing into something I can't see, you know."

"Well... Avoid the fireball from blowing up the next cannon, then. They're attached to the *surface* of the thing once they extend."

Abigail stifles another laugh. "Point taken. I'll see what I can do about that."

As Major Albright continues her dizzying dance with the blasts from the remaining two cannons below them, Nyx brings Abigail's darter into position for the second dive. It's a touch easier this time, although they're still having to will their hands to stop shaking from the combination of nervousness and potential imminent death. Their tail, rather than twitching, is now firmly coiled around the supports of the copilot's chair. They know that being so anchored won't do much to protect them, but it's still comforting in some small way.

"Okay, Abigail," Nyx says, pushing the throttle a little themself now that they have the darter lined up with the next plasma cannon. "It's all yours!"

Once again, just as soon as she takes the controls of the small craft back, Abigail has them speeding as fast as they can in a rolling dive towards the target. Like before, she fires as soon as she comes into range of the camouflaged communications jammer, blasting the plasma cannon away before it can reorient itself to fire on her instead. This time, she pulls up faster, at a far more comfortable meter or so away from the burning remains of the cannon.

"That's two!" Abigail cheers as she maneuvers back up into the higher circles Nyx has come to expect. "You want to try taking the third one out yourself, Nyx?"

"Oh, no," Nyx replies, unable to keep themself from laughing with her this time. "I'll stick with playing 'autopilot guidance system'—you have to do all of the death-defying laser-y parts yourself!"

"Aww..." Abigail teases as she releases the darter's controls back to them, "you're sure? Defying death and setting Novan tech on fire is *fun*!"

"And who am I to deny you your fun, Abigail?" Nyx's nervousness is giving way to a sort of adrenaline-fueled reflection of their friend's jovial mood, although they're not entirely sure why. "Ask me again when we're on the final melon of the day—maybe I'll have changed my mind by then."

"I will! All set? I'd like to get this one taken out before poor Penny makes herself spacesick."

"I somehow doubt that *anything* could make your sister spacesick, considering the way she's flying." Nyx pauses to push down into the dive at the final plasma cannon. "There you are!"

"And away we go!"

In short order, the last of the melon's defensive weapons is gone. Much to Nyx's relief, it doesn't show any signs of having further weaponry. Abigail pulls her darter back up into its waiting position circling above the camouflaged Novan device while the other three pilots get themselves lined up with the boulders.

"Let's try this again!" Abigail calls over the radio. "Full blast this time, Musketeers! Forward to immortality!"

With another static-overlaid echo of their now-familiar battle cry, the other three darters each dive at a boulder just as Abigail had at the plasma cannons. They fire their pulse lasers at a rapid, high-charge blast, vaporizing the boulders and the support struts with them before pulling up into a sharp upside-down loop away.

"That's done it!" Nyx exclaims, pointing at the now rapidly rising melon with their upper hand. "Just like Major Toussaint said it would! And the camouflage is flashing! Can you see it now, Abigail?"

"I can!"

With an elated laugh, Abigail pulls her darter into position and begins firing on the melon before it has a chance to reach the ground. Soon, the other three pilots have joined her in formation, also firing on the now-falling object. Under their combined attack, it vaporizes in a cloud of debris and briefly flaming gases.

All of the pilots cheer over the radio.

Abigail cheers with them, then turns around to Nyx. "You know, Nyx? I think you're just as much of a good luck charm as Wyndi is—and a good copilot to boot!"

Nyx can't help laughing. "I'll take that as a compliment, Abigail—but as soon as this whole thing is over, forgive me if I *never* want to get into a darter again."

"Fair enough!" Abigail's grin tells them she doesn't believe that at all.

MIRAWYND HAS BEEN CONTENTEDLY SNUGGLED inside Reba's half-zipped jacket ever since their human helped her strap into the copilot's seat and asked them to watch over her. It's not quite the same as flying in their human's familiar pocket, but sitting with Reba is far more comfortable than trying to sleep under the seat with their collection of shiny things. Reba, after all, is *warm*. Even better, she's been lightly petting their head and ears ever since they took off. It's a very cozy way to fly, indeed.

"Ugh," Reba mutters, rubbing at her temples with her free hand. "I *really* should have taken a dose of that sedative cocktail meself..."

Mirawynd looks up to her slightly-paler-than-usual face with a curious squeak. They give her other hand an affectionate nuzzle and begin purring more loudly again in an attempt to make her feel better. The hand lightly resumes stroking their ears in return. "Don't worry, Reba," their human says from the seat in front of them, "we've only got three more of these melons to deal with after this, and then we can be done with the acrobatics for a while."

"I wish I could believe ye about that, Julian." Reba sighs softly. "I don't know how any of ye can still walk after ye land, flying like this."

"You get used to it!" Mirawynd's human chuckles. "Lucky us, though—since I've got you back there, we don't have to play cannon bait like Major Albright's been today. Usually that's *my* job."

"Why am I not surprised?" Reba turns to look out the canopy polyglass towards the object she can't see and the darter that's zooming around it like a particularly agitated pollen-bot.

Mirawynd's eyes follow her gaze. They can see the shiny object their pilots are flying around. It's big and spiky and shimmery in a weird way, and currently it's spitting blasts of white fire at the darter circling its base. They've been watching Penny dance with it for a while now, and it's down to only having two spiky mouths to spit at her with. High up above Penny and the shiny thing, they can feel Abi's darter making a circle and getting ready to fly in and make another one of the mouths stop spitting.

After a moment, Mirawynd yawns and turns their attention back to snuggling Reba's hand. They've watched the dance enough that they're almost ready for a nap now, and their job today is to keep Reba company while their human is busy flying, anyway.

A bright dinging sound from one of the little holoscreens in front of Reba catches Mirawynd's attention just as they're starting to fall asleep.

"That'll be the timer ye had me set, Julian." Reba taps the screen to make the dinging stop. "From the look of things, ye should have just enough time to attend to it before ye have to put us through another of ye attack runs."

"Thanks, Reba—and I've been *trying* to go easy on you, you know."

"I know." She lets out a small, tired laugh. "Now call in before ye make them wonder if ye went and got yeself killed."

Mirawynd perks their ears up when they hear their human activate his radio on the special frequency that has the soft whistling sound in the background. They squirm out of Reba's jacket and push off gently from her chest. In the microgravity of the darter's cockpit, this small movement sends them flying at precisely the right speed and angle to gently land on their human's shoulder. They give his bearded cheek a nuzzle just under where his flipped-down microphone bar is sitting.

"Wyndi! I thought I told you to stay back there with Reba. You can't keep doing this every time I have to call in." Their human scolds them with a tone of affectionate amusement coloring his voice that tells them that they're only a little bit in trouble.

Mirawynd nuzzles him again and takes their usual seat on his shoulder anyway, holding onto the collar of his jacket with the curl of their tail and both right hands. It's worth a small scolding to get to listen.

"Oh, just wait 'til all of this is over and I tell Celadon what you've been up to..." Their human shakes his head lightly, then taps on his microphone bar. "Speaking of whom—This is Julian Potts of the Musketeers calling Celadon Toreval and *Aegolius*. Are you where you can hear me, Celadon? I've got our hourly report ready for you."

After a few moments, Mirawynd hears their favorite Entile's voice coming out of the earphone of their human's headset. *"Hearing you just fine, Julian! And you have good timing; I just got all of my landmarks in place. How are things at Mayview?"*

"Plan's running smoothly for the moment. We're going to be down to three melons in a few minutes—just waiting for Majors Ioane and Albright to finish taking out the plasma cannons on this one."

"That's good to hear. Have you met with any other complications yet?"

"Not yet, thankfully. Whereabouts are you?"

"About three more jumps out, if Li lets me keep pulling doubles like this. Otus, Ketupa, and Gymnasio are about the same distance too now—they were set to rendezvous with us anyway in a few days before we had to divert to pick up certain hitchhiking darter pilots, and Jenny's finally got word to them about the change in plans."

"The more the merrier!" Mirawynd's human quips, chuckling softly. "Anything else you need to pass on to us before I get back to work blowing stuff up? It looks like the girls are done teasing the thing."

"Only that you had all better still be alive by the time I get us there!"

"We'll do our best, Celadon. Safe jumping to you too."

With a click, the sound of comforting bell-toned laughter is replaced by the regular static of the darter's short-range radio. Mirawynd immediately loses interest in favor of returning to Reba's nice warm jacket and the nap that their human's call to their favorite entile had interrupted. They give him another nuzzle and then lightly bounce themself off of his shoulder and back over to Reba.

"Ye done with ye eavesdropping, Wyndi?"

Mirawynd yawns softly and snuggles back down into the nice half-zipped-up nest that Reba has made for them out of the front of her jacket. She's pleasingly warm to snuggle with.

"It's a good thing they are," they hear their human say. "I didn't have to get onto them about securing themself for the run this time."

"I take it that's ye way of telling me to hold on and try not to give up me breakfast?"

"It is at that, Reba! Forward to Immortality!"

Mirawynd falls asleep to the sound of their human laughing and the darter's engines speeding up. For them, it's almost as comfortable and home-like a sound as the very human heartbeat of the woman holding them.

They're not sure how much later it is, or what *exactly* is going on, but when Mirawynd wakes from their nap it's with a jolt of awareness that makes all of their fur stand on end. They slip up out of Reba's jacket with a litany of squeaks replacing the words they can't remember how to say at the moment, doing their best to point her eyes in the right direction to see the things that they can so clearly feel.

"Ah, what's got ye so upset, Wyndi?" Reba asks, sputtering a little as their tail accidentally swishes against her mouth. "I know ye can't possibly be getting nightmares—even though ye man flies like he's having one."

Mirawynd tugs on her ear and continues to try to turn her head in the right direction so she can see. "See! *See*!" That's the only word they can come up with that isn't frantic squeaking.

"Which way are they pointing you?" Their human sounds serious enough that he must understand this time what they mean.

"To ye rear and upper left and—yes, Wyndi, I *hear* ye, settle down—I don't see anything yet, but—"

"—*Incoming!*" they hear Abi's voice calling over the radio. "*Nyx says to—your tail and—*"

Mirawynd sees the sky move around them as their human pulls his darter up out of its holding pattern around the big shiny thing on the planetoid's surface. They cling onto Reba's shoulder, keeping their eyes fixed on the spot among all of the stars where they can feel that something that *shouldn't* be there *is*.

"Sarge! Tarantara!" they call, swishing their tail frantically. Finally, they've remembered the other word that their human has taught them that goes with the things they can now see instead of just feel coming towards them. "*Tarantara!*"

"I get the message, Wyndi!" he replies, "now settle down back there so I can get us away from the strikers, will you?"

Mirawynd makes a little salute and squeaks an affirmative, then dives back into the warm security of Reba's jacket so they can keep her safe while their human is focused on flying. It's a nice change to have a second human to snuggle with when they have to be quiet.

"Julian—"

"—Don't worry, Reba, I've got this!"

"I *know* ye do," says Reba, turning in her seat as far as the safety restraints will allow her to look out the back of the canopy bubble. "But ye've also got *three* strikers trying to get on ye tail and I can see them now."

"Only three?" Mirawynd's human laughs. "That's not too bad."

Looking up out of their nice secure Reba-jacket-nest, Mirawynd sees the rest of their pilots pulling into a neat formation with their human's darter. Something else catches their attention. They swivel their ears in the appropriate direction, then squeak in alarm and point up for Reba to see.

This time, she immediately looks where they're pointing.

"Three *behind* ye, Julian—and what looks like another dozen coming in after them!"

"*Stars*, it's turning out to be one of those days..."

A S A TEENAGER, IOANE HAD EARNED HER WINGS
flying resupply missions with her father to the
various small mining and scientific research stations
scattered around Mayview's surface and minor moons.
Her first and only love has always been *flight*, whether
it be within the bounds of a planetary atmosphere and
gravity well or out in the deep void between stars. She'd
never wanted to do anything else—and had sat through
more than a few reprimands for her "unscheduled practice
flights" and "accidental landings" from Mayview's security
team as a result.

She'd gotten her start with the Fleet, too, after one
of those "unscheduled" tours of Mayview's airspace
happened to coincide with an incident involving a visiting

ship's transport shuttle losing its guidance computer. Funnily enough, the local kid out with a not-quite-regulation antique single-rider skimmer craft had turned out to be the only one close, skilled, and *foolish* enough to try to dock onto the shuttle and safely bring it down from orbit before its engines overheated. Two days later, the high-ranking Fleet engineer who'd been unfortunate enough to be *on* that transport shuttle at the time sent off a recommendation letter for her and promised Ioane a career with the Fleet beyond anything her arguably backwater hometown could have offered her. At sixteen, she'd been the youngest among the test pilots involved in Project Snail-Darter prior to the onset of the Novan War. The work suited her *perfectly*.

Now a grown woman, Ioane finds herself back to zipping around the heavily cratered surface of Mayview's innermost moon at speeds that would have made poor Heb have a fit if she'd ever admitted to trying to reach them in that skimmer they'd once helped her rebuild—and pulling maneuvers that are just inside the range of what her darter can handle without blaring all sorts of structural integrity alarms. If it weren't for the pack of Novan strikers on her tail trying to shoot her out of the sky, she'd be of a mind to bask in the nostalgic symmetry her life has taken on this week.

There are, though, *far* too many strikers on her tail for her liking at the moment, so thoughts of the old days and childhood misadventures are only the dimmest of undercurrents in her mind.

"There's another wave coming down from orbit, Abigail!" Nyx calls from the copilot's seat behind her.

"Seriously?" Ioane can't help laughing, although why the situation strikes her as abruptly hilarious, even she couldn't say. "How many of these strikers *are* there?"

Nyx is silent for a moment, although Ioane can dimly hear the sound of one of their hands tapping rhythmically on the armrest. "Twelve or eighteen, I think? Forgive me, there's so many things moving around us now that I'm having trouble keeping track."

"No worries—that's more warning than I'd get otherwise!" Ioane pauses to blast one of the bright yellow Novan strikers in front of her that have been trying to separate Sarge's darter off from the rest of the group with her pulse lasers. Once she's clear of the debris, she taps into her radio to pass their warning on to the rest of her squadron. "Look alive, Musketeers, Nyx says we've got more company inbound!"

"*Oh you have—to be—ing kidding me!*" Penny's voice calls back.

Ioane counts it as a point in their favor that taking out all but two of the melons has cleared up the short-range radio channel enough that she's able to make out most of what her fellow pilots are saying.

"*This is what we get for—spider's web!*" Anna adds in.

"*Reminds me more—hornets,*" she hears Sarge quip. "*If Eddie has any spiders—act like this, I don't want to know—*"

"*Holy—on a cracker!*"

"What is it, Anna?" Ioane asks, pulling up into a high loop to set her own pursuers into position for her wing-sisters to take out. The resulting fireball behind her flashes bright enough that she sees a reflection of it in the polyglass of her darter's canopy.

"He's right! We've got—number of strikers than I've ever—outside of major battlefield." Anna pauses, probably because she's having to concentrate on spiraling her way back into the defensive formation alongside Ioane's own darter. *"Hornets have—ing nests! Where's the—"*

Ioane glances down at the warning lights that have just come on to remind her that her darter only has an hour's worth of charge left if she keeps going the way she's been. It's not a comforting thought in the slightest. For the sake of her semi-conscripted Florivan copilot's nerves, she decides not to say anything about it just yet. Anna's pointed out something far more important anyway.

"Nyx," she asks, not taking her eyes off of the scene ahead of her, "did you catch all of that?" Ioane knows her Florivan friend's hearing is good enough that they've been able to hear the others' voices on the speaker of her headset so far.

"I did—give me a moment to focus..." A long pause. "Do you know what the flight range of the hornets is?"

Ioane waits to finish maneuvering out of the way of one striker so she can fire on it before it gets in line with her tail. "Interplanetary for sure, but there's too many of these for it to be one of their long-range attacks—and they came too soon after we started busting melons. They can't safely outrun us, if that helps any!"

"It does!" Nyx goes quiet again.

Ioane focuses her own attention on staying in formation with the other three darters as they continue to make practiced circles in the area just outside outer limit of the firing range of the melon's remaining plasma cannon.

"Ah!" Nyx's upper hand points out the canopy glass. "Somewhere up that way—on a line between Sirius and the last moon! It's just come close enough now that I can feel it."

"Bigger or smaller than the moon?"

"Smaller, maybe eight hundred meters? That's still the biggest ship I've ever felt!"

"Let's hope our help gets here before you have to take a good look at it!" Ioane knows all too well what it must be, but she can't look to see it for herself at the moment. She taps into her radio. "Anna! Your hornet's nest is coming into far orbit on the other side of the outermost moon. If Nyx is right, we've got one of their striker-carriers on our hands."

"*I hate being—ing right sometimes!*" Anna calls back.

"*Well,*" says Penny's voice, just as her darter breaks formation to loop up and take out another striker that had tried to get too close into range of their collective tails, "*you did give us the odds—one show up! Let's see—taking this—ing melon out of—anyway. I'm tired of looking—where it isn't.*"

"*Agreed!*" Sarge chimes in. "*Might as well—what we started!*"

"*I'm in! Might improve—odds in the end.*"

"Sounds good to me!" Ioane chuckles. This, she knows, is not necessarily the *safest* plan they could have come up with, but it's certainly the one that'll put the Admiral and the captains of the other three Fleet starships in the best position once they show up. The more they can open up the communications channels around Mayview, the better their chances—assuming they all live long enough to see those starships arrive. She doesn't allow herself to dwell on that last notion too long. Ioane has been flying darters long enough that it only registers as a possibility and not something to be fearful about.

"Abigail! Point's yours!" Penny calls cheerfully. *"Tell Nyx—too long lining—up! We'll make the run—soon as you fire."*

"Roger!" Ioane pulls up as high as she dares from the moon's surface and starts circling towards the melon. The other three darters rearrange their formation around her. "Nyx, I know you aren't going to like this, but—"

"—But we don't have much of a choice. I heard." Nyx hesitates, then takes a deep breath and seems to take on a more determined tone. "Line us up with the boulder and start the dive, I'll fine-tune the trajectory on the way down. Keep control of your weapons—I won't be the one to shoot down anyone who gets in our way."

"I wouldn't ask you to." Ioane nods, although she knows they can't see her. She adjusts her course so the darter is aimed in the right direction. "Ready?"

"No," says Nyx, almost laughing this time as say the same thing they do every time she hands over the controls. "But go ahead anyway."

"All right! She's all yours!" Tapping the buttons to switch to copilot control and activate her radio at the same time, Ioane calls out to her fellow pilots with a whoop. "Forward to immortality!"

"One of these days," she dimly hears Nyx say over the other pilots echoing of the rallying cry, "you're going to have to tell me what that *means.*"

"Just as soon as we're safely out of the bird!" Ioane laughs and readies her pulse lasers. "Trust me when I say you *don't* want to know until all of this is over."

As Nyx pulls her into the dive, the other three pilots break formation, leading the pack of strikers off in different directions. Ioane feels the tell-tale vibrations of her engines being pushed towards full throttle as they hurtle towards the surface and the object she knows is at the center of the three large boulders but can't see.

"There!" Nyx calls behind her, "good luck!"

"Thanks!" Ioane laughs as she takes back control of her darter and pushes the throttle the rest of the way. They've been pulling this maneuver all day, but she still can't help but find it absolutely *thrilling*.

Within moments, she's close enough to begin firing on the plasma cannon—and going fast enough that it hasn't had a chance to target her or charge up yet. Two direct hits and it explodes in a brief flash of fire and debris in front of her. She lets out a celebratory whoop and pulls up as sharply as she dares to avoid crashing into the object beyond the cloud of white-hot fragments and gases.

"You did it!" Nyx cheers, sounding far more excited than they had the first time the two of them did this.

"I'd say *we* did!" As soon as she's clear of the melon, Ioane pulls back around into position for the second step of the plan to destroy it.

"The others are making their run now! But there's still strikers following them—ah! And us!"

"Why am I not surprised?" Ioane shakes her head and speeds up, doing her best to make herself a less convenient target without losing her position for firing on the melon. "Anything else you're picking up out there?"

"I think—" Nyx is interrupted by the perfectly-timed destruction of the three boulders beneath the camouflaged melon. "—Ah! It's rising towards us, Abigail! Do you see it?"

"I do!"

The heat-shimmer of the camouflage on the rapidly moving object has just begun to flash off and on. Ioane dives towards it, firing full-blast as she comes into range. Soon, she's dodging a cloud of burning gases and large debris fragments and pulling back high away from the moon's surface.

"*Woo! Good shot there—two!*" Penny calls over the radio. "*Let's push back towards—and see if we can't make a dent in—strikers while we wait.*"

"*Sounds like—ing good plan to me!*" Anna chimes in.

"*I doubt we'll run out of strikers—chase before anyone shows up!*" she hears Sarge's voice teasing.

In her peripheral vision, Abigail catches the motion of something pulling into line on either side of her darter. A quick glance—and the lack of Nyx frantically trying to warn her—tells her it's the rest of her squadron forming up. She grins and taps into her radio. "Let's just get there in one piece and worry about the rest after, hmm? We've still got one melon left, after all!"

"Abigail!" Nyx interrupts with a particularly relieved note coloring their wind-chime-toned voice. "They're here!"

"Really?" She scans her whole field of view, but sees nothing. "Where?"

"Far side of Mayview—one, two… no, four ships just crossed the veil!"

"Stellar!" Ioane grins broadly and taps back into her radio. "Penny! You can send out your 'tarantaras' now!"

"Finally! I was beginning—wonder if anyone would ever—up to hear them. Lead us home, Abigail!"

Ioane fires at a striker that's made the unfortunate choice to attack her head-on, then deftly dodges the debris left of it when her pulse lasers prove faster than its own weapons. "Will do!"

"Do you think we'll be able to make it there?" Nyx asks her, hesitating slightly.

"Nyx, my friend," Ioane says, unable to hold back a laugh, "as far as I'm concerned, we're going to make it there with bells on! Don't let yourself think otherwise."

"**D**O YOU SEE ANY MORE ON OUR TAIL, REBA?" Potts calls over his shoulder, dodging striker fire and doing his best to pull back in line with the rest of the Musketeers' formation. He'd only come out of it for a moment to take care of a striker that had gotten close enough to clip Major Toussaint's wing; that had, unfortunately, proved long enough for another set of the swift yellow Novan craft to cut him off and try to separate him from his unit altogether.

"Aye, one—and another two coming on ye wing from the right!"

Potts curses under his breath and turns, rolling to the left just in time to dodge the shots that would have taken out his wing. Combined with a loop down and a speedy corkscrew back up, and he's in a perfect position to fire on the offending striker. He dodges the debris from the resulting explosion and banks back towards the rest of his unit. They're almost into Mayview's orbit, now, but considering how many Novans have come out of the woodwork already, he's not holding out any hope for it being an easy flight back to a friendly ship.

"The one's still on ye tail, Julian!"

"I am *trying* to shake it *off*—just hang tight back there."

Potts hears Wyndi squeaking, and then Reba muttering softly under her breath. He can't make out the words, but he has a distinct impression he doesn't want to know what she's saying. He's used to this sort of thing, of course, but his oldest friend is a *doctor* who's been stranded on a deserted planetoid for years. Expecting her not to be alarmed by the situation would be just plain stupid.

He zigzags back and forth in an attempt to catch the striker off-guard so he can put a bit of healthy distance between them. It stays right on his tail the whole time. Potts recognizes now that it's chasing him further and further away from the Majors. It's either that, or that the strikers the three of them are dealing with are chasing them away from *him*.

"Y'know, I could use a friendly assist over here," Potts calls into his radio, hoping at least one of the Majors will hear him.

The request coincides with the familiar sensation of Novan laser fire striking one of his wings. He rolls the darter again to counteract the force of the blast, then turns towards the planetoid again and pushes his throttle as far as he dares.

"I don't think that were meant as friendly," Reba says behind him. She's lost the usual teasing brightness in her voice, but at least some part of her sense of humor seems to be intact.

"Friends!" Wyndi repeats excitedly. "Friends!"

"No, ye wee silly beastie, folks what shoot lasers at us *ain't* friends."

"Friends!" he hears the kitten squeaking again.

"Wyndi, settle down back there—Reba, can't you do something about them?" Potts keeps the majority of his focus on dodging further blasts. The Novan on his tail is *annoyingly* close now.

"I'm trying. Just fly, Julian, leave the kitten to me."

"Friends," Wyndi says once more, quieter but still insistent.

Potts shakes his head and adds that to the list of lectures he needs to give his little counterpart later—assuming they all survive long enough for there to *be* a later.

He's just about settled on diving towards Mayview's atmosphere and trying to loose his pursuer there, since he's nearly close enough now, when suddenly, he catches a glimpse of a streak of green-and-ivory motion speeding past on either side of his canopy from somewhere up ahead. A moment later, he sees the distinctive flash of a striker exploding reflected in the polyglass in front of him.

"And when the trouble's near—manage to appear!" Potts hears a younger man's voice singing over his radio as the streaks go past and the striker meets its end.

He knows the words well, too, and can't help laughing in relief: it's one of the final verses of the darter pilots' anthem. "About *time* you appeared!" he calls through the radio to the singer. "Who do I have to thank for the rescue?"

As a darter pulls into formation on either side of Potts, a lightly accented baritone answers his question over the top of the radio signal from the young singer, who doesn't seem to realize he's transmitting at all. "*You called for the cavalry, young—didn't you? 6th's Colonel Vasquez here—your left, and... Tarnation, Breezy! Tell that Navigator of yours to—it out already and clear the channel!*"

"*Yes, Colonel!*" a distinctively Florivan voice giggles. Potts is first startled, then puzzled to hear it. He's never heard of anyone from the Fleet's small corps of volunteer jumpers to ever leave their ship during a battle.

A moment later, the singing stops.

"*Sorry, Sir,*" the young singer's voice calls. "*Thought it was appropriate and—carried away.*"

"*Anyway!*" Colonel Vasquez says to Potts over the radio, "*That's Corporal Barker on—right. His copilot's—honorary Mustang—call them Breezy.*"

"Well, then, thanks to all three of you!" Potts stifles a chuckle. "2nd's Sergeant Potts here, and I don't have her on the radio, but I've got a civilian doctor in the back seat. Mind escorting us over to the rest of the Musketeers, sir?"

"*Happy to oblige!*" says the Colonel. "*I still owe the ladies—from last time we played cards. Saving your tail's—to count for something.*"

"Friends!" Potts hears Wyndi squeaking cheerfully behind him. While he's too busy to turn and look, if he knows his little counterpart they're probably up on Reba's shoulder waving out at the two new darters.

"Aye," Reba says with a sigh that's halfway between relieved and resigned, "ye were right, Wyndi, dear, they be friends. Now get back in me jacket and settle yeself down before ye silly man has to shake us around again."

Potts finds himself grinning. "Don't worry, Reba, we should be landing on a nice stable starship before long."

"Ye say that, but I *know* ye'll find more trouble to get into on the way there. Ye always do."

Normally, Potts would protest, but at the moment he's too busy flying around the debris of the strikers the two pilots from the Mustangs had taken out on their way to rescue him. Thankfully, it doesn't take long before he's falling back into formation with the rest of his own unit, Colonel Vasquez and Barker right along with him. Two more unfamiliar darters have already pulled into place with the Musketeers by the time he gets there—he assumes these must be the rest of the Colonel's own wing.

"*Howdy—Miss Penny, gals!*" Colonel Vasquez calls over the radio, "*You—a stray yearling?*"

"*Not anymore!*" Major Albright replies with a laugh. "*Thanks—rounding him up, cowboy. Rest of your—ponies cutting a path for us?*"

"*They are, and don't you—on that pony talk, now, señorita. We're in the middle—saving your hides, you know.*" The Colonel's tone betrays enough amusement even through the remaining static on the channel to give Potts the impression this is a very old joke the two of them have going on.

"*Fair enough!*" Major Albright replies. "*You got a plan— us, Esteban?*"

"Admiral's orders are—get y'all back to Aegolius alive. 1st's guarding our ships while—sort you out, 14th and 8th are—that Novan battle cruiser for us."

"Anything about—jamming station?" Major Toussaint asks.

"No," says the Colonel, *"why? Did y'all leave us—fun to blow up after all?"*

"Just one!" Major Ioane chimes in. *"It's down on—surface. Invisible, though. Did they get word—you about that?"*

"They did, Miss Abigail!" the Colonel replies. *"Don't worry, I brought a good set—eyes along. We'll head down and—care of that once we've passed—off to my second wing."*

"Sounds good to me," Potts says, glancing at his gauges. "I'm low enough on charge I'd rather not risk another run for the last melon."

"Same here," Major Albright agrees. *"I'm flying—fumes, what with all—dancing I've done."*

"We should come with—though," he hears Major Ioane say as another set of four darters comes into formation below all of them. *"Nyx and I know right where the melon— and how to take it out quick. I've got just—charge left to do that and still get home."*

"You've got a point—Esteban? Keep—sister safe or I'm giving—that judo demo when I catch you and I won't—nice about it." Major Albright makes a slight motion with her wings, signaling for him and Major Toussaint to follow her down to join the escort waiting below them.

Potts obliges.

"Will do, Miss Penny! Y'all heard—Major. Forward to Immortality!"

The radio rings with voices echoing the Colonel's battle cry. Potts adds his voice in, and as usual has to try not to laugh too much when Wyndi tries to do the same.

"T'immt'ality!" the kitten squeaks behind him, muffled by Reba's jacket. They still haven't mastered the words, but it's unmistakable what they're trying to say.

"Settle down," Reba chides, clearly stifling a laugh herself. "Ye ain't a pilot yet."

"No," says Potts, more to himself than to his friend, "but at this rate they just might live long enough to earn their wings…"

As Ioane and her escort from the 6th Squadron edge down into the haze of Mayview's atmosphere on their way to the final melon of the Novan signal-jamming resonance network, she glances up at the reflection of her copilot in the polyglass of her darter's canopy. "How are you holding up back there, Nyx?"

Nyx hesitates, twitching their ears lightly but not turning their eyes away from the view of the planetoid and four of the eight darters that have formed a defensive ring around Ioane's own. "Well enough, but I'll be *so* glad when this is over."

"And here I thought you were starting to enjoy flying with me," Ioane teases.

"Oh, I *was*," Nyx replies, letting out a half-nervous chuckle, "right until folks showed up and started shooting at us. I'd even admit to enjoying the experience if it weren't for that."

"Fair enough! I'd prefer a few less strikers in the sky myself—but hey, the strikers will all be someone else's problem just as soon as we pop this melon and get back to *Aegolius*." Ioane holds back a giggle of her own and taps into her radio. "All right, cowboy, we're almost there. Did they brief you on the plan to take these melons out, or do I need to?"

"*We got the notes on it, Miss Abigail! That's why—let Breezy tag along.*"

"You'll need them to aim the darter and start the dive at the cannon," Ioane cautions. "Can you handle that, Breezy? The more speed you pick up on the way down, the better."

"*I certainly can! Don't—about me, Major, this bird's my friend.*" The Florivan's voice is colored not with nervousness, but *excitement*, she realizes, just like any of the other darter pilots. Whoever they are, they clearly have more flight experience than the average jumper.

"*Breezy's one of my best,*" Vasquez crows through her radio, "*and the kid's not—bad himself either. The two—them will pull it off, no sweat.*"

"Good to know and glad to be flying with you, then!"

"*Barker,*" Vasquez orders, "*stick with—Major. The rest of us—handle defense and distraction 'till—rid of those cannons. My wing's on—boulder run; Hawkins, yours—keep us covered.*"

A chorus of affirmatives sounds over the static.

"Sounds like a plan to me," Ioane chimes in. "We'll show you what to do with the first one, Barker; we can save some time taking the other two out together."

"*Roger, Major!*" the young pilot's voice replies. "*We'll— your tail clear 'til then.*"

"*I see a shimmer ahead of—now,*" the equally young-sounding Florivan says. "*Is—our melon?*"

"I'd say it is. Nyx?" Ioane asks.

"It is. Right where we left it yesterday, but with a whole swarm of strikers around it."

"Now those I can see. Don't worry, our friends will take care of that." Ioane tries to sound reassuring as she begins leading her Mustang escort in wide circles around the melon. "That's the target all right," she says into her radio. "Those three boulders between the craters are your marker, cowboy. Cannons will track you from a hundred meters in."

"*Roger, Miss Abigail!*" Vasquez laughs. "*Just like our old—of tag back at Teegarden.*"

"That it is!" Ioane laughs too. Vasquez is another of the remaining survivors of the test pilot program and an old friend—the urge to tease him back about how often he'd failed to catch her back then is strong, but they have other business to attend to at the moment. "All right, pony express, let's take this melon out. Follow my lead!"

"*—To Immortality!*" The other pilots cheer as she pulls up into position above the melon.

"Ready, Nyx?" Ioane asks, once she's circling high above the boulders with two of the defense team beside her and Barker's darter on her tail to observe. Far below, the rest of Vasquez' wing is already playing tag with the plasma cannons and the strikers that have appeared to guard the melon.

"No, but let's go anyway."

"One of these days," Ioane chuckles, tapping the button to pass control of the darter to her Florivan friend, "you're going to give up and say yes when I ask!"

"Oh, where's the fun in that, Abigail?" She hears Nyx force a laugh. Somehow, she has the impression that they're genuinely starting to get used to doing this, even to the point of *almost* being comfortable flying with her— although she's sure they won't admit that anytime soon.

Nyx pulls the darter sharply into line with the boulders and starts the dive at a steep angle, throttling up to nearly full speed. Ioane keeps her pulse lasers at the ready the whole time, taking back control just when she needs to fire on the first plasma cannon and pull back up to avoid hitting the melon.

"*Nice shooting there, Major!*" she hears young Barker's voice calling over her radio.

"Think you can match it?" Ioane calls back, circling around to come back into formation with the younger pilot and dodging a rather persistent striker all the way up.

Barker's darter pulls out of formation and corkscrews around her just in time to blast her pursuer away and then take position on her left wing. "*We think so!*" he crows.

Ioane grins. She's not met this kid before, but she gets now why Vasquez seems to have so much confidence in him. "Okay, then! Together, now. You're taking the cannon to the left of the one I just shot, we'll get the one on the right. Remember to pull up *immediately* after you blast it or you'll crash into the melon. Clear?"

"*Clear!*" the Florivan's voice replies. "*Don't worry! I can see what not—crash into.*"

"Good. Get into position and be ready to go on my mark."

"*Roger!*" Barker and his copilot call back in unison.

Ioane checks her gauges quickly while they're getting back up into the high circles. She has just enough charge left to make this run and get out to *Aegolius*, but that's it. There's barely a safety margin, but it's enough that she's not too concerned yet. After all, she has a third of a squadron running interference for her so she won't have to do as much dancing with the strikers herself on the way to the ship.

"Nyx?" she asks, glancing back over her shoulder with a grin. "You ready to get this last run over with so we can get out of the sky for a bit?"

Nyx gives her a genuine laugh in return. "Now *that*, I'm ready for!"

"Bird's all yours, then!" Ioane chuckles and taps in to her radio again. "Here we go! Forward to Immortality!"

"*—To Immortality!*" the young pilot and his Florivan friend echo.

At once, Nyx and Breezy pull into position and begin the dive down towards the final two plasma cannons. Ioane readies herself to fire and take back the darter's controls. The dive goes smoothly and *fast* as Nyx pushes her all the way to full throttle in line with her target.

"*Major—out!*" Ioane hears one of the other Mustangs calling to her just as she fires on the plasma cannon. "*You've got strikers—on you!*"

"Just what I need." Ioane curses under her breath. "Nyx?"

"Diving on us and coming from both sides!"

The warning comes too late.

Ioane's already had to pull up to avoid getting caught in the explosion from the plasma cannon and she can't turn for risk of running into the melon or to one of the other darters that are zipping around it. Too late does she see the strikers running full-throttle down at her, two firing on her wings and one on a direct collision course. She has no room left to dodge this time.

In the moment just before the inevitable impact, she has an impulse to turn and apologize to her new friend and unintentional copilot for having broken her promise to keep them safe. She doesn't have time, though.

"Abigail!" Ioane thinks she feels Nyx's hand settle onto her shoulder. She tries to reach up to set her own on it, but the flash that comes a moment later is so *bright* that she doesn't know if she does. "Close your eyes—"

Darter pilots know from the start that they can't outrun their end forever. They sing about death as if it's an old friend. Still, for all her years flying, Ioane has never entertained the thought that *her* end would smell so much like jasmine and fresh rain.

"See, Reba?" Potts asks, standing on the wing of his darter and reaching in to offer her a hand as she climbs out to join him. "What did I tell you? Safe and sound and none the worse for wear."

"*Safe*, I'll grant ye." Reba wobbles a touch as she tries to stand up on the wing beside him. "I ain't so sure about the 'worse for wear' part."

Potts stifles a chuckle and hops down to the hangar floor to offer his hands to her again so she can get down more easily. "It wasn't *that* bad flying with me, was it?"

Reba smirks at him when he catches her, lingering for a moment in his arms while she recovers her balance. "I ain't going to answer that, Julian. Ye don't want to know."

Potts smiles, brushing a stray red curl out of her face and gently tucking it behind her ear. "I'm sure you'll tell me once you recover from the adventure regardless."

"I might."

"Home?" Wyndi asks sleepily, squirming up out of Reba's jacket. They look around the hangar he's landed in with a curious flick of their ears.

"*Aegolius*," Potts tells them. He reluctantly lets go of Reba so she can un-rumple herself and stretches the flight stiffness out of his arms. "But it'll be home for a while this time."

Wyndi's eyes brighten and the long fluff of their silver tail starts dancing excitedly as they leap to his shoulder. "Aunt Jenny!"

Potts chuckles and pats his little counterpart on the head to settle them down. "Yes, this is the Admiral's ship. I'm sure she and Lt. Hsu and Celadon are all pretty busy right now—so you *stay put*, you hear me? No going off and pestering people until the battle's over."

"Wyndi stay," the kitten agrees, although their tail is still swishing excitedly. Potts is well aware why. There are enough people on this ship who Wyndi clearly counts as part of their odd little family that they always get like this when he happens to bring them to *Aegolius*.

Two seconds after promising to stay on his shoulder, Wyndi is already bouncing off to greet Major Albright as she climbs out of her darter.

"Wyndi!" Potts calls, chasing after them, "what did I *just* say to you?"

"Oh really, Julian." Reba laughs as she follows him. "Ye didn't really expect that to stick, did ye?"

"One of these days," he says, slowly shaking his head as he reaches Major Albright's darter. When he looks up, Wyndi is happily snuggling her and trying to help her get her white hair back into its usual pair of poofy ponytails. "Well, Major? How much charge did you have left?"

"Right down to the line!" Major Albright grins broadly. "Coasted in on the landing, but here I am. What about you?"

"I think I'd have twenty minutes left at the most." Potts looks back to where his own darter is sitting. Two of *Aegolius*' own darter maintenance personnel are already hooking the bird up to the ship's mains to recharge. "Glad we had someone show up to take over when they did, that's for sure."

"Agreed." Major Albright hops down from the wing and nods in the direction of Major Toussaint's darter. The canopy's just started to rise, as it was the last to land. She hands Wyndi back to Potts. "Come on, Sarge, let's see how Anna made out—I'd say whichever of us has the most charge left has to be the one to get the first round of the night once Abigail and Nyx get back and we celebrate having lived to fly another day."

"Sounds like a plan to me!" Potts matches her grin, then turns and offers his arm to Reba. "Besides, I'm sure you want to see what's become of your patient?"

"I do at that," Reba says, taking his arm and lightly leaning on him as they walk. "Although considering what all I put into that sedative cocktail I dosed him with, I ain't so sure he'll even be awake yet."

"That's probably better for us," Major Albright teases. "If Rudy's awake he'll be all grumpy about the state of our darters—this way, he won't be getting onto anyone until tomorrow night at the earliest!"

"Considering where we are," Potts quips, "we might get *two* days before he notices how much of a mess we've made for him."

They've just reached Major Toussaint's darter when Wyndi bounces off of his shoulder *again* and makes a beeline for the door leading to the rest of the ship. Potts is about to chase after them when he sees a familiar dark-haired man in an officer's crisp emerald-green uniform and long double-wrapped ivory scarf walk in. The officer scoops the overjoyed kitten up on his way over without ever slowing down.

"Lt. Hsu!" Major Toussaint calls, waving from the wing of her darter as she climbs out. "Thought you'd still be up in Nav, but I've got your cargo right here—and not a scratch on him, I promise!"

"I appreciate that, Major." Potts catches the slightest hint of a rolling motion in the Lieutenant's eyes as he reaches them and extracts a now-somewhat-disappointed Wyndi from his scarf. "Stay with Elias for me, Mirawynd. I need to borrow your Navigator, and Celadon's going to need your help when we get back."

Wyndi squeaks happily and tosses the Lieutenant a cute little salute before they bounce up into the cockpit of Major Toussaint's darter.

Potts tilts his head to one side and tries his best to gauge the expression the Lieutenant is wearing. It's *serious*, whatever's going on. "Borrowing me? What's up, sir?"

"How much charge do you have left?"

"Twenty minutes? Why?"

"Good." Lieutenant Hsu turns on his heel and gestures for Potts to follow back to his own darter. "That should be enough if we hurry. Come on, we've got an emergency to deal with."

Potts goes with him, confused but alert. "What's the situation, then?" he asks, climbing into the cockpit after he's waved *Aegolius'* maintenance techs over and told them to unhook his darter so he can launch.

The Lieutenant has already finished strapping himself in and connecting the Nav headset he's wearing into the darter's systems. "We have a lost jumper to retrieve. I need to use your radio to reach them."

"And you can't do that with us sitting in the hangar?" Potts quickly secures and seals the canopy bubble and begins running through his launch checklist.

"Too much interference from *Aegolius'* systems—and I need you to make sure we get them back here and landed safely once we have them on the right side of the veil." Potts hears the distinctive click over his own headset of the Lieutenant tapping into the darter's standard short-range radio system. "*Aegolius* Navigator Hsu calling Ocean Marbree: we're launching now. I'm with *Surnia's* 2-M-4. Where are we meeting you?"

"*We're heading your way up from Mayview,*" the Florivan the Mustangs had called Breezy answers just as Potts clears the hangar bay doors. With the last melon gone, the signal is nearly crystal clear. "*Escort should be joining you now to bring you to us at 5 by A and 1E—that's the jump-out point we've got to work with.*"

"Good," Lt. Hsu replies. "I'll start trying to reach them on our way."

"Hello again, d'Artagnan!" the leader of the same wing of the 6th that had brought Potts over safely to Aegolius not ten minutes ago calls to him as the defensive formation takes shape around his darter. *"Breezy warned us you'll be out of contact for a bit. Don't worry, just follow us and we'll take care of you."*

"Roger that," Potts says, pulling down his own microphone bar. "I've got... ah! 23 minutes worth of charge, so try not to make me pull anything fancy to keep up with you."

"Noted!"

"Switch us over to Elias' system now, Sergeant, we don't have time to waste." Lieutenant Hsu sounds even more crisp and business-like now than he had in the hangar.

"Yes, sir!" Potts taps through the activation buttons, cutting the sounds of his fellow darter pilots off in favor of the soft hum of the imaginary intercom system he'd been using to keep in contact with Celadon a few hours ago. "Who are we looking for?"

"Your friend Nyx, assuming Ocean's right that they're alive somewhere. I may need your help getting through to them, if they can't hear me easily."

"Nyx? But they were with Major Ioane—"

"—With any luck, Sergeant, they still *are*. She doesn't have time for you to get a proper explanation." The Lieutenant takes a deep breath. When he speaks again it's with all the distinctive resonant clarity Potts still can't manage to imitate when he's supposed to be using his Nav voice. "This is Elder Celadon's Navigator, Hsu Li of *Aegolius*. Wherever you are, Nyx Yrital, answer me so I can give you your jump-out coordinates."

There's a brief silence. Potts' mind fills it with the startling realization of what must have happened for Nyx to need to be led back across the veil and the alarming question of what could be happening to Major Ioane right now. He focuses himself on flying instead of thinking about it. He does, after all, still need to keep up with his escort.

"Beacon?" Finally, Nyx's voice rings out on the channel, just as it had when they were helping Rudy tune the system. *"I hoped... I managed to turn the imaginary system on, but I didn't know if anyone would find us..."*

Potts breathes a sigh of relief. He hears Lieutenant Hsu do the same.

"Hello, Nyx," says the Lieutenant. "You can hear me okay?"

"I can, Beacon, sort of... You're coming through on Abigail's headset, so I'm having to keep my good ear turned that way so I can hear you—Abigail! She's unconscious, but I need to get her out, and—"

"—I know, Nyx, don't worry." Lieutenant Hsu's voice remains calm and somehow reassuring. "Celadon's waiting for her. Now, I've got points for you so you can jump back out. You'll have a full squadron waiting around you once you make the jump. Ready?"

Potts hears Nyx take a deep breath of their own now. *"Ready. Cardinals?"*

"Your primal is going to be Mayview itself. Max Up is *Aegolius*, 5 by E and 1E," the Lieutenant begins, "and your Down is *Gymnasio* at 4 by E and 1A..."

While Lieutenant Hsu and Nyx are going through a somewhat rushed version of the routine a Navigator uses to orient their counterpart in Quantum Space, Potts continues carefully keeping pace with the Mustangs. They lead him to a spot that's relatively clear of the action of the ongoing battle at the moment, right between *Aegolius* and the planetoid itself. The rest of the 6th is waiting there, circling widely around a single near-motionless darter to keep the area for almost two hundred meters around it clear of strikers. Potts' escort leads him down into the center of the circle, where the slow-moving darter signals with a particular waggle of its wings for him to come alongside it.

Potts has enough of a grasp of what's going on now to understand why: that must be the darter with the Florivan copilot, and he's to wait there along with them to guard the jump-out point. Likely, the two of them are going to have to help guide poor Nyx in, considering how little his new friend knows about flying darters in combat.

"*I have the space sorted now,*" he hears Nyx say to the Lieutenant. "*What's my exit?*"

"Jump-out point is 5 by A and 1E. We're in position now. Switch to your short-range radio as soon as you've made the jump."

"*Thank you, Beacon, I think I remember how to do that. Jumping in ten... nine...*"

When Nyx's countdown reaches one, Potts sees an odd shimmering flicker in front of him. At first he thinks it's just his eyes, but then the flashes slow down and ultimately stop, revealing Major Ioane's darter sitting just ahead of his own.

"Switch us to short-range, Sergeant. Now it's your and Ocean's turn to get them the rest of the way home."

"Yes sir." Potts taps the button and then calls into his short-range radio, "Nyx? This is Julian—can you hear me?"

"*I can! Thank you!*" He hears Nyx let out a nervous but clearly relieved laugh. "*Now, can you tell me how to land this contraption? Abigail didn't get around to showing me and she's... not going to be able to help right now.*"

"*Don't worry, Cousin Nyx!*" Potts hears the Florivan whose public name is apparently Ocean chime in, "*We'll talk you through it. Landing from the copilot's controls isn't as hard as you think!*"

"*Ocean Marbree,*" Nyx replies, genuinely laughing this time, "*if my Nida could see us right now...*"

"*They'd have a lecture for both of us for sure! You should have heard them the first time George let me land and I crashed us right in front of them and River—*"

"*—Hey, now, Breezy,*" the young pilot, Barker, cuts in, "*do you have to tell everyone that story?*"

"I seem to recall we're on a time limit, but *I'm* looking forward to hearing the story later." Potts chuckles and pulls in on one side of Major Ioane's darter, just as Barker—or more likely Ocean themself, he's starting to suspect—does the same on the other. "First thing is to ease your throttle back up so you're *going* somewhere, Nyx. We'll be right here beside you all the way. Colonel Vasquez and the rest of the Mustangs will keep the strikers away from us, so just head towards *Aegolius* and we'll deal with landing once you get there."

"*Right. Throttle is... ah! Got it.*"

Nyx slowly gains speed and pulls the darter around gently so it's heading in the right direction. Potts and the assorted members of the 6th Squadron keep pace with them, following right along without getting out of position.

"How's the Major doing, Nyx?" Lieutenant Hsu asks, once they're flying smoothly enough to be able to answer.

"She's... stable for now, I think? It's hard to tell from back here, but I can hear her breathing. The miasma should all be gone from the darter by the time we get there, at least."

"Good. Let's get the two of you home."

Potts keeps flying. He can't do anything for his friend now except help Nyx get her safely back to *Aegolius* and hope she'll be okay.

The whole world smells of jasmine and new rain.

The brightness of chaotic color and sound gives way to soft sunlight filtering through tall, endlessly tall trees.

The canopy of leaves above is every shade of black and purple. The bark of the tallest trees—thick-trunked, wider than she is tall, traced with lighter-shaded vines that stretch up high and bear soft smelling yellow flowers—is dark too, peeling away in patches to reveal lighter cinnamon-cream layers underneath.

She walks down a path through the jungle alone, following the trail of dappled sunlight along the path of a slow-flowing stream.

She does not know, does not remember, how she came to this place, or if she has ever been anywhere else. The warm humid air scented with growth and a rainbow of petals clouds her thoughts, her mind, her memory.

The jungle, the stream, the sunlight through translucent layers of shimmering leaves—safe, but strange; familiar, but not. She cannot remember if the feeling is to be lost or to be going somewhere.

She does not know how long she walks along the stream in the dappled sunlight of the endless jungle where time is a thing she cannot remember. All she knows is walking.

Walking, and perhaps feeling like someone is looking for her, like they will be there when she finds the end of the water.

A new sound echoes in her world, a vibration that is soft and warm and felt in her chest even more than it's heard in her ears. The sound that is a feeling pulls her onward through the sunlight, gives shape and form to her self that is more than just her walking along the stream in the jungle.

"Follow the water home. Follow the path of the light from our stars."

A voice calls to her in the stream by her feet, in the trickle of water flowing over smoothed stones, the sound of small wind-chime bells ringing.

She knows the voice of the water, or it knows her; her soul knows, but her mind can't remember. It feels like warmth and the sparkling black sand of a beach, the taste of sour fruit and salt, a shining shell placed in her hand.

Did she ever know a beach, a moment like that?

She walks through the jungle, along the path by the slow-moving stream. The jungle is all she can see and hold in her mind; the stream and its clear sweetly-fresh flowing and grey-pebbled bed are all the water she knows. The vibrating sound that is a feeling too is still there, echoing in her ears and warming her chest with a softness like the edge of a memory.

There is a difference between lost and wandering, and she cannot remember what it is.

"Come back to us," says another voice like the first, the voice of the wind rustling the leaves around her, the song of the soft breeze tousling her hair. "You're safe now."

The second voice is younger, somehow, not quite so familiar as the voice of the stream, but familiar still—it feels like motion, like soaring, like joy and freedom and flight far above the trees whose tops she cannot see.

Was she ever up above, beyond the treetops like the wind's voice makes her feel is the place she belongs?

Following the stream, treading softly on the fallen leaves that are all shades of purple and black, that and the sound in her ears and her being is her world. She is alone and not-alone, but she does not know why she feels someone else is there in the voices of the wind and the water. All she can see is the jungle.

"Please." Another voice, this one coming up from the small leaves of the ferns by the stream, from the trees above and all the vines and flowers all around her. "We're here, come back to us."

The voice of the jungle warms her, makes the vibration of the sound of softness grow to touch her entire being just as the warmth of the sunlight streaming through the trees does. It is the voice of growing things and the greenness that is missing around her, the wind-chime sound that smells always of jasmine and new rain.

"Please, Abigail," says the voice of the jungle, calling her by the name she had forgotten was hers, bringing her fully into herself where her memories can find her, "come back to me."

The world fades away into warm, soft light and the sound of the vibration on her chest...

Ioane's first awareness as she awakens is that she's not alone.

Her eyes don't want to open immediately, but she can still feel a cool, alien hand holding one of hers and the familiar sensation of a small purring creature curled up on top of her. She realizes she's laying on her back, and as she gathers the strength to persuade her sleep-heavy eyes to open, she learns that she's certainly not in her quarters on *Surnia*, nor her old room in her Dad's suite at Mayview where she's been bunking for the last few days that she remembers.

She's not entirely sure *where* she is, only that the room and the bed she's laying in are softly furnished and the lights are dimmed down most of the way. She doesn't know how she got wherever she is. Her memories are foggy with sleep and dreams she only half-remembers that are already slipping further away.

A motion from the curled-up creature purring on her chest catches her attention. She turns her eyes and as much of her head as she can manage down to look. A small, familiar face pops out from underneath the soft amber-shaded quilt that's draped around her, three wide and almost relieved-looking golden eyes meeting hers.

"Hey there, Wyndi," Ioane tries to say, but her voice comes out as less than a whisper. Her lips form the words, but the sound doesn't want to happen. She finds enough strength returning to her free hand to reach up and ruffle the kitten's ears instead.

Much to her surprise, just as she's gotten her hand into place on Wyndi's head, two more Florivan kittens pop their faces out from under the quilt. These are much smaller than Wyndi—smaller than she remembers them being when Sarge introduced her, even—and even their tall catlike ears are still covered in a soft coating of fluffy silver fur. Like Wyndi, both of them are purring quite loudly.

One of the new kittens widens its eyes and makes a soft, curious trilling sound at her. The other tries to nestle its little fuzzy head under her hand with Wyndi's.

"Abi," Wyndi tells the two smaller kittens amid a litany of other soft squeaks, giving each one of them a small nuzzle for emphasis. They point up at her face with one of their upper hands. "Friend!"

The two small silver fluffs squeak excitedly in response and slip out of the blanket entirely now, coming up to nuzzle against her neck.

"Oh, now, where did you two cuties come from?" Ioane tries to whisper, wanting to laugh but her throat unable to make that sound either just yet.

She feels the hand holding hers, still, and on an impulse gives it a gentle squeeze.

"Abigail?" Looking up to the source of the familiar voice, she sees Nyx's relieved-but-concerned face looking back down at her.

Ioane smiles up at them.

Her friend gives her an impulsive hug, much to the squeaky annoyance of the disturbed kittens. She wraps her own arms around them after a moment, unsure why that feels so natural any more than why she thinks she feels the warm wetness of tears falling on her shoulder where their face is buried.

"Hey, Nyx," Ioane does her best to say, lightly patting their back. "What did I miss?"

"I AM SO SORRY, ABIGAIL," NYX SOFTLY MUTTERS into Ioane's shoulder when they finally speak again.

"For what?" Ioane asks, finally releasing them from the hug. Her voice is little more than a breath, but she hopes it's enough that her friend can still understand her. She reaches up as Nyx starts to return to their chair beside the bed she's laying in and wipes a stray tear off their cheek. She hadn't been certain that they were crying, but it seems they were—and she has no clue as to why.

"I..." Nyx slowly leans back in the chair and seems to be choosing their words carefully. Their tail twitches with a slow agitation in the silence, finally settling onto their lap so their lower hand can work at straightening out the silver fluff at the end of it. "You were... hurt. Because of *me*."

Ioane doesn't understand, nor remember, what they could possibly be talking about. She weakly tries to sit up, but manages only to turn her head and shoulders partway to look at them more directly. The kittens snuggling her neck reposition themselves accordingly, with no small amount of protesting squeaks. She tries to speak again, with little success. "Where...?"

"*Aegolius*. These are Elder Celadon's quarters. It was the best place to keep you while you recovered, considering the circumstances... oh!" Nyx turns their eyes to Wyndi, who's started to snuggle themself back under the blanket. "Mirawynd, would you go tell Elder Celadon that Abigail's awake for me?"

Wyndi squeaks cheerfully and makes one of their adorable little attempts at a pilot's salute. They bounce out of the blanket and down past Ioane's limited field of view.

"I'm so glad you're awake, Abigail," Nyx says to her now, reaching up with their upper hand to brush away another hint of tears from the corners of their third eye. "It's been a *week*, and I was starting to think..."

"Hey, now." Ioane tries to whisper. She reaches over to set a hand on Nyx's lower one, since it's within reach. She dimly remembers crashing into *something*, now; at least, the confusing fragments of memory seem to indicate that. "Not my first crash—I'll be up and flying again tomorrow, you'll see." It's too much to try to say, though, and leaves her in the middle of a coughing fit.

The kittens on her neck squeak and dive back under the blanket to get out of the way.

"Abigail?" Nyx helps her sit up so she can catch her breath, clearly alarmed.

Ioane weakly gives them a reassuring smile and a thumbs-up once she's gotten through the worst of it. "I'm... okay," she breathes, mouthing the words more than saying them.

"Try not to talk so much just yet, please." Nyx's face is still one of nervous concern.

The two kittens peek up out of the blanket at her, then squeak cheerfully and climb up to her shoulders. One kitten drapes themself on either side of her neck, purring contentedly once they've settled into place.

"Abigail..." Nyx begins, hesitantly, "to be honest, it wasn't—"

"—Good morning, Abigail!" Celadon comes into the room with Wyndi on their shoulder and a vaguely familiar-looking adolescent Florivan close behind them. The younger Florivan is a deeply teal-green shade of blue beneath their silver stripes and has their hair cut shoulder-length and held back from their face with intertwined braids, a notable contrast to Celadon's own ice-pale coloration and the elaborate ribbon-entwined braided buns they keep their hair in. Both are in casual tunics like Nyx's, with Celadon's in a cozy-looking amber and the younger Florivan in white with an amber sash tied as a belt under their lower pair of arms.

Both of the kittens snuggled against Ioane's neck perk up and make excited little squeaks in the direction of the visitors. They start to purr even louder than before.

Ioane waves to Celadon. She pats one of the kittens on the head with her free hand, then looks questioningly to her old friend. "Yours?" she manages to ask, although what little voice she'd had before her coughing fit is gone.

Celadon sits down on the edge of the bed beside her and nods. "Surprised me too, when it happened, but yes—and I'm glad we had them and Wyndi here, for your sake." They smile and make a soft trilling sound towards the kittens. "Teryin? Tesnee? I think Abigail can manage without you for a few minutes while we talk."

The two kittens seem reluctant to leave their posts snuggling Ioane's neck, but a repetition of Celadon's beckoning trill and a matching gesture convinces them. They give her a last nuzzle on each cheek, then scamper down and across the blanket and disappear under the hem of Celadon's tunic.

"Cute." Ioane tries to say, wincing softly when her reflexive chuckle proves too much for whatever's wrong with her throat.

Wyndi takes the opportunity to slip down from Celadon's shoulder and back under the blanket to snuggle with her instead, giving her hand a sympathetic nuzzle as they do.

"They are." Celadon beams momentarily, then takes on a familiar tone of concern. "But please don't force yourself to talk—from what Dr. Kiely and I can tell, your lungs and windpipe were rather badly damaged. Straining your vocal cords won't help matters." They pause, pulling out their pocket-com. They set the little device's holoscreen up in front of her with a text-to-speech program running on it. "Here, this will help for now. How are you feeling?"

Ioane nods. She fiddles with the holoscreen interface for a few moments, then taps the button to make the program read out her response. *"Tired. Sore. Feels like I've been gargling salt and fire. Musketeers okay? What happened with melon and Novans?"*

"They're all well and elsewhere on the ship waiting for me to say it's safe to visit you." Celadon stifles a laugh after they answer. "Your fellow pilots are off getting into some sort of trouble or other by now that I'll be held responsible for, I'm sure."

"Well, George is *my* responsibility, if he's getting into trouble hanging out with your pilots," the younger Florivan says cheerfully, looking to Celadon and now taking a seat on the bed beside them. "So that's one less for you to worry about having to take care of."

Celadon turns to the younger Florivan with a wry look and raise of an eyebrow that Ioane knows all too well. "Need I remind you that as a Fleet volunteer, *you* are part of my household, Ocean Marbree? Your Navigator is as much my responsibility as you are—and I still haven't finished drafting my explanation for your Nida of why the two of you were out flying through an active combat zone..."

"...Point taken, *Elder*," says Ocean, with only a momentary playful hint of a sheepish tone. They turn their attention to Ioane with a wave of their tail and a not-at-all-subtle attempt to change the subject. "Anyway, Major, the last melon's gone! We blasted it out of the sky and it was *stellar*—and the Novans are all gone or dealt with! So nothing to worry about on either front there. The Valkyries and Thunderbolts managed to take out that battle cruiser of theirs too, even, since it was just the one that showed up to try and stop y'all destroying their resonance network. *Otus* is staying behind at Mayview to clean things up while they wait for the Fleet to get some other folks there to take over. *Ketupa* and *Gymnasio* are flying with us, since the Admiral was heading to the base at Luyten's Star to begin with and we were already tagging along for that."

Ioane nods, relieved to hear that the parts of the battle she seems to have missed went well. She's never encountered a Florivan who sounded so much like a fellow pilot when describing such things before, though. *"You're the Mustang jumper?"* she taps out on the holoscreen.

"I am!" The young Florivan giggles softly, offering her one of their lower hands. "You can call me Breezy, if you like—most of the other pilots do. I think we met once before?"

Ioane gives their hand a brief squeeze rather than a shake, thinking about it. She *had* thought their voice over the radio was familiar somehow, but she can't quite place their face.

"Ocean attended Elias and Li's wedding," Celadon explains, setting a hand on the younger Florivan's shoulder. "You'll remember their littermate better, I think. River was the one of Elder Caeruleus' apprentices you and Anna escorted down to visit Kapteyn's Agricultural Research Institute for me while they were here."

Ioane nods again. *That* had been an interesting little unofficial mission for sure, particularly once the quail got involved. She'd forgotten that there'd been some drama or other going on in the background about little River's littermate having signed to the Fleet straight out of their apprenticeship, but it's easy to connect the dots now.

"I remember! Thanks for the assist with those plasma cannons, Breezy."

"Anytime!" Breezy's tail swishes cheerfully. "I normally only get to fly with George when the Mustangs are training, though. Colonel Vasquez doesn't like getting lectured for letting me put myself in danger any more than my poor Navigator does—"

"—Or than you do yourself, so don't keep giving me a reason to repeat it." Celadon rolls their third eye dramatically. "It worked out well *this* time that you were there to help, Ocean, but do *try* to remember what your role as a volunteer is supposed to be."

"Yes, Celadon." Breezy sighs softly and then looks up to them with wide, innocent eyes. "I'll try to be just as good and rule-abiding as *you* are from now on, I promise..."

"Cheeky kitten." Celadon shakes their head and reaches up to ruffle the younger Florivan's ears with an almost sibling-like affection. "If you do that, your Nida will be lecturing *both* of us before long."

Ioane taps out another question that's come to mind, then settles into petting Wyndi while she waits for an answer. *"I think I remember crashing. If I was hurt, why am I here? Sick bay full?"*

"Ah, no, it's a bit more complicated than that." Celadon and Nyx briefly exchange a look. For some reason, Nyx seems uncomfortable; they've started running the fluff at the tip of their tail through their lower hand's fingers again, at least. "You didn't crash, exactly, and there's plenty of beds open in the infirmary, thank the stars... but we needed to keep you sealed away from the rest of the ship until the kittens had done their work. It wasn't safe to let any of the human doctors even examine you in person when you were brought in."

"*I don't understand.*" Ioane's used to her friend being a bit cryptic. That's their usual way of talking, even. This, though, makes little to no sense. "*How did I get here?*"

"Li carried you for us." Celadon seems to be going for a record level of cryptic today.

Ioane gives them a confused look.

"You're too tall for either of us to carry alone, and one of us had to focus on keeping the air around you clear," Celadon clarifies with an enigmatic twitch of their ears. "Li's the only human on this ship who could risk coming close to you at the time, so he stepped in to help us." There's something in their tone that suggests they weren't entirely happy with that arrangement, although Ioane doesn't understand why.

"We had to put a respirator mask on you and wrap you up in a blanket with the kittens so it'd be safe to take you through the ship to get here at all," Breezy adds. "But it all worked out okay! You're here, you're awake, and my big brother's hangover from helping us was easy to fix." Young Ocean, as it turns out, is every bit as good at being cryptic as Celadon is.

Ioane looks between the three Florivans again. Nyx can't seem to bring themself to meet her eyes now, and she doesn't understand that at all. "*Why?*"

"After what you'd gone through," Celadon answers, "your lungs were still filled with clinging miasmas and there was a bit of it soaked into the layers of your clothing as well. We couldn't risk exposing the rest of the ship. My Navigator's a bit of a special case, but just the amount of the Strange that was sticking to you when Nyx landed your darter would have been *deadly* to most humans." They sigh softly. "There's still quite a bit around you that the kittens haven't dealt with yet, I'm afraid, so we've been keeping this room and the rest of my quarters sealed as much as we can."

"*Miasmas?*" Ioane taps out on the holoscreen, "*I don't understand. If I didn't crash, what happened?*"

"You don't know?" Breezy looks over to Nyx, all three eyes wide with surprise. "I thought you would have told her already."

Nyx takes on an almost ashamed tone, turning their eyes down to the fluff at the end of their tail that they're still so methodically straightening. "I was trying to when you came in."

"*Now you're all being cryptic,*" the computerized voice of the pocket-com comments on Ioane's behalf. She reaches over and pats the nearest one of Nyx's arms that she can reach, shooting them a gentle smile. She's still incredibly confused, but that's mixed considerably with concern because of how her recently-acquired friend is acting. "*Tell me what?*"

Nyx looks to her, hesitates slightly, then sighs. "That you were *going* to crash into that striker, Abigail, and I... well..." They trail off, looking to Celadon.

"Nyx here saved both your lives by jumping your darter into the Strange," says Celadon, as matter-of-fact as if they were simply saying that the galaxy is *large*. "It was something of an instinctive action on their part, and you're quite fortunate that you've proved more resilient to exposure than the average human." They nod to Nyx with a reassuring flick of their ears. "Considering that you *are* both alive and relatively well now, and what the alternative was? I'd say it was the right instinct to follow."

Ioane's incredulous stare encompasses all three Florivans. It takes her a few minutes to process what she's just been told enough to even have a question to ask. *"That's possible? How? And how am I alive at all?"*

"It's possible, yes," Celadon replies, waving their tail in an almost amused gesture. "It's similar to what happened to Julian when Mirawynd's parent died—although they *threw* him several light years, from what we can tell. Nyx only took you from one side of the planetoid's orbit to the other once Li was able to coordinate points so they could return to the Normal safely."

Ioane thinks about it, then nods. It's only slightly less confusing than things already were, of course. Considering that in her experience, Florivans always seem to be holding back a bit on how much they're really capable of, it makes a strange sort of sense. The implications, though, are staggering.

"As for how you've managed to *survive* the experience," Celadon continues, reaching out to ruffle Wyndi's ears momentarily, "you can chock that up both to your own natural resilience and the fact that we had kittens on hand to soak up the miasmas that were stuck to you once we got you safely here. The three of us could have managed something without them, but it wouldn't have been nearly as quick or easy a thing to do."

Wyndi purrs more loudly and nuzzles Celadon's hand before settling back into a neat little curled-up ball in Ioane's lap.

"Kittens like quantum space miasmas? I know you and Sarge mentioned it was important for Wyndi to go jumping now and again with you or Indigo, but I never asked about it."

"It's good for them!" Breezy chimes in with another cheerful swish of their tail. "Little kittens need a bit of the Strange around them while they're growing—and since they absorb miasmas easily, it makes them perfect to help with humans who've been seriously exposed."

"It's also something spacefaring Elders *don't* explain to the humans we work with very often," Celadon adds, their lower pair of hands almost unconsciously settling over their abdomen as they make a vague gesture with the upper two. "We're aware that it would make people feel... unsafe, I suppose is the best word, if they knew what we carry for our kittens."

Ioane nods slowly. She's been friends with this particular Florivan Elder for *years* now. Even though the information is new, the idea that they have secrets they keep for the sake of safety for the rest of their species isn't. Celadon is the Fleet's only Elder, after all. Beyond that, they're one of a very small handful of the reproductive members of their genderless, asexual species who their governing Council has allowed to leave the Florivan Sanctuary planet at Procyon at all. Ioane's also well aware of the dangers of exposure to quantum space miasmas— personally so, now, it seems—and of how frightened some of her fellow humans are about the possibility just of minor leaks during Quantum Space transit. She can't imagine those people being pleasant to be around if they knew what her friend has just told her.

"I'll keep that to myself, then." Ioane taps out on the holoscreen. *"Thanks for letting me borrow the cuties."*

"You'll be borrowing them for the next few weeks, I think," says Celadon, reaching over and lightly setting their hand against Ioane's cheek. They look into her eyes with an expression of gentle concern and careful consideration. "The Strange liked you well enough that it's settled into your blood as much as it did your lungs."

Ioane cracks a smile at them and manages a soft chuckle. *"Is that a good thing or a bad thing? I can't tell."*

"Hm." Celadon looks into her eyes more closely. "Are you in any pain, Abigail?"

Ioane considers it before she answers. *"Bit of a headache, maybe, but other than that? Only when I try talking. I've had worse after a night out with the girls."*

Breezy giggles. "She sounds like your Navigator, Celadon."

"She does, doesn't she? I will never cease to be amazed at how quickly some humans adapt... and how resilient some of you are." Celadon shakes their head, smiling softly as they withdraw their hand from Ioane's cheek. "Then I'd say it's just a thing that is, and that hopefully will pass with time."

Ioane nods, taps something else out on the holoscreen, then looks over to Nyx with a smile while the program reads it for her. *"Thanks for saving me, Nyx. I'll take this over the alternative any day."*

"I *am* sorry there wasn't another way, Abigail..." Nyx hesitates again to meet her eyes.

It takes Ioane a minute or two to finish tapping out what she wants to say this time. She reaches over to give

Nyx's closest hand a squeeze while the program reads the words for her. "*Don't go feeling guilty because of this. Darter pilots take off knowing we might not come back, every time. That's what we're trained to do. That's what I volunteered to do when I first put on my Fleet colors: to fly off and fight and die if I have to so that civilians like you and everyone I care about who used to live at Mayview can be safe from the Novans or anyone else who might want to harm you. Any flight where I come back alive in the end is a good flight, and I only came back alive because you were with me. Not just from jumping out of that crash, either. You spotting strikers for us is what kept me and the rest of the Musketeers alive long enough for help to arrive. I might have gotten hurt, but I'm alive, and I'm grateful to be alive so I can fly another day to protect you. That's all that matters.*"

Nyx nods and squeezes her hand back. "I'm glad you're alive too, Abigail." Their voice catches slightly on the words.

"That's what that whole 'immortality' business is about, you know," Breezy interjects brightly. "It's from their song. George explained it to me as sort of a joke that means 'we know we're going off to die and it's terrifying but we're going to do it anyway!' so that hopefully everyone else will get to live safely to remember them." They make air quotation gestures with their lower hands as they speak, then lightly rest one upper hand on their chin. "It sounds a lot more exciting and noble when George says it, though."

"*That's* what it means?" Nyx looks between Breezy and Ioane with an expression that's best described as shocked amusement.

"Breezy's right, it does. I told you that you didn't want to know while you were in the bird with me!" Ioane can't help laughing, even though it comes out as little more than a pained squeak or two. She deals with the resulting small cough while the text-to-speech program reads her words.

"...No, I wouldn't have wanted to." Nyx shakes their head, showing just a hint of amusement in their eyes. "No wonder Cousin Elias calls you and your sisters madwomen."

Ioane shoots Celadon a knowing smirk while her response to that little comment is spoken for her. *"Don't let him fool you, Nyx. Rudy's just as mad as the rest of us. Keeps us flying, after all! Speaking of: He recovered yet?"*

"Mostly," Celadon replies, with an amused twitch of their ears. "Whatever it was Dr. Kiely gave him before you left Mayview took the better part of a day to wear off. He got into an argument with Jenny again this morning, though, so I'd say he's back to his usual self."

Ioane shakes her head. One of the Fleet's great mysteries is whether Admiral Marvin *actually* still disapproves of Rudy's existence or if the two of them just get on like oil and water out of habit at this point. *"Do I want to know what it was this time?"*

"He and our Mister Sidney have started talking about making some adjustments to George's darter because I fly with him!" Breezy takes on an unmistakably excited sparkle in all three of their eyes. "So we'll have a com system like you and Sergeant Potts have on your darters, but modified to connect with *Gymnasio* and *Aegolius'* Nav/ Quan intercom mains, and some other things fixed up so that if I ever have to jump George's tail out of harm's way he won't be exposed—"

"—Which *ideally* will not be a thing that you ever have to do in the first place." Celadon sets a hand on Ocean's head and ruffles their hair like Ioane's seen them do to settle Wyndi down. "And we're still discussing all of that. The Admiral will agree to it after *I* decide what I think of the plan."

"Yes, Celadon..." Breezy lets out a reluctantly acquiescent sigh. "But it'll be neat if it works."

"Hm. We'll see." Celadon ruffles Ocean's hair again and smiles at them in a way that, knowing them as well as Ioane does, suggests to her that *they're* just as interested in the project as the younger Florivan is. "Now, since Abigail's awake, would you do me a favor and go get Dr. Kiely and let her know?"

Breezy nods and scampers out of the room.

"Are they really old enough to be a jumper?" Ioane asks, amused but curious.

"Yes, believe it or not—although you should see their Navigator. His file may say he's of age, but it's hard to believe he's any older than Ocean is, if that." Celadon twitches an ear, then grins at her. "You'll like him. He's just as much a magnet for trouble as you and Julian are."

Ioane shakes her head again in an effort not to laugh. *"No wonder you let them keep him."*

"What can I say?" Celadon quips. "If I've learned anything since I left Procyon, it's that the most troublesome darter pilots make some of the best Navigators. You're already used to maneuvering in three dimensions... and mad enough that working with the Strange isn't all that jarring of a transition for you."

Ioane can't help giggling, even though no sound comes out. She knows most of the other pilots Celadon's volunteers have picked out over the years for their counterparts, and "troublesome" is putting it *mildly* as a description for some of them.

She taps out a teasing quip on the holoscreen and looks over to Nyx as it's being read. *"I know you're not in the market for a Navigator, Nyx, but if you want a trouble-magnet of a darter pilot for a pet of your very own, I promise I'm mostly housebroken."*

Nyx's eyes widen, not with shock this time but with something Ioane can't help but interpret as hesitant elation. "I'm not joining the Fleet," they say after a moment with a slow swish of their tail. "Still... since I'm going to be traveling with *Aegolius* until we get to Luyten's Star, I wouldn't mind watching over you until then so you don't get into any more trouble."

Ioane grins. *"Deal. I'll try not to need saving again anytime soon."*

"Would that be all right, Elder Celadon?" Nyx asks, looking up to them. "I know we already talked about how I can't be a proper ship's jumper as I am... and I still think I'd rather stay a civilian for now... but would a temporary compact with one of your pilots be acceptable?"

Celadon grins at both of them in the way they usually do when one of their cryptic little schemes is coming together exactly the way they want it to. "I can sort that out, yes, if that's what the two of you want. I'd rather you did have a counterpart of some kind while you're with us, and Abigail here *will* need one of us with her at all times until she's fully recovered. It would certainly simplify things if I could count on the two of you to look after each other."

Ioane looks up to Nyx with a smile. *"Sounds good to me. You're the best copilot I've had in a long time."*

"Thank you, Abigail, but don't expect me to fly again anytime soon. I've had my fill of excitement for the *month* at least." Nyx laughs genuinely this time.

"Fair enough! I doubt they'll let me fly again anytime soon as it is." Ioane does her best not to laugh too, if only because laughter hurts at the moment.

"All the better that you have a companion, then," says Nyx. "I've been told bored pilots tend to get themselves into *trouble*."

Celadon stifles a giggle, although their tail is waving with clear amusement to make up for it. "Oh, they do..."

"Well, then, companion," Ioane taps out on the holoscreen, *"I don't think I'll be up for tag anytime soon. How would you feel about a walk through hydroponics once they let me out of here?"*

Nyx smiles softly and reaches over to pat her hand. "I'd like that."

Somehow, even though she knows it's only temporary, Ioane can't help but be pleased with the arrangement. She's already looking forward to getting to know her recently-acquired Florivan friend better.

MIRAWYND IS RATHER RUDELY AWAKENED from the nap they were taking comfortably curled in a ball under Abi's blanket by the sensation of a pair of hands picking them up. They squeak and squirm in the hands for a few moments before they're awake enough to recognize the person holding them. *Why* she's picking them up, they don't know, but Reba is, so they settle down a bit and give her a curious head-tilt.

They also don't know why she has her face covered completely with a pair of tinted goggles and the funny sort of mask that Abi was wearing when Entile Celadon brought her to their nest a few days ago and asked Mirawynd and their little cousins to look after her.

"That's right, ye sleepy wee beastie, it be me," Reba says, her voice lightly muffled. "Now be a good kitten and sit here with Celadon and Nyx while I finish seeing to me patient."

Mirawynd relaxes and allows themself to be handed over to their favorite entile. They are rewarded with snuggles and a gentle scratching of the itchy borders of the places where they no longer have fur, so they don't mind in the end at all. They watch with interest while Reba holds some sort of humming hand-scanner tool over different parts of Abi's body and then gets out one funny-looking shiny thing to listen to her lungs and another to stare down the inside of her throat. After a few minutes, Reba puts her tools away and sets her hands on her hips.

"Well, for a woman what likely shouldn't be alive? Ye be doing rather well. Celadon here's right that most of the damage be in ye lungs and windpipe—I'll be talking to Dr. Baxter about setting up seals around the roboscanner chamber so we can see more of what be going on with that. If ye start feeling worse or having trouble breathing, ye have Nyx send for me. Clear?"

Abi nods. So does Nyx.

"Other than telling ye to keep quiet and prescribing some lozenges to help with ye cough, there ain't much more I can do for ye at the moment." Reba shakes her head. "Ye darter pilots have all the luck of a cat what don't care to know which life he's on."

"They really do, don't they?" Entile Celadon asks, chuckling. "And here Jenny's gone and made me responsible for a whole squadron of them..."

Abi grins at them and taps at her little holoscreen for a few moments. *"Luckily for you, Commander, there's only four of us in your little honor guard! Well, and Rudy, but you already might as well have been in charge of him."*

Mirawynd squeaks curiously in her direction. They're still not used to Abi using the voice of a shiny thing instead of her own.

Abi makes a sound that's more of a rough squeak herself rather than her usual chuckle and taps at the holoscreen again. *"Right. And Wyndi, but they're more the one who takes care of Sarge than the other way around."*

"And ye be lucky enough now that ye silly little squadron of self-destructive fools has its own doctor for the next few months," Reba adds with a smirk. "And a first-rate mad botanist to keep one of ye two most troublesome pilots out of harm's way."

Entile Celadon laughs. "Yes, yes, you're all *wonderful* and I couldn't ask for better. I'll just be glad when all of my charges are well and able to play with each other safely again. I know what darter pilots get like when they're bored and lonely. They're just as bad as kittens in that respect."

Abi makes her most innocent face, but doesn't say anything.

"That they be, Celadon. My Julian were like that long before he got his wings, even." Reba shakes her head. "Ye'll have ye hands full with the lot of them, but Nyx and I will do what we can to help ye." She turns to Nyx with a softer smile. "And as for ye, Nyx, dear? Try to eat something and get some sleep now that ye've no cause for worry? I know how ye be, and *ye* know I won't let ye get away with forgetting to take care of yeself any more than ye have."

"Yes, Reba," says Nyx, swishing their tail with amusement.

"Good. That goes for ye too, Celadon—ye Navigator and I had a rather long conversation about ye, since I'm tasked with *ye* too now..." Reba gives them a knowing look.

Entile Celadon laughs again and leans down to ruffle Mirawynd's ears. "Do you hear this, kitten? My Navigator is conspiring with *doctors* now to make me take better care of myself."

Mirawynd doesn't entirely understand, so they settle for giving their favorite entile a nuzzle. "Mine," they say, contentedly.

"Seems they agree with you, Dr. Kiely. Okay, then, I will *try* to be good." Entile Celadon grins and stands up, taking Mirawynd back up in their hands and offering them to Reba. "Mirawynd, I think you can go back to Julian for tonight. Teryin and Tesnee can help Nyx handle things here while I go join Ocean and see to the jump shift. I'm sure you're eager to check on your counterpart by now."

Mirawynd leaps to Reba's shoulder and gives her an enthusiastic nuzzle too. "Sarge?"

"Yes, Wyndi, dear, I'll take ye to him. Our man's been all out of sorts missing ye, too, not what he'd ever admit it." Reba laughs, although the sound is muffled by the mask she's wearing. "I'll be in to check on ye in the morning, Major."

"Thanks, Dr. Kiely. Say hi to the girls for me?"

"I will." Reba says her goodnights and slips out the door, Mirawynd still perched on her shoulder.

When Reba gets down the corridor to her own cabin, she pulls the respirator mask and goggles off and sets them on a small table built into one wall. Once that's done, she plops down on the small window seat under her open, star-filled viewport and pulls out her pocket-com. She taps some sort of message on it and then sets it aside on a shelf before, leaning back against the cushioned side-wall of the bench and stretching out her legs. She kicks off first one boot and then the other, leaving them with a rather satisfying plop on the floor.

Mirawynd, still sitting on her shoulder, does their best to sort out all of the tangles that the straps from her mask and goggles have put into her hair. It's not easy, since she has so much hair to begin with and it doesn't like being tamed.

"There we are, Wyndi," Reba says, reaching up to ruffle their ears. "I've told our silly man to come collect ye—but I don't mind cuddling with ye for a bit while we wait for him."

Mirawynd contentedly slips down to snuggle against Reba's chest and lets her pet them as much as she wants. They like Reba. She's warm and very good at ear-scratching and she seems to make their human happy, which in turn makes Mirawynd happy. They're pleased to count her as the latest human addition to their small family.

A few minutes later, just as Mirawynd is about to fall asleep again, the door makes a chiming sound. Reba looks up from whatever it is she's pulled up on her holoscreen to read while they were cuddling. "Come in, Julian—door's unlocked."

The door opens. Mirawynd's human steps into the room, his pilot's jacket hanging loosely over the clothes he wears when he's off-duty.

Mirawynd immediately scampers over and leaps up into his arms, squeaking excitedly as they try to tell him all about what they've been helping their Entile Celadon with for the last few days even though they don't know all of the words to say it with and performing their usual checking for injuries nuzzles all at the same time. Thankfully, he seems to be okay and uninjured. They suspect that's because Reba's been taking care of him while they were busy.

Their human laughs and gives them a warm hug, lightly rubbing their ears. "I missed you too, Wyndi. Now settle down, will you?"

"If the two of ye ain't the cutest thing, I don't know what it be." Reba is smiling softly at the two of them from the viewport bench.

"Thanks, Reba…" Their human laughs awkwardly and rubs at the back of his hair while Mirawynd takes their usual post on his shoulder and snuggles up against his neck, purring even louder now than they had while Reba was cuddling them. "How's the Major?"

Reba pats the seat next to her. Mirawynd's human smiles and takes it.

"She's doing better than I'd thought she would. Celadon were right about the kittens helping her—stands to reason, too, now that they've explained things to me about what happened to ye and Wyndi." Reba shakes her head. "It's nothing short of a miracle, and I ain't claiming I fully understand... but me patient be living and recovering. I'll take that as a win."

Mirawynd's human nods, busying his hands with petting their ears now. Mirawynd is most pleased to have him back where they can snuggle with him. They love Abi too, of course, but as nice to snuggle with as Abi is, she's still not their human. He's their *home*, after all.

"Glad to hear she's going to be okay," he says. "How's Nyx holding up?"

"Finally relaxing a bit, now that the Major's awake and able to tell them she ain't mad for having her life saved." Reba lets out a small laugh. "And according to Celadon, she be serving as their counterpart until we get to Luyten's Star. I'd say that be good for both of them."

"I can see that working out." Mirawynd's human chuckles too, then his eyes soften and he looks to Reba with a lightly concerned curiosity. "What does that mean for you, then? It was just you and Nyx down there at Mayview for *years*... will you be okay?"

Reba shrugs. "It ain't like it means we be going separate ways entirely, Julian. Nyx be the sibling I never had, and we've been through hell and back together. That's something what stays forever, no matter where either of us be. Besides, we still be on the same ship—and while I'll admit I ain't used to sleeping alone anymore, much less during Quantum Space transit... I'll be fine, and they know my nest be theirs to share whenever they need it."

"I think I can get that." Mirawynd's human nods.

"And... well." Reba hesitates, then scoots over closer to him with a smile. "It ain't like I be alone now, ye know."

Their human smiles and lifts his arm up so she can slip in underneath it.

Mirawynd contentedly repositions themself so *both* of their humans can reach to pet them, nuzzling Reba's hand so she gets the idea. She obliges with a gentle scratch behind their ears.

"No," their human says, "and I don't think Wyndi has any intention of leaving you alone either."

Mirawynd looks up at him, then shrugs and relaxes into a comfortable stretched-out position over both of the nice warm laps. "Mine," they agree, yawning softly at the end of the word. Their purr starts up again.

"Julian…" Reba says softly after a few minutes, just as Mirawynd is starting to drift off to sleep again. "I *am* glad it were ye what came to find us. I… I'd put a lot of hope in seeing ye again."

"I don't know how to even begin to tell you how glad I am that you're alive." Mirawynd's human sighs lightly. "Or how much I *never* want to lose you like I thought I had."

"I know what ye mean."

There's another long silence, and then Mirawynd feels their human shifting positions like he's about to stand up. "I should probably take Wyndi back so you can sleep—"

Mirawynd slips out of the way, intending to climb up to his shoulder, but then they notice that he stopped talking because Reba has pulled him close and is nuzzling his face in that weird way humans do sometimes. With anyone but Reba, Mirawynd would put up a fuss about this and try to rescue him, but they trust her not to hurt their human or try to eat his brains. Besides that, he seems to be quite happy to set his hands on her waist and lean in to nuzzle her back.

Mirawynd contents themself with scampering over to investigate how soft the blankets are in Reba's new nest. It's similar to the bunk their human has on the ship that is their home, and cozy enough in their opinion. Still, they much prefer the layers and layers of soft nest that she and Nyx had assembled in their plant-filled room. They make a note that they should see if they can find Reba an extra blanket so she won't get cold here. Aunt Jenny's ship is much colder than Reba's home was, after all.

When Mirawynd finally pops their head back up out of the blankets a few minutes later, both of humans are standing next to the viewport, just staring at each other for some reason.

Reba slowly withdraws her arms from around their human's neck. "I've been meaning to do that since ye left Teegarden," she says, softly. "Do ye mind?"

"Not at all. I'd... well, I'd been meaning to *myself* ever since you stepped out of the vines and put down that laser stunner, you know."

Reba giggles. "Will ye stay, then?"

Mirawynd sees their human is smiling brightly now. He leans down and nuzzles Reba's forehead. "Tonight, and as long as you'll have me."

"Then I'll be keeping ye forever."

"I'd be okay with that." Mirawynd's human gives Reba a long hug, then looks over to them. "Well, Wyndi? Looks like Reba's keeping us."

Mirawynd squeaks cheerfully and takes this as an invitation to bounce back over and join the hugging.

They're always pleased to have a chance to snuggle with their favorite humans, after all.

"That's right," says Reba, lightly stroking Mirawynd's fur. "I be keeping *ye* too, Wyndi, dear. I know ye and Julian be a package deal—and I need all the help I can get looking after him."

Mirawynd looks up at their human with a pleased squeak. A thought occurs to them, and they turn their eyes back to Reba with their most hopeful expression. "Snack?"

"What, this time of night?" Reba laughs. "Oh, ye be just a wee fuzzy bottomless pit, Wyndi, I swear..." She hands Mirawynd back to their human. "Here, Julian, hold ye counterpart while I get me shoes back on—but we be bringing our snacks back here. I still ain't used to the chaos the Fleet calls a dining hall."

"Sounds good to me, Reba." Mirawynd's human is smiling more broadly than they've ever seen him before. They decide that must be because he was ready for food too.

Some time later, after snacks have been found and a nice game of "chase the knotted sock" has been played, Mirawynd contentedly curls up on the pillow between their human and Reba and falls asleep. They are warm and safe and can sleep easily, secure in the knowledge that they've done a good job taking care of the person their parent told them to protect and that their small family is *together* and happy.

They couldn't ask for a better end to an adventure than this.

★ The End ★

Appendix

Timeline of *Strange Space Adventures*

The following timeline lists all of the published *Strange Space™ Adventures* and Short Stories in roughly chronological order. Where stories feature major time skips, they have been placed based on the earliest events of that story.

Short Stories marked with *[1] can be found in *Tales of the Navigators: Volume 1.*

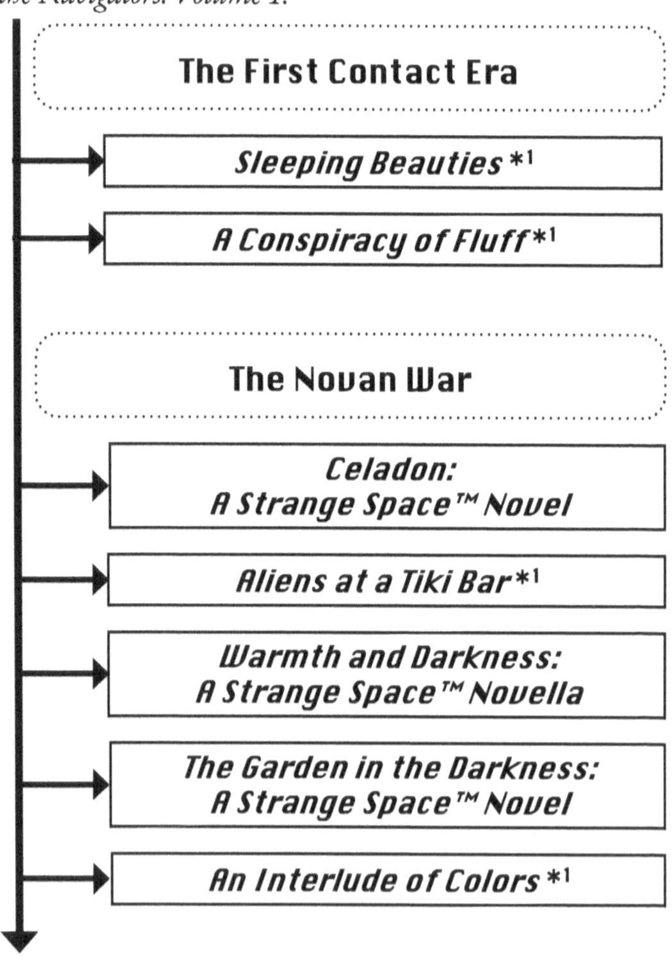

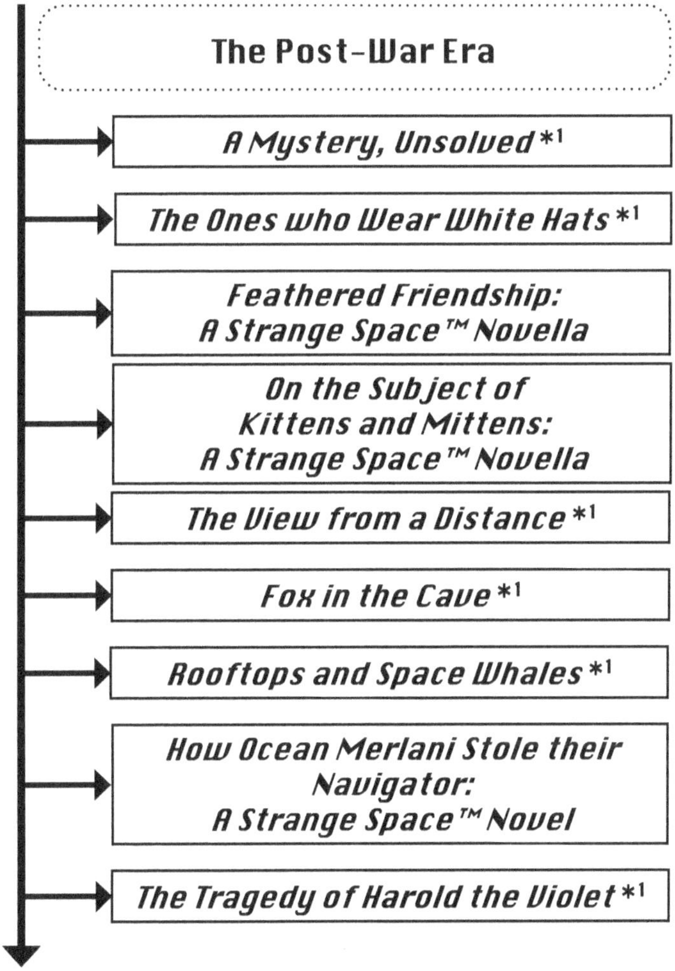

The Post-War Era

A Mystery, Unsolved *1

The Ones who Wear White Hats *1

Feathered Friendship:
A Strange Space™ Novella

On the Subject of
Kittens and Mittens:
A Strange Space™ Novella

The View from a Distance *1

Fox in the Cave *1

Rooftops and Space Whales *1

How Ocean Merlani Stole their
Navigator:
A Strange Space™ Novel

The Tragedy of Harold the Violet *1

On Character Identities and Pronouns

The Garden in the Darkness takes place in a far future setting in which human society has long since reached the stage of accepting and celebrating all varieties of diversity. This is a sort of world that I, personally, would like to live in. I don't claim it to be a *perfect* setting, but I do take an optimistic view of our potential as a species.

Several of the human characters presented in this story would, in today's terms, likely identify with one or more communities under the LGBTQIA+ umbrella. While the narrative of this story did not call for the characters to specifically state which labels they would use, and I like to imagine that a lot of who they are can be inferred through their interactions, as a member of the LGBTQIA+ community *myself*, I'm aware of the importance of clear representation. Seeing characters like ourselves in stories where they are valued for who they are and able to live without being marginalized for their nature is, in my opinion, *powerful*, and a big part of my philosophy as a writer.

Please note that at the same time, it is impossible to represent an entire community in the form of one character. My characters are simply themselves, and while they draw on my own experiences and those of people I know, they are not meant to be "perfect" renditions of one thing or another. Just like every human, their various identities are *aspects* of them, rather than the entirety of their personality.

That all being said, the following characters who feature in this story would like to "come out" to you and share this aspect of their lives:

Pilot-Major Abigail Ioane would describe herself as asexual and aromantic.

Dr. Reba Kiely would describe herself as "demi-attractional," or both demisexual and demiromantic.

Elias Rudolph would describe himself as homosexual/homoromantic. (In his words: "a man who happens to be attracted to other men." Rudy has never been all that interested in labels of any sort.)

Lt. Hsu Li would describe himself as pansexual and demi-romantic.

(Note: Please keep in mind that this is not an exhaustive list of the LGBTQIA+ characters who appear in this story, any more than it is a full description of each of the characters in question. These are simply the ones who feature most prominently and asked me to clarify their identities.)

On behalf of all of my characters, humans and Florivans alike, I'd like to thank you, dear reader, for being accepting of them and respecting their preferred sets of pronouns.

I hope that we all will one day live in a world like the one these characters inhabit, in which a person can openly be themself without fear. I do believe it's possible for us to get there, too; every small step we make in the right direction matters.

—Katie Silverwings

On Florivan Names

Florivan names consist of two parts: the 'public' name and the 'personal' name. The 'personal' or 'kitten-name' is given to a Florivan when they first open their eyes, while the 'public' name is chosen for them when they are old enough to be presented to the Council of Elders. Personal names come from the ancestral Florivan language, and are largely untranslatable. All of the kittens in a litter will usually be given names with the same or similar initial sounds.

Public names are always words from human languages which connect somehow to the individual's coloring. Kittens, therefore, receive their public names once they have shed enough of their fur to show a large patch of a recognizable color. Elders will often carry a theme through the public names of their kittens such as different stones, plants, or a specific language of origin.

Florivans are most often addressed by their public names. Only Elders, family members, or the closest of friends will address or talk about a Florivan by their personal name, and then only in private. (Private, in this case, also extends to situations where only other Florivans or close friends of the family are present.) Florivans also commonly take on nicknames which are used by their families, friends, and colleagues. Who can use a certain nickname for them depends on the situation and origin of the nickname. Ocean Marbree, for example, is called "Breezy" publicly by the personnel of the 6th Darter Squadron and their other human friends. Elder Celadon Toreval is called "Val" in private, but only by their Navigator.

Florivan Elders are addressed and referred to formally with their title, although most of them will grant close friends and colleagues permission to address them by their public name alone outside of formal situations. The Eldest of the Council is a particular exception to this rule, as they are never referred to by name after assuming the role of Eldest, save by their siblings in private. Younger members of an Elder's line will call them 'Nida' ('Parent') or 'Ai-Nida' ('Grandparent') as appropriate in most situations. Apprentices to an Elder typically use their title as a sign of respect regardless of whose line they belong to, although the Elder may ask them to do otherwise in private.

On the Defense Fleet's Darter Squadrons

The Sol Coalition Defense Fleet's squadrons of darter pilots are either legendary for their bravery or infamous for their love of danger, depending upon whom one asks.

The technology for small, two-person craft capable of maneuvering both within a planetary atmosphere and in the zero-gravity environment of outer space was already in development prior to the beginning of humanity's involvement in the Novan War. At that time, the inherently pacifist Florivan Council of Elders was still restricting the use of their all-important Quantum Space Drive to civilian and Ranger Corps vessels only. Without the Drive to allow their ships to use the veiled dimension of Quantum Space as a shortcut around the physical distances between planets and stars, the Sol Coalition Defense Fleet was left to come up with other means of protecting the eight star systems in its charge.

The concept of short-range fighter craft serving as a mobile force which could be placed on individual inhabited worlds or space stations as a final line of defense against potential invaders was the Defense Fleet's best option at the time. The danger of invasion was primarily theoretical at the onset of Project SnailDarter's development, as the only alien species humanity had thus far encountered were the neighboring Sol-based Europans (who were unable to leave their moon of origin without assistance) and the charismatic and friendly Florivans who had become humanity's closest ally and begun a process of peaceful societal integration.

When humanity found itself suddenly in the middle of the ongoing war between the Novan Imperium's conquest force and the Prelvee and T'irsh-fel Alliance, the development of Project Snail Darter was sped up in order to provide a serviceable defensive and expeditionary force.

Notably, the representatives of both senior member species of the Alliance were reported to be "horrified, but thoroughly impressed" by the demonstrations held for them of the capabilities of the "darters" and their pilots in combat scenarios against long-range particle weapons and unmanned drones. While the Alliance's strategists were familiar with the live-piloted "strikers" used by the Novans to overwhelm their enemies with seemingly endless waves of disposable attack craft, neither species had ever *dreamed* of placing live pilots at the controls inside similar spacecraft themselves. The idea of a single human being responsible for operating an object operating at the very limits of what the laws of physics and understanding of human science would allow and sending them out to attack the enemy directly was as completely alien to them as humans themselves were. Nevertheless, the Alliance quickly recognized the value of the Defense Fleet's darters as a counter to the Novan Armada's striker forces.

Initial plans for the use of these unique small fighter craft centered around forming squadrons of darters to be stationed as the defense of individual inhabited worlds within the Sol Coalition's territory. Additionally, a number of these squadrons would be selected to serve as an expeditionary force on the Alliance's ships in nearby battle sectors. The so-called "defection" of the Florivan Elder Celadon Toreval and the arrival of their household as the Fleet's "Florivan Volunteer Corps" made several changes to the Alliance's core strategies possible. The newly formed squadrons of darters were instead posted on the Defense Fleet's brand-new QSD-equipped starships, where they could more easily be mobilized to defend the Sol Coalition's territory and aid the other members of the Alliance when possible.

The first nine darter squadrons were formed by the time the Fleet's ships were ready, and each was placed under the command of one of the veterans of the Project Snail Darter test pilot program. While eight of these squadrons were immediately assigned to starships, the 9th remained stationed at the Teegarden Shipyards to defend the base there and assist in the training of additional pilots.

At the time of *The Garden in the Darkness*, there are a total of twenty-eight darter squadrons in service. Each is composed of sixteen pilots, divided into four "wing teams" during maneuvers. The wings of a squadron are subdivided into patrol pairs. Each wing is led by one of the squadron's most experienced pilots, with the "lead wing" being that of the squadron's commanding officer. A darter squadron also includes a number of maintenance technicians responsible for repairing and updating the darters as needed. Typically, there is one of these technicians assigned to each wing, with a "chief mechanic" overseeing all of them.

The 2nd Darter Squadron is a notable exception to this standard personnel arrangement. The 2nd began as a typical squadron, albeit as the only one with more than one former test pilot in its ranks. After its commanding officer and the majority of its members were lost along with SCV *Athene* during the first Battle of the Teegarden Expanse, the decision was made to allow the remaining three pilots to reform their unit as a single-wing squadron retaining their initial designation. At the time of *The Garden in the Darkness*, the resulting smaller 2nd squadron is assigned to SCV *Surnia* as an attachment to the ship's own recently-formed 18th Darter Squadron.

THE SONG OF THE DARTER PILOTS

The "Darter Pilot's Anthem" dates back to the early days of Project Snail Darter's development. Reportedly, the original version of the song was little more than a lightly modified rendition of "When the Foeman Bears his Steel" from Gilbert and Sullivan's The Pirates of Penzance performed by the test pilots during a talent show at the Teegarden Shipyards Shell Island base for the amusement of their coworkers. Head test pilot Colonel Gunther Hannemann himself took on the role of the Police Sergeant, while then-Lieutenants Andrea Bell and

Morelia Darcy sang the female parts while doing their best impressions of Admiral Marvin. (The Admiral, it should be noted, was in attendance at this event. She reportedly sat through it with a good-humored stoicism, but did not state her opinions at the time; her former personal assistant and the base psychologist who organized the event can both attest to her having kept a recording to watch on occasions when she needs a good laugh and a reminder not to take herself too seriously.)

After the initial performance, Colonel Hannemann and his fellow test pilots made the song something of a running private joke amongst themselves. The chorus phrase, "forward to immortality", in particular, became their battle cry, while the word "tarantara" took on the status of a warning or distress call. Before long, a full set of modified lyrics for a simpler solo or duet version of the song had been assembled. With the onset of the Novan War and the swelling of their ranks, this "Darter Pilot's Anthem" and the associated phrases spread throughout the squadrons and became firmly ensconced as one of the pillars of the common culture of the pilots. It is commonly sung by the pilots as part of their recreational activities, seemingly as a tongue-in-cheek celebration of their continued defiance of death.

With apologies to Gilbert and Sullivan, what follows are the full lyrics of "The Darter Pilot's Anthem." The tune remains mostly the same, if you wish to hum along.

THE DARTER PILOT'S ANTHEM
(FORWARD TO IMMORTALITY)

Opening:

Now, let we darter pilots lion-hearted
Be gathered to declare our common courage,
Ere we depart upon our dread adventure.
Onward, we fly!

Verse 1:

Though we know the danger's real,
(*Tarantara! Tarantara!*)
And we uncomfortable feel,
(*Tarantara!*)
Still we find the wisest thing,
(*Tarantara! Tarantara!*)
Is to slap our chests and sing:
Tarantara!
For when gravity refutes,
(*Tarantara! Tarantara!*)
And your heart is in your boots,
(*Tarantara!*)

There is nothing brings it round
Like the trumpet's martial sound!
Like the trumpet's martial sound:
Tarantara!

Chorus 1:

Tarantara-ra-ra-ra-ra! Tarantara!
Tarantara-ra-ra-ra-ra! Tarantara!
Tarantara, tarantara!
Tarantara, tarantara!
Forward to immortality!

On, we pilots, on to glory,
On to face the combat gory,
We shall live in song and story.
Forward to immortality!
Go to death, but go with laughter;
Die, but pilots ever after
Shall our bravery long remember.
So, forget death—live and fly! Tarantara!

So, forget death—live and fly!
So, forget death—live and fly!

Verse 2:

Though to us it's evident,
(*Tarantara! Tarantara!*)
Words of caution are well meant,
(*Tarantara!*)
Such expressions don't appear,
(*Tarantara! Tarantara!*)
Calculated folks to cheer,
(*Tarantara!*)
Who are off to meet their fate
(*Tarantara! Tarantara!*)
In a somewhat nervous state.
(*Tarantara!*)

We can't worry on the wing,
So instead we'll cheer and sing!
So instead we'll cheer and sing:
Tarantara!

Chorus 2:

Tarantara-ra-ra-ra-ra! Tarantara!
Tarantara-ra-ra-ra-ra! Tarantara!
Tarantara, tarantara!
Tarantara, tarantara!

Forward to immortality!

Go and do our best endeavor,
And before all links we sever,
We will say farewell forever.
Forward to Immortality!
Though our foes are fierce and ruthless,
False, unmerciful, and truth-less;
But we simply couldn't care less,
As we fly to save the day! Tarantara!

As we fly to save the day!
As we fly to save the day!

Verse 3:

We won't put too great a stress,
(*Tarantara! Tarantara!*)
On the risks that on us press.
(*Tarantara!*)
For we know there is a lack
(*Tarantara! Tarantara!*)
Of our chance of coming back.
(*Tarantara!*)
And we know it isn't wise
(*Tarantara! Tarantara!*)
As we take unto the skies,
(*Tarantara!*)

For the need is evident
We won't let our fears torment.
We can't let our fears torment!
Tarantara!

Chorus 3:

Tarantara-ra-ra-ra-ra! Tarantara!
Tarantara-ra-ra-ra-ra! Tarantara!

Tarantara, tarantara!
Tarantara, tarantara!
Forward to immortality!

On, we fly into the unknown,
On, where no one ever has flown!
We shall meet the foe together.
Forward to immortality!
Whether death, or to a new day;
Onward, onward, that is our way!
So fly we into the fray.
Even if our end is nigh! Tarantara!

Even if our end is nigh!
Even if our end is nigh!

Verse 4:

Though in body and in mind,
(*Tarantara! Tarantara!*)
We aren't cautiously inclined,
(*Tarantara!*)
We're anything but blind
(*Tarantara! Tarantara!*)
To the danger that's behind.
Tarantara!
Yet, when the danger's near,
(*Tarantara! Tarantara!*)
We manage to appear!
Tarantara!

As insensible to fear
As anybody here,
As anybody here.
Tarantara!

Final chorus:

Tarantara-ra-ra-ra-ra! Tarantara!
Tarantara-ra-ra-ra-ra! Tarantara!
Tarantara, tarantara!
Tarantara, tarantara!
Forward to immortality!

Ever onward, ever flying,
Ever we are death denying!
Ever joyous are we calling:
Forward to immortality!
We'll face death, but we'll remember;
As we mock it in our banter
One day our stories they'll gather.
So once more now, hear our cry! Tarantara!

So once more now, hear our cry!
So once more now, hear our cry!

Tarantara-ra-ra-ra-ra! Tarantara!
Tarantara-ra-ra-ra-ra! Tarantara!
Tarantara, tarantara!
Tarantara, tarantara!
Forward to Immortality!

Katie Silverwings is a glassblower, visual artist, and writer, originally from Texas and now a nomadic creative spirit. She holds a BA in English and History from McMurry University in Abilene, Texas, with minors in Art, Arts Administration, and Biblical Greek Translation, as well as a BA (Hons.) in Glass from the University for the Creative Arts in the UK. Silverwings identifies as aromantic, asexual, and genderfae; "she/her", "they/them", and "fae/faer" pronouns are all welcome.

Long fascinated by nature and space, Silverwings' speculative fiction work centers around notions of optimistic futurism, friendship, found family, and adventurous journeys into the known and unknown. Her characters do most of the driving, and she does her best to keep up and negotiate pleasing stories with them.

Silverwings' two cats are commonly found staring over her shoulder while she's writing. The small cloud of dark matter with eyes likes to sit in her lap and interfere with typing, while the calico makes operatic editorial comments from across the room.

www.KatieSilverwings.com

@KatieSilverwings

MORE BOOKS
BY KATIE SILVERWINGS

Celadon

✦ A Strange Space™ Novel ✦

The Novan War has just begun. All that stands between Humanity and utter destruction are the ships of the Sol Coalition Defense Fleet.

The only problem? None of those ships are equipped with the all-important Quantum Space Drive which allows humanity to travel between planets and stars at a reasonable scale of time. The Drive needs Florivan QSD Engineers to run it, and Florivans are pacifists. Their Council of Elders has never allowed service on military vessels.

The Fleet can do little more than sit at the edges of the Coalition's seven member systems and *wait* for the Novans to attack.

Celadon Toreval is the Youngest of the Florivan Council of Elders. If anyone can come to Fleet Admiral Marvin's aid and help her save her people—and theirs—it's them.

Celadon, though, has their own reasons to get involved...

Available now from Amazon and Barnes & Noble and at
www.KatieSilverwings.com

Warmth and Darkness

✦ A Strange Space™ Novella ✦

Admiral Jennifer Marvin used to think she'd seen everything the galaxy had to throw at her. That, though, was before she met the Florivan Elder Celadon Toreval. She can sum up this Quantum Space Drive Engineer and dear friend of hers in two words: *cryptic chaos*. Their preference for the company of the most troublesome humans they can possibly find in the Fleet's ranks doesn't make matters better.

These days, Admiral Marvin is just grateful that the galaxy occasionally sends her a sign that something unusual is about to upset her carefully laid plans. Whether she manages to see those signs in time to do anything about it, though, is always a gamble.

Join Admiral Marvin's crew aboard the starship SCV *Aegolius* as they face the next chapter in the tales of the Novan War, and find out what new adventure waits for them in the darkness.

Even in the depths of space, you can find warmth...

Available now from Amazon and Barnes & Noble and at
www.KatieSilverwings.com

How Ocean Merlani Stole their Navigator

✷ A Strange Space™ Novel ✷

Every starship wanting to use the veiled dimension of Quantum Space as a shortcut around the physical distance between planets and stars needs a Florivan to run the Drive.

Every Florivan QSD Engineer needs an Astral Navigator to orient them and keep them anchored to Normal space. Finding the *right* human to be their life-long counterpart is one of the most important choices a young Florivan ever makes.

What happens, then, to someone like Ocean Merlani Barker, who can't seem to click with *any* of the highly qualified Navigator prospects their instructors have to offer? Ocean themself seems content to spend their second year in the Nav/Quan training program alone and taking extra classes for their secondary degree in geosciences.

Content, that is, until a chance encounter with a certain graduating student from the Security/Tactical program changes the course of their life forever...

Available now from Amazon and Barnes & Noble and at
www.KatieSilverwings.com

Feathered Friendship

✦ A STRANGE SPACE™ NOVELLA ✦

Dr. Ariadne Salzar-Newman is *not* a mad scientist.

She *is* a scientist—a brilliant one at that—but she's hardly *mad*. If one asks MSS *Venture's* staff psychologist and QSD Engineer, the Florivan Elder Navy Irleeim, she's only "amusingly eccentric, with a bit more of a fascination with the Strange than is healthy for a human."

That fascination has her once again working with the dangerous miasmas of Quantum Space, in hopes of making travel through that veiled dimension safer for human starships. It's not particularly safe for a scientist, for sure. Still, having taken Navy's apprentice under her wing as a part-time assistant, she's safer than usual. Working with her is good for Cobalt Mereday, too, if only because her unique brand of oddity seems to be the only thing capable of helping them.

Even Dr. Salzar-Newman has no reason to suspect just how much of an effect this particular project will have on her family and her protégé, nor how far-reaching the consequences will be.

Little Bernadette is *not* an ordinary budgerigar...

Available now from Amazon and Barnes & Noble and at
www.KatieSilverwings.com

On the Subject of Kittens and Mittens

✶ A Strange Space™ Novella ✶

Ranger Captain Taimri Hämäläinen loved playing in the snow as a child. Now, on a vacation with her family in the snow-covered mountains of a certain planet in the Beta Centauri sytem, she has a chance to share all of her favorite winter games with her own children.

Taimri's three adopted Florivan kittens, of course, have never seen snow before; they live on a space station with her husband, George Barker. That only makes it more fun to dress Sky, Storm, and Ocean up in their warmest clothes and take them out into the frosted wonderland, in Taimri's opinion.

While her Florivan counterpart, River Myrval, stays behind in the cozy comforts of the lodge, Taimri and her kittens are in for a bit of an adventure they hadn't expected...

Available now from Amazon and Barnes & Noble and at
www.KatieSilverwings.com

Tales of the Navigators (Volume 1)

✦ A Strange Space™ Short Story Collection ✦

The world of *Strange Space™* is full of stories of all sizes.

This first collected volume Katie Silverwings' *Strange Space™ Short Stories* includes ten tales from the lives of the enigmatic Florivans and their human Astral Navigator Counterparts:

- *Sleeping Beauties*
- *A Conspiracy of Fluff*
- *Aliens at a Tiki Bar*
- *An Interlude of Colors*
- *A Mystery, Unsolved*
- *The Ones who Wear White Hats*
- *The View From a Distance*
- *Fox in the Cave*
- *Rooftops and Space Whales*
- *The Tragedy of Harold the Violet*

The Strange is calling you...

Available now from Amazon and Barnes & Noble and at
www.KatieSilverwings.com

www.ingramcontent.com/pod-product-compliance
Lightning Source LLC
Chambersburg PA
CBHW061337310726
48974CB00001B/90